KOSINSKI

"One of our most significant writers."

—**Newsweek**

"Jerzy Kosinski is considered one of the best writers in the English language."

—Tom Brokaw,
"Today Show"

"One of the foremost psychological novelists in the world."

—Gail Sheehy, author of
Passages, in **Psychology Today**

"Jerzy Kosinski's books are an unusual hybrid of adventure-thriller . . . that create the pinball effect of a work in perpetual formation."

—**Saturday Review**

"Kosinski's vitality and inventiveness are as irresistible as ever."

—**Time**

"Jerzy Kosinski is one of the most important and consistently entertaining people writing today."

—**Literary Guild**

BLIND DATE

BLIND DATE

Jerzy Kosinski

BANTAM BOOKS · TORONTO · LONDON · NEW YORK

BLIND DATE

*A Bantam Book / published by arrangement with
Houghton Mifflin Company*

PRINTING HISTORY
Houghton Mifflin edition published November 1977
Literary Guild of America edition published February 1978

Bantam edition / October 1978
2nd printing .... October 1978
3rd printing .... September 1980

ISBN 0-553-14661-0

Published simultaneously in the United States and Canada

PRINTED IN THE UNITED STATES OF AMERICA

12 11 10 9 8 7 6 5 4

FOR KATHERINA

"Remove me from this land of slaves,
Where all are fools, and all are knaves,
Where every knave and fool is bought,
Yet kindly sells himself for nought;—"

JONATHAN SWIFT

"But henceforth who is to define crime?
Who shall decide what is good and what
is evil? All the traditional systems have
placed ethics and values beyond man's reach.
Values did not belong to him; he belonged to
them. He now knows that they are his and
his alone . . ."

JACQUES MONOD

BLIND DATE

When he was a school-boy, George Levanter had learned a convenient routine: a four-hour sleep in the afternoon enabled him to remain mentally and physically active until the early dawn, when he would again go to sleep for four hours and wake ready for the day.

Now, years later, this pattern helped him maintain the energy he needed for his business activities in the city; in the mountains, it allowed him to pursue his strenuous skiing without giving up the equally strenuous resort night life.

The restaurant owner came out onto the terrace, asking in French for someone who could understand English. Behind him, dressed in the latest ski gear, trotted a chubby young Arab who was clearly ill at ease.

Levanter considered volunteering his services, but he realized that in ValPina, as in most Swiss resorts, there were undoubtedly numerous bilingual guests who could do better.

One of a group of Americans got up and offered to assist. The owner gestured toward the Arab, saying in French, "Please tell him I can't cash his check."

The American spoke to the Arab, who handed him the check. The American gasped.

"It's for twenty-seven thousand," he mumbled to his companions. He looked at the Arab, then at the owner, then once more at the check. "Twenty-seven thousand dollars!" he said again.

"I just received it this morning from Barclays Bank in London. It is my weekly allowance from my uncle, Sheik Zaid. It is good, I vouch for it!" the Arab insisted in his high-pitched, British-accented voice.

"That's a lot of money for a weekly allowance," remarked the American, handling the check with obvious reverence.

The young Arab glanced at him defensively. "That's after taxes," he said. "My allowance changes every week, depending on the price of oil."

The American looked puzzled. "What do you have to do for it?" he asked.

"Do?" said the Arab. "There is nothing to do. Oil keeps gushing up from under the sand, whether or not my family wants it to." He giggled nervously. "You are from the U.S.?" he asked.

The American nodded.

The Arab reflected for a moment. "My country has a population of seven million," he said. "Yours has two hundred and twenty million. Yet my country has more money in U.S. banks alone than all of America's own monetary deposits! That's oil! Think what we could do to any bank in America that refused to cash our checks!" He smiled. "Now, what about my check here?"

"You really want him to cash it?" the American asked.

"How else can I pay for my lunch?" asked the Arab, who still seemed not to comprehend the astonishment of the others. "I left all my cash at the hotel. This check is the only money I have with me."

The American relayed the message to the owner.

"This is a mountain restaurant, not a bank!" the owner exclaimed. "All he had was a regular skier's lunch. Tell him I can't accept his check. And we don't give credit here!"

2

It was afternoon and Levanter was getting drowsy as he sat on the terrace: it was nearly time for him to ski down to the hotel for his afternoon sleep. He dozed off for a moment and when he awoke he saw a little girl, about four or five years old, playing with a doll next to his chair. A woman reclined on a deck chair, basking in the sun with her eyes closed.

"What's your name?" Levanter asked the girl.

"Olivia," she answered guardedly.

"Olivia? But that's a girl's name, and you're a boy. Your name must be Oliver," Levanter said.

"I'm a girl, not a boy." She giggled and moved closer to him.

Levanter leaned forward and drew the child gently toward him. "You're a boy. Don't be ashamed—you're Oliver, a handsome boy."

"I am not a boy. I never was a boy. I'm a girl." She was upset and was almost shouting. "You can ask my mother."

The woman in the deck chair opened one eye, smiled at Levanter, then spoke to the child. "You must convince this gentleman yourself," she said. "If I tell him you're a girl, the gentleman might not believe me either." She shut her eyes once more.

"You see, Oliver," Levanter lectured, "even though you think you're a girl, you're really a boy. Ask anyone."

The girl looked over at a nearby table, where a group of young men and women sat drinking wine and beer. Some of them had turned to watch Levanter and the child. They smiled but no one said anything. For a moment the girl looked uncertain, then she became playful.

"All right, I'm Oliver. So what?" Now she was challenging Levanter, letting him know she was ready to pursue their game.

At that moment a couple came out onto the terrace from the restaurant. The man, heavy and balding, appeared to be in his late fifties. Clinging to his arm was a platinum blonde, half his age, wearing a blouse which revealed her plump breasts. One of the young men rose respectfully.

"How are you, Professor?" he said, extending his hand to the man.

Levanter's attention was distracted from Olivia as he watched the professor and the young people.

The little girl was obviously annoyed that her game had been interrupted. She accosted the professor, saying in a loud voice, "How are you, Madame?"

He looked down at her. "I am Professor or Mister," he said, "not Madame."

The girl smiled precociously. "You're not Mister. You're Madame," she said. "Even if you think you're a man, you're really a woman. Ask anyone, ask this gentleman," she urged, pointing to Levanter.

Levanter closed his eyes, to appear to be napping.

"You're wrong, my child," the man insisted, his lips tightening. "You've made a mistake. Now be a good girl and run along."

Undeterred, the girl patted his hand. "You know you're Madame, even if you don't want to admit it. There is nothing to be ashamed of, Madame!"

The girl sat down primly next to Levanter. Everyone at the neighboring tables laughed.

Levanter woke from his afternoon nap. He bathed, dressed, and went down to the hotel dining room. After dinner, he wandered into the hotel bar for a drink. Sitting alone in the bustling cocktail lounge, he watched as a woman entered with two small girls; all three had thick blond hair and pale green eyes. The woman scanned the room for an empty table, and quickly navigated a path through the crowd to the vacant table on Levanter's left. Once she was seated, she began to inspect the room. She glanced briefly at Levanter, but

4

when she saw that he was looking at her, her gaze quickly shifted.

In a few minutes, the girls left the cocktail lounge, and their mother was alone at the table.

Levanter felt awed by the woman, but his feelings seemed to be triggered by something he could not define. He and the woman did not look at each other, yet he knew she was aware of his attention to her. They both kept their eyes fixed on the pianist, a man with the resigned air of a musician who has been playing popular songs for forty years. When he took a break, the woman got up and walked through the crowded room to the piano. She sat down and began to play an intricate Chopin nocturne.

Within seconds, her professional style had captured the attention of everyone in the lounge. As her fingers moved over the keyboard, she looked around at her audience, occasionally meeting Levanter's gaze. Levanter studied the shadows her lashes cast on her cheeks and stared at her lips, parted slightly as she concentrated on her music. He tried to imagine her face contorted in a spasm of pleasure or of pain, but he could not. As unobtrusively as possible, he made his way out of the lounge.

In the lobby, Levanter saw the woman's daughters playing. He went over to them and asked their ages.

"I'm eight," the older girl said, "and my sister is six."

"What are you going to be when you grow up?" Levanter asked her.

She looked closely at him and, without hesitation, said she wanted to be an actress.

"An actress? I know many actresses," said Levanter. "Do you want me to audition you for a role?"

The girl nodded, a serious look on her face.

"Let's pretend I am your husband," said Levanter, "and this hotel is our home. I have just returned from a trip abroad. While I was away, our dog died. His name

5

was Frecky, and we loved him very much. You didn't write me that Frecky had died because you didn't want to upset me. Now you have to break the news to me. Ready?"

As her sister watched with envy, the girl assumed the pose of an anxious wife. Levanter stepped away, then came back, his arms outstretched in greeting.

"Darling, how I've missed you," he said, embracing the girl. "I'm so glad to be back with you and Frecky." He paused, looking around. "But where is Frecky? Frecky, Frecky!" Levanter managed to give the impression of shouting without raising his voice. "Where is my sweet little dog, Frecky? Come here, your master is home!"

The girl was flushed and perspiring. She took Levanter's hand and patted it. "Sit down, my love," she said quite firmly. "Sit down. I have something to tell you."

Levanter pushed her aside. "In a minute, darling. Let me find Frecky. Frecky!" he shouted.

"Sit down," the girl insisted. "It's about Frecky. You see" —tears welled up in her eyes—"Frecky is not here."

"Not here? Where is he?"

"You must sit down," pleaded the girl. Levanter sat down, and she moved closer and embraced him tenderly. "But if I tell you the truth about Frecky, will you love me just the same?" she whispered. She could no longer hold back the tears.

"Of course I will. You and Frecky are all I have!" exclaimed Levanter.

"Now you have only me," she sobbed, "because Frecky—Frecky is dead." She covered her face.

He was about to pretend to faint when the younger girl ran over to him and pulled at his sleeve. "I can play it better than she did," she said. "I'm a better actress!"

Levanter smiled. "We'll see. I'll give you a tryout. Are you ready?"

The girl jumped up and down excitedly.

Levanter repeated his routine. "Frecky, Frecky, where are you? Where is Frecky, my dear little dog?" he exclaimed.

Under the critical gaze of her older sister, the little girl began to panic. She searched for words.

"Frecky, Frecky!" continued Levanter. "I'm home. Come here right away!"

She hesitated, then came closer, focusing her gaze on Levanter. "Frecky won't come," she said tensely. "He's in our bedroom. Upstairs." She stressed each word.

Levanter frowned. "You were supposed to tell me that Frecky was dead. Instead, you said he was upstairs. You forgot your lines."

"I didn't forget my lines," said the girl firmly. "If I'm your wife, I love you too much to tell you just like this that Frecky is dead. So I'm telling you he's upstairs. You'll go upstairs and find Frecky there—dead! Now can I be an actress?" she asked, tears forming in her eyes.

Levanter attempted to distract her. "If you are going to be an actress, you must learn not to cry when you are not acting. People won't believe that an actress really cries. They'll think you're just acting."

The girl stopped her tears and smiled.

"All right, you two," said Levanter, embracing them both, "let's see whether you are good storytellers. Tell me about your mother. Maybe someday she will play with us. Start with her name."

"My mother's name is Pauline," said the younger girl. "She is a famous pianist. Ever since she was a little girl, my mother wanted to play the piano."

When Levanter went down to the hotel lounge the next afternoon, Pauline was there. Her daughters were playing near the table. As soon as they saw him, they asked him to make up another game. Levanter promised to play with them after he talked with their mother.

He introduced himself to her, and she responded courteously, inviting him to sit down. After a short exchange about children, skiing, and resorts, he complimented her on her performance the previous evening. She thanked him.

"You're very talented," said Levanter. "I admire that."

"My piano teacher warned me that insufficient talent is nature's most cruel gift." She laughed.

"My mother was also a pianist—and she used to say the same thing! Who taught you to play the piano?"

The children came over and begged him to play another game, but Pauline gently sent them away. He asked about her musical training and she began to talk about the teachers she had studied with. Levanter was only half listening, until he heard her mention a Russian name.

"That's the name of a professor my mother had at the Moscow conservatory," he said. "In fact, she even told me she was his mistress."

Pauline reflected, a mischievous smile on her face. "My professor was the only pianist in his family," she said. "It must be the same man. He was probably about thirty when he taught your mother in Russia, and he was in his sixties when I studied with him in England. If he were my lover too, would I be linked to your mother?"

"Yes, and if I had been my mother's lover," said Levanter, "I then would be linked to you."

Her eyes met his, but she said nothing. Then she lowered her glance.

"It's too bad you don't play the piano," she said. "You have beautiful hands—the hands of a pianist."

Levanter's mother was twenty years younger than her husband and twenty years older than her only son. She and her husband had emigrated from Russia and settled in Eastern Europe shortly before Levanter was born. A tall, slender woman with delicate features, she had a fair complexion that contrasted with the lustrous black hair that billowed around her long neck.

When Levanter was in high school, it was his mother, not his friends, who arranged most of his dates. Any time she met a pretty girl—whether it was someone who came backstage after a recital to ask for her autograph or someone who was simply sitting beside her on a city bus—she would ask her to tea to meet her son. In each case, the young woman would report to Levanter later, his mother had been so charming that probably no one—not even a married woman—could resist her invitation.

If Levanter happened to meet a girl on his own and bring her home, his mother would praise the girl politely at first and then begin to point out her faults. One girl was undoubtedly beautiful and graceful, she conceded, but not quite clean. Another, she admitted, was elegant and pleasant to talk to, but not in any way physically attractive.

As Levanter's father aged, a heart disease forced him to retire early. He withdrew almost entirely from social life into the seclusion of his room and his study of ancient languages. Levanter's mother, still young and attractive, continued to be active socially and often came to the parties her son or his friends gave.

Eventually, Levanter's father suffered a severe stroke and had to be hospitalized. Every morning, the nurse on duty telephoned Levanter's mother to report on her husband's condition. From his room, Levanter could hear the phone ring in his mother's bedroom and then, almost immediately, the sound of her anxious voice. One day, the ringing went on and on. Levanter jumped out of bed and, without even putting his bathrobe over his naked body, ran to answer it. He was picking up the receiver when his mother rushed into the room, her skin wet from the shower, and took the phone from him. She made no attempt to cover herself with the towel in her hand or to reach for the robe hanging over the foot of her bed. As she listened, she stood erect, facing Levanter, who had sat down on her bed.

She hung up the receiver and told Levanter his father's condition remained unchanged. Then she dried herself and lay down on the bed, just inches away from him.

Levanter was aroused, and he was afraid to stand up because he would be embarrassed if she noticed. He did not move. Attempting to appear at ease, he reclined a bit, only to feel her thighs against his back. Without a word his mother reached for him, and without a word he responded.

She pulled his face to her neck, her shoulders, then her breasts. She held him at her nipples, then slid partially under him. As he began caressing her body with his tongue, she pushed herself farther under him and gripped his shoulders, pulling his body upward. He ceased to be aware of anything but his need for her and entered her, eager and abandoned.

Levanter and his mother remained lovers for years, although she continued to find women for him. They were together only in the morning. By sleeping in the nude and making love with him only when she had just awakened, his mother never undressed especially for him. She never allowed him to kiss her on the mouth and, despite her animated discussions of the sexual proclivities of other women, always insisted that he caress nothing but her breasts.

He never talked with his mother about their lovemaking. Her bed was like a silent, physical confessional: what happened between them there was never talked about.

Once Levanter left Eastern Europe, he could not return, and the authorities would not permit his mother to travel abroad. But when she had had several unsuccessful operations for cancer and all the doctors agreed that her end was imminent, she was allowed to meet her son in Switzerland. They had been separated for twenty years.

Levanter waited in the arrivals building and watched as the passengers came through immigration. He noticed a nurse and an airport steward pushing a wheelchair with a small, shriveled woman wearing an ill-fitting wig. This was not what he was expecting and he started to turn away when the woman raised a frail hand and waved at him.

He ran toward her. She embraced him and looked hard at his face. He kissed the hollow cheeks and loosely fleshed hands, trying not to cry. Her wig slid sideways. Levanter, pained to see that she was bald, held her closer. He commented on her perfume, and she was pleased that he recognized it after so many years. She whispered that she had met a beautiful young woman on the plane and had arranged for the three of them to meet for tea one day.

The day never came. The excitement of preparing for the journey, the stress of the trip itself, and the meeting with her son took all her remaining energy. On the second day in Switzerland, she collapsed. Her awareness waned and she began to fear that she would not regain it; she asked the doctor and nurse to let her spend her last moments alone with her son.

She gestured for him to lie down beside her, and he obeyed. The arm that reached toward him was covered with bluish patches around veins which had been pierced by repeated injections. Yet as she touched him, her face took on the indulgent transfixed expression that had been so familiar to him. She guided his hand through the opening in her robe and when he stroked her breasts, her eyes glazed over, as if her thoughts were miles away.

Just before Pauline left ValPina, Levanter invited her to visit the underground lake of St. Leonard. The lake had been discovered when a huge boulder was displaced by a rockslide in an earth tremor that shook the valley just after the war.

When they arrived at the narrow opening to the rectangular cavern, the custodian, a young man in a sheepskin coat, seemed surprised to see them. Although the fifty-foot-deep lake was a popular tourist attraction, visitors seldom came to St. Leonard in the winter because the cavern was too cold. He sold them tickets, and they followed him into the grotto, leaving the daylight behind.

The narrow walkway was lit by dim electric bulbs. They reached the edge of the lake, but could not see the far end, a thousand feet away. The custodian untied one of the three boats moored to a rock and steadied it as first Levanter and then Pauline stepped in and sat down.

Levanter started the boat moving with one powerful pull of the oars. They glided noiselessly into the shadowy space, breaking the still water and upsetting the reflection cast upon it by the bulbs attached to the rock roof. In seconds, the lights of the mooring site disappeared as Levanter rowed around a curving wall of rock. The cave opened before them, revealing massive walls of limestone, iron, and marble. Elsewhere, nature surrendered these raw materials to man, but here they seemed appropriated solely for nature's own use. Levanter had the sense of intruding in the domain of an artist who worked hidden from the world.

A school of albino fish flashed in the translucent waters around the boat. The custodian had told them that salmon were brought in; after weeks of being deprived of natural light, the fish lost their orange coloring and turned chalk-white.

Levanter folded the oars, and the boat floated slowly. They were in the center of the cave, hardly moving. The light that reflected in the water seemed to be shining up from below the surface. Pauline's shadowed face looked unfamiliar in the strange half-light.

"If the mountain above us collapsed and cuts us off here—" she began. She waited for him to finish her thought.

Levanter said, "We would just wait here together until they came to blast away the rocks."

"For how long?" she murmured.

"A few days, I guess. Maybe more. It would depend on how much rock fell over the entrance."

"What would we do while we waited to be rescued?"

"Talk."

"Talk about what?"

"About ourselves," he told her. "Possibly for the last time."

"Then this could be our last talk," she said, huddling down in the boat, drawing her long fox coat tightly around her.

"It could," he agreed. "Still, this cave has brought us close to each other."

The fish darted from under the boat, their white bodies glittering in the faint light.

"A baseball player I once knew," said Levanter, "fell in love with a teen-age waitress in a small town where his team sometimes played. Soon the girl was in love with him too. Each time he came to town, they would lock themselves in his hotel room after the game and make love until they were exhausted. Some months later, he was bought by a major-league team and became a big star, playing only in large cities."

"Why are you telling me this?" Pauline asked.

Levanter smiled. "This is how we get close to one another. Besides, you're a performer, like him. In any case, the baseball player didn't get back to that town for a year. When he looked for the waitress, he learned that she'd become a hooker. He went to the club she hung out at and asked her to come to his hotel room. She said she didn't like him anymore and refused to go with him. He thought she was teasing, so he assured her that he wanted her then as much as he had always wanted her—it was simply the circumstances of his life that had changed. Again she said she wouldn't go, and when he offered to pay her, she said no money would make her sleep with him again. This time he believed she meant it."

The boat bumped against a rocky ledge. Levanter set it gliding again. Pauline's attention was on him, but she said nothing.

"Later in the evening," he went on, "the baseball player called the owner of the club. Using a made-up name, he claimed to be an old customer of hers and promised to pay double the regular price if she could be sent to his suite. He left the door unlocked and waited in the bathroom. When she knocked, he shouted for her to take the money from the dresser and make herself comfortable. Seconds later he ran out and locked the door. Once again he told her that he'd always loved her. She threw the money at him and started to dress. He put his arms around her. As she tried to struggle free, he reached into a drawer for his gun. She laughed at him. She died of two bullet wounds. After a short trial, he was acquitted."

In the morning, Levanter drove to Aratus, a three-story chalet with several garages, a tennis court, and iron sculptures adorning acres of private park. The driveway appeared to have been swept and sanded recently, and everything about the chalet suggested constant care.

Levanter parked just outside the entrance to the grounds and waited. The ValPina postman pulled up to the house in his small car. He placed a stack of mail on the front doormat, rang the bell, and, without waiting for a response, drove away again. Levanter left his car and walked to the door with the confident stride of an expected visitor. At the door, he bent down as if to brush the snow off his boots and trousers, and, certain he could not be seen from any of the windows, he quickly perused the mail. He spotted a large manila envelope, looked at the return address, and deftly tucked it under his coat. Then, in case anyone in the house had seen him approach, he stepped far enough back to be visible and slapped his forehead as if he had just discovered that he was at the wrong house. As he was about to drive away, he saw the chalet door open. A black woman in a maid's uniform picked up the mail and, without looking around, took it inside.

An hour later, Levanter telephoned Aratus. A butler answered and Levanter asked for Clarence Weston, Sr. It was a matter concerning Pacific and Central Enterprises, Inc., he said.

Weston came to the phone. Levanter introduced himself and asked for an appointment.

"What is it you want from me, Mr. Levanter?" asked Weston in the manner of a man accustomed to fending off requests.

Levanter was not deterred. "Some highly confidential information about Pacific and Central has leaked. I think you should know about it."

"I know my company, Mr. Levanter. If something has leaked, it wasn't confidential. If that's all, then——" He was ready to hang up.

"It's about the Monaco deal," said Levanter. "And the results of the talks Rashid, Omani, and Young held in Lake Tahoe."

Weston was silent.

"I'm sorry to have troubled you, Mr. Weston," said Levanter, his tone indicating he too was now ready to end their conversation.

15

"Where are you calling from, Mr. Levanter?" Weston asked quickly.

Levanter gave the name of his hotel.

"My car will pick you up in twenty minutes."

When Levanter arrived at the chalet, Weston was waiting for him in a large living room. Apparently in his sixties, he had gray hair and a ruddy complexion. As he gestured Levanter to the soft leather chair beside him, Weston's bright eyes seemed to be making a careful assessment of his visitor. The black maid whom Levanter had seen picking up the mail now brought in coffee, cognac, and a plate of biscuits.

"What do you do, Mr. Levanter?" he asked.

"I do as I please."

Weston laughed, displaying the unnatural whiteness of denture enamel. "Many men can say that. But how do you make a living?" He leaned forward.

"I have always been an investor," said Levanter. "A self-employed idea man. A few times a year I come across an idea and try to sell it to people who might need it."

Weston picked up a biscuit and bit at it delicately. "How do you get these ideas?" he asked, openly ironic.

"Any investor knows that ideas are traps," said Levanter. "But only one who knows how to set the trap will make a catch."

"And you, Mr. Levanter, decided that you knew how to set one for me—and figured you could make a killing. Is that so?" He did not wait for an answer. "Well, not yet, my friend. The Monaco deal is someone else's trap. You couldn't have come across it all by yourself. Someone must have helped you set me up or worked for you." He leaned closer. His expression was hard, almost hostile. "Isn't this simply blackmail, Mr. Levanter? You tell me who is selling the secrets of Pacific and Central and I pay you for the tip?" He looked into Levanter's eyes. "How much?"

Levanter got up and walked across the room, the

thick, furry carpet muting the sound of his steps. He stopped and gazed out of the large window. The snow glittered in the sun, its smooth, vast surface broken here and there by fox pawprints. Below, he could see the valley of Valais.

"When are you going back to California?" he asked Weston.

Weston looked impatient. "If you don't know that, Levanter, your insiders didn't tell you much," he said sternly. "Now, what's your answer?"

"You are still the chairman of the board and chief executive officer of the company, aren't you?" Levanter asked. "I want to be sure I'm talking to the right man."

"That's what the corporate letterhead shows," answered Weston. "But for some time now I have been performing my duties from here, by remote control, you might say. A self-imposed semiretirement of sorts."

"How come?"

"Age. Some arthritis. To save remaining energy." His smile looked forced. "It's a multibillion-dollar company, Levanter. Thousands of employees. Shareholders. As long as I'm here they can't keep track of the state of my health. No one bothers me. You're the first." He chuckled.

Levanter pointed out the window at the extensive grounds. "And all this is yours?"

Weston nodded. "It sure is. But don't be too impressed," he added quickly. "It's just twenty-five acres. The Arab next door owns four times as much land, and he's building eight separate villas on it—one for each of his wives."

Levanter returned to his chair. "If I were to tell you how I obtained a detailed account of the Monaco deal and those talks in Lake Tahoe, what would you do?"

Weston became animated. "I would fire the person who allowed the information to get out. I would teach the bastard a lesson he'd never forget."

"Why?"

"Why? This is a publicly owned corporation. A leak like this could have serious consequences." He stopped.

Levanter spoke. "Yes, it could. It could force the resignation of your top men, a loss of confidence in Washington and on Wall Street. The company's stock would plummet, millions of shareholders would lose their savings. And all this as you sit here in the comfort of your mountain estate, enjoying the fortune that you have accumulated over the years. Meanwhile, many of the investors, contractors and subcontractors, and dozens of companies that depend on your conglomerate would go out of business."

Weston rose from his chair, his face flushed. "Now wait a minute." He raised his voice. "I owe nothing to anyone."

"Now you wait," Levanter countered. "I'm the one who discovered the man responsible for the leak."

"How much do you want to name him?"

"I haven't said that what I know is for sale, or that I intend to reveal it to anyone else," said Levanter. "But if another man came to you with what I know, how much would you pay him for telling you how he got the information?"

Weston sat down. "Is this bastard at Pacific and Central the only one responsible for the leak?"

"As far as I know, he is," said Levanter with conviction.

"And he can be stopped?"

"He can. Very easily."

Weston picked up a pencil and wrote something on a small pad. He tore off the slip of paper and passed it to Levanter.

Levanter glanced at it. "Are you sure you're not too generous?" he asked.

"You don't have the check yet," said Weston with a laugh.

Levanter stood up and walked out to the hall. He took the envelope from his coat and went back to the living room and handed it to Weston. "Here it is, all intact," he said. "And the addressee is the bastard whose negligence allowed me to obtain it."

Weston looked at the name. His face turned red as he anxiously enptied the envelope. "What do you mean 'negligence'?" he demanded.

"I picked up the envelope outside your door this morning."

"How did you know this would be in today's mail?" Weston asked.

"I didn't. But I'm sure you receive something like this almost every day. I assume you do only the unimportant transactions by phone since it is likely to be tapped, and certainly you don't trust messengers. Anyway, how do you know I haven't been picking up and resealing your mail for weeks?"

Weston was angry. "Stealing mail is against the law. I can have you arrested."

"You can," said Levanter. "But is what I've done worse than Monaco?"

Weston did not respond. He had turned his attention away from Levanter and begun to sort through the papers.

"Well, everything is in order," Weston said as he slipped them back into the envelope. "You haven't made any copies?" he asked.

"What for? I'm a small investor," said Levanter. "That's what I'll always be."

Weston got up again and paced for a moment. "Wait here," he ordered and left the room with the manila envelope. He came back a few minutes later. "This is for you," he said, handing Levanter a check.

"You don't have to," said Levanter.

"I know I don't," said Weston.

Levanter looked at the check. The amount was

twice the figure Weston had written on the paper. "Why?" Levanter asked.

"You could get twice as much from any of our competitors," said Weston. "Besides, you've just given Pacific and Central an idea. These days new ideas are tough to come by."

Levanter stood at the cable-car window, pretending to enjoy the view but in fact reveling in the admiring glances of the other skiers. Not every one of the hundred or so people in the car could have noticed his modish ski suit, American racing boots, and Japanese-made skis, but he knew he looked striking. He always selected his apparel and equipment with an eye to creating this effect, as did many of the fashionable skiers who came to ValPina. The attire was, after all, a part of the sport itself. Levanter was paying little attention to the babble of French, Italian, Swiss, English, and German until, over the cacophony, he distinctly heard the sound of Russian. He looked across the car and spotted a man and two women in city clothes who contrasted markedly with the colorful, animated skiers around them. They had the drab appearance and repressed bearing of Soviet officialdom.

Levanter inched his way across the crowded cable car and maneuvered a place in front of the trio. From their remarks, he learned that they were indeed Soviet officials on their way from Geneva to Milan, stopping for a day of sightseeing in ValPina. Their conversation was a series of judgments on everything they saw: the skiing was imperfect, the slopes badly maintained, the view less than beautiful, and the Western ski equipment garish and extravagant. Levanter expected some comment about himself. Then, surprised that they hadn't noticed his outfit and gear, he shoved his elbow against the man, stumbling as if the sway of the cable car had upset his balance. The man tripped, then regained his balance and looked at Levanter with disdain.

One of the women glanced at Levanter's boots. "Interesting design," she said to her companions.

The man looked down at the boots. "Cheap plastic garbage. Not an ounce of leather," he muttered.

Levanter stared out of the window.

The other woman looked at Levanter's skis. "Ya-ma-ha," she read aloud.

"Japanese trash," the man said.

"Still, the parka is vivid," the other woman said.

"Gaudy," commented the man.

The Russian man turned to get a better look at Levanter, who continued to stare out of the window. "I know his type," said the Russian. "Spaniard, from the looks of him. Works at a lodge in some menial capacity, no doubt. Kitchen boy. Or a porter. Or a waiter. That's it. A little Spanish waiter! The Swiss import these poor bastards and work them like dogs. Fourteen, sixteen hours a day. So when he finally gets a day off, he puts on his flashy outfit and parades around like a big shot."

Levanter turned to face them. Assuming the manner of an authoritarian Soviet bureaucrat, he addressed the Russians in their language.

"Excuse my intervention, Comrades," he said, pausing to gauge the effect. The Russians stared at him, stunned. "I am Lieutenant Colonel Romarkin, Soviet Armed Forces, temporarily abroad with the Soviet Ski Team in the Alpine Competition." He paused again. Other skiers in the cable car were watching the strange scene, understanding nothing of what was happening but spellbound by the formal tones of the voices and the Russians' sudden subservient attitudes. "I could not help overhearing your remarks about me," Levanter continued, stressing each word. "As, let me remind you, I am here on behalf of our beloved motherland, the Union of Soviet Socialist Republics—"

"But, Comrade," the man stammered, "in no way did we mean to—"

"Do not interrupt," Levanter commanded. "It does not matter that you don't know that my equipment is the very finest obtainable for our Soviet sportsmen to appear in at this competition. What does matter—"

"But, Comrade, in no way did we mean to undermine—"

"I haven't finished yet." Levanter looked sternly at the man. The official, silenced, turned ashen. "What matters," Levanter went on, "is that you, Comrade, unmasked your true feelings: to you the term 'Spanish waiter' is derogatory. Yet such poor Spaniards desperately fought in Spain against the forces of fascism." The official, his mouth dry, muttered something incoherent.

Levanter turned to the women. "As for you, Comrades—"

The women, visibly upset, gave him stubborn looks. "I merely commented upon your parka, Comrade," one of them said, licking her lips as she spoke.

"And all I said was 'Ya-ma-ha,'" pleaded the other, small droplets of perspiration rolling down her cheeks.

" 'Parka' and 'Yamaha.' That's all you could say? Neither of you felt it necessary to object to this comrade's fascistic remarks?" Levanter enunciated every word. "Enough. We will resolve the matter in Moscow. Now, please: name, profession, and position?"

The man spoke first, and the women quickly answered after him. As Levanter had suspected, they were minor functionaries, employees of the Moscow Ministry of Trade. The man offered his passport with a trembling hand, a gesture of utter servility and guilt. Levanter studied the document long enough to give the impression that he was memorizing the man's name, then turned away without speaking, as if he were disgusted by the sorry affair and eager to end it.

The cable car arrived at the midstation, from

which point skiers either continued up on the PicSoleil gondola or skied down. The door opened. In the confusion of skiers pouring out, the Soviet trio scurried away.

As he went through the passageway to the gondola, Levanter saw the Russians sitting at one of the most secluded tables on the terrace. They nervously shuffled their passports and other papers, no doubt preparing themselves for the investigation that would await them at home.

For a moment he felt sorry for them and considered going over to apologize and tell them the truth, to shake hands with them and laugh at the masquerade in which they had all taken part. But he knew they would not laugh: he would only be frightening them more. They would then be convinced that a man who spoke perfect Russian and knew Soviet jargon must be an émigré spy for the CIA, donning still another disguise to find out more about them.

Then he felt ashamed and somehow unnerved by his deception. To his surprise, the short encounter with the Soviets had resurrected a part of himself he had believed to be buried, the enjoyment of having certifiable power. When he had terrified those three Russian mice, he had actually felt himself being transformed into a Soviet lieutenant colonel; no real-life Soviet lieutenant colonel could have carried it off better.

He promised himself to remember to tell the whole incident to Romarkin, his friend in Paris whose name he had borrowed. He could already imagine Romarkin laughing uproariously, repeating over and over, "And all I said was 'Ya-ma-ha'!"

Only when he skied was Levanter able to recognize the subtle changes brought about by age. While his mind retained its ability to consider circumstances and issue commands, his body, which had once reacted automatically, was now frequently unable to respond as expected. Refusing to acknowledge this breakdown, his mind kept supplying the images of past performances but, no matter how hard he tried, Levanter could no longer repeat them. He was becoming conscious of a division between what he knew he had done once and what he could actually do now.

For a boy who had not learned to ski until he was twelve and could practice only during school vacations, Levanter had shown considerable aptitude for the sport. By the time he was in high school, he had entered a few local ski competitions and collected some equipment as prizes. He loved being on the slopes and saved up his money to take lessons to become a certified ski instructor. This certification proved to be an asset.

To demonstrate to the world that pleasures once reserved for the privileged were now enjoyed by the masses, the Party had instituted a program of ordering peasants to the mountains for winter vacations about the time Levanter was a university student. Most peasants rarely left the agricultural flatlands, and few had ever seen mountains before. The twenty-four-hour railroad ride to the high-altitude ski resort often left many of them lightheaded, and a few older ones would faint or vomit as they stepped from the stuffy, overheated train into the thin, cold air. Overwhelmed by the towering mountain peaks that loomed like prison walls, the disoriented peasants would become querulous about everything from dizziness to dangers underfoot. They consistently refused to walk alone, even on the sloping village streets, for fear that they would lose their footing and plummet down the side of a cliff, rolling over and over all the way down to the valley. With arms tightly linked, small knots of these unwilling vacationers would be seen stumbling forward, trying to keep their bodies upright, always looking down at their feet, never up at the mountains. Many of them actually believed the mountains were man-made, like the massive government buildings they had seen on their obligatory visits to the capital, and they wondered why the government had built them so high.

The ski instructors were mainly sons of local artisans whose families had lived in the region for centuries. They had all been on skis from the moment they could stand, and many of them were regional and even national champions. But skiing was all they knew. Their only other interests were drinking, playing cards, and seducing vacationing females. As children, they had gone to the local parish school to learn how to pray, write, and read, but most soon forgot what little they had managed to learn. None of the instructors had any notion of what "ideology" meant; few had ever heard of Marx or Engels; and all they knew about Lenin was that after his death Stalin began to take care of the world's working people.

This lack of knowledge made local Party authorities apprehensive. Since ski instructors had contact with the workers and these vacationers might return home with embarrassing stories about ignorant mountain men, the political consciousness of the ski instructors had to be raised. The authorities decided they needed a university-educated certified ski instructor at each resort to indoctrinate the local ski teachers. Since Levanter was qualified, the university released him for four months each winter to teach skiing to peasants and to conduct a biweekly class in ideology for his fellow instructors. He was also required to test their progress at the end of each one-month course; those who failed the simple finals twice in a row had their skiing instructorships suspended, and those who failed three times were fired. Levanter was to be the only judge of his students' ability.

During his first lesson, Levanter made a reference to the end of the nineteenth century. Someone asked how a person could tell when one century ended and another began, and no one in the class had an answer. In a class about Trotsky, they wondered how the same man who had founded the workers' state had so quickly turned into its dangerous enemy.

To keep their athletic standards as high as their newly imposed ideological ones, all the instructors had to compete every December and March. The widely publicized Ski Instructors' Championship combined downhill and slalom with jumping and cross-country races. The first time Levanter participated, he was the only skier not born in the region and his entry received a great deal of attention. He felt he was in good shape and had ample reserves of strength. Confident of his stamina and form, he assumed he would place among the first ten or fifteen skiers in the meet.

At the start of the cross-country race he was determined not to tire himself in the first few miles. The forty-five participants soon stretched out along the course, and Levanter found himself skiing alone. Toward dusk he arrived at the finish line. The area was deserted: there were no judges, no press and no radio commentators, no other skiers, and no crowds. Levanter realized that he had come in last, but not a soul was waiting for him. He assumed he had lost his way somewhere during the race, and everyone must have thought he had dropped out. That night he talked with some of the others and learned to his dismay that he had not been lost—he was simply that much slower than all the other instructors.

In his class the next morning, Levanter began with a question. "What, according to Comrade Stalin, are the five factors that determine victory in war?" The instructors, intimidated as usual, sat in gloomy silence. "No volunteers?" asked Levanter, scanning the bored faces.

"The last volunteers died in the First World War," someone shouted from the back row. The class guffawed.

"Let's be honest with each other," said Levanter.

"I no more enjoyed finishing the race so far behind you than you would enjoy being asked such questions on your final exam."

To emphasize the confidential nature of what he was about to say, Levanter stood up and closed all the windows and locked the door. Then he moved his chair into the middle of the room and motioned the instructors around him.

"I am not a winner," said Levanter, "but no man was born to be a loser. There are forty-five of us here, and there will be forty-five of us competing in the March championship. I won't mind if I finish forty-fifth, but I will mind if I finish hours after everyone else. Understand?"

The instructors nodded.

"While it would be hazardous for me to try skiing faster, it would not be hazardous for you to ski slower. Thus, for our mutual safety—mine in the race and yours in the exam—I propose that all of you slow down so that I can finish the race within sight of the last ten racers. You have until March to think it over."

The day of the March cross-country race dawned clear and windless, with crisp, well-packed snow. This last championship of the season was held during a holiday weekend and attracted unusually large crowds of spectators, including the capital's café society and the wives and children of government, Party, and diplomatic dignitaries.

In the early stages of the race, Levanter felt in great form; by the middle stretch he began to lose time, but discovered he was not alone. Each time he hit a rough patch and lost speed, the six or eight instructors just ahead of him slowed down as well. From time to time, he would see one of them turn to look over his shoulder and hear him shout ahead to the others, "I see him! I see him!"

Levanter again finished last, but this time he was only thirty seconds behind the forty-fourth contestant.

Surrounded by reporters and fans, Levanter overheard a radio broadcaster telling his listeners that the skiing conditions must have been extraordinarily tough, since the winning time was almost an hour longer than the previous cross-country race.

Levanter liked skiing alone. Often he carried a small camera in his parka and stopped to photograph the dramatic high-mountain scenery that changed from moment to moment. One day he decided to ski the Aval, ValPina's longest run. For a mile the Aval offered a straightforward, gently sloping descent, although the top tended to be very windy because the glacier PicSoleil loomed alongside. At the foot of the initial descent was a narrow ridge, which opened onto a plateau just above the first of five downward slopes, all so steep that they made this one of the most challenging runs in the Alps.

When Levanter reached the plateau, he came upon four skiers slowly making their way down, moving in a winding course. One of them, a young woman dressed not in ski clothes but in a sheepskin jacket and woolen slacks, appeared to be having great difficulty. She was clearly terrified of the steepness of the slope below the plateau and of the run stretching before her. Each time she started to gain downward speed, she would try to slow herself by heading away from the dropline. Her momentum would carry her uphill, in a zigzag pattern, onto the side of the slope, where, in a desperate attempt to stop, she would throw herself down into the deep snow. Her ski bindings opened and released the skis, but the safety straps kept them attached to her ankles so the loose skis continued to strike her body. Levanter saw this happen several times, and he wondered how long it would be before she was seriously hurt by the steel-edged skis.

The three men with her wore regular ski gear and handled themselves competently. Levanter was close enough to hear that they spoke with pronounced British accents and to sense that they were annoyed by their companion's falls.

One time the woman fell into soft, unpacked snow. She was about one hundred feet above Levanter, but he could hear her breathing and moaning. With each move she made, the snow collapsed under her, yet she continued the struggle to regain her footing, as though afraid she would suffocate in the powdery depths. She appeared desperate as she squirmed and flailed like a wounded insect, unable to fit her boots back into the ski bindings.

Quickly, he pulled out his camera and took several shots of her snow-covered form. Then he photographed her companions. The three men first stared at him and then ignored him.

"Cheer up, dear, you're doing fine!" one of them shouted to the woman.

"Just lean downhill, go with the slope!" screamed another.

Finally, she managed to get to her feet. As the men were helping to dislodge the sodden lumps of snow from her slacks and coat, Levanter skied over and, without a word, photographed the four of them.

He smiled politely. "Beautiful day, isn't it?"

The men nodded uneasily.

"Do you ski the Aval often?" asked Levanter.

"This is our first time here," one of the men answered.

"It's a lovely run," Levanter commented. "Tough, but lovely." He looked at the young woman. Her cheek was bruised, her forehead cut and bleeding. "And you," he asked her. "Have you skied it before?"

"No. It's only my second day on skis, you know," she added apologetically.

"Your second day on skis?" Levanter asked. "You

mean to say that you only began to ski yesterday, and today you're on the Aval, at eleven thousand feet?"

The woman nodded, attempting a smile.

Levanter moved closer to her. "Tell me," he said softly, "how long have you known these three gentlemen?"

She looked at them hesitantly, then at Levanter. "I met them skiing yesterday."

"Yesterday! And, knowing that you can hardly stand up on skis, they brought you to do the Aval, one of the toughest runs in all the Alps?"

"Yes. Why do you ask?"

"I'm curious. Did they tell you that they expected you to kill yourself today?"

One of the men glided forward. "I say there, hold on," he shouted angrily. "What kind of stupid question is that?"

Levanter disregarded him and continued to address the woman. "They didn't?" he said. "This is just the beginning of the run and by no means the worst of it. Surely you realize you don't stand a chance of making it alive."

She listened without responding.

"Perhaps you didn't understand that each slope becomes more treacherous as you descend," Levanter went on.

"You've no right to scare a person like that," one of the Englishmen intruded.

Levanter turned to the men. "Now you all listen," he said. "This young lady will walk all the way down, and you will carry her skis. I'll be around to make sure that nothing happens to her. If she is hurt, I have taken enough photographs to have all three of you arrested and charged by the authorities in ValPina."

"And in whose name are you doing this?" snapped one man.

"Simple humanity will do for the moment," Levanter replied. Then, raising his camera, he quickly photographed them again before they could raise their hands to cover their faces. Without a word, the girl took off her skis and handed them to her companions. They all started the long walk down.

By late afternoon, the four finally reached the midstation. Levanter was waiting for them in the restaurant. At first they all ignored him. After the meal, as the men gathered their skis together, the woman slipped over to his table.

"I wouldn't have made it without you," she whispered. "You saved my life." She leaned forward, drew his face close to hers, and kissed him. Her lips, chapped by the wind, felt dry.

Levanter was still in his robe the next morning when his breakfast was brought to his room. He opened the door and found himself facing the chest of an enormous man holding a breakfast tray. The waiter walked in and placed the tray on the table. Then, instead of leaving, he remained in the room, leaning against the wall, looking out of the window. Levanter assumed that the black-haired giant was waiting for a tip, and he handed him some change from the bureau. The man pocketed the tip but did not move.

"That will be all, thank you," said Levanter, but the waiter paid no attention. Levanter then walked to the tray and bent over it, as if checking the contents. "Two soft-boiled eggs, bread, butter, coffee, milk," he murmured out loud. "Sugar, salt, pepper." Then, "Marmalade, jam," he continued. "Of course, napkin, fork, knife, spoon. Everything's in order." He looked at the waiter to indicate that nothing else was needed from him. Again the man did not react. Levanter, annoyed, spoke directly to him. "I think that's all, thank you," he said in a louder voice.

The man turned slightly and looked down at Levanter. "Eat! No talk," he said gruffly, motioning with his chin toward the breakfast try. "Eat!" He turned back to the window.

Levanter's first reaction was to back away, but he stopped himself. "Whether I eat or not is my business, not yours!" he said.

As if he were reprimanding a capricious child, the giant looked at Levanter and pointed at the tray. "You no talk. Eat! Eat!" he repeated, raising his voice. He stood with his arms folded.

Levanter thought for an instant about this strange behavior and the man's abnormal height, and it occurred to him that the waiter might be insane. He thought of running out of the room but was afraid to provoke the man. Still, he was unwilling to give in. The waiter noticed the delay.

"Eat!" he commanded, unfolding his arms and dropping his hands, each of which, Levanter thought, could squeeze his head like a soft-boiled egg.

He decided to obey rather than irritate the madman. He sat down and started to eat. The waiter, satisfied, resumed his post at the window. Every few minutes he glanced at the table to see what progress was being made. Levanter had barely managed to swallow his last mouthful when the man picked up the tray and calmly left the room.

Angry and humilated, Levanter dressed and went to see the hotel manager. "One of your waiters, a very tall, black-haired—"

"Oh, yes, Antonio," the manager interrupted, smiling politely. "He's from Barcelona."

"I don't care where he's from," Levanter said. He suddenly thought of the Russians in the cable car. "He brought me my breakfast and refused to leave the room until I had eaten it."

The manager looked at Levanter expectantly. "Did he in any way prevent you from eating the breakfast, sir?"

"No, but why should he stay in my room while I eat?"

"Guests who call for room service often make the hotel's cutlery into souvenirs," said the manager. "And if the waiters don't notice and report such thefts, they are all required to pay for the missing pieces at the end of the week."

"What does this have to do with me?" Levanter asked.

"As a Spaniard," the manager explained, "Antonio is a man of honor, and he will not pay for the mistakes of others. He personally guards all cutlery used in the meals he serves." The manager paused. "You know, Mr. Levanter, you are the first guest to object to his presence. Perhaps you just don't like Spaniards!"

Upon the midstation terrace, Levanter sank deeper into the deck chair. An indefinable, boundless dread came over him. First it flowed slowly, like a gray snow cloud; then it surged and gained in strength, compelling Levanter's heart to beat with double force.

He panicked, and lost a breath. Until a few years earlier, he had believed that his heart merely responded to his mind, that it acted in uncomplicated, clockwork response to the sovereign brain. But at times like this he knew the heart dictated sensation and that if the crude, simple pump faltered, Levanter could not make it work properly; his brain could do nothing more than react with intense terror.

He had tried to fashion his existence to accommodate the whims of this organ, as he always accommodated the demands of his flesh. He never went against its rhythms. When his heart was restless, he crowded his schedule with events and people. When his heart was calm, Levanter enjoyed living day by day, unconcerned about either chance or necessity. Rather than perceive

his being in intellectual terms, he chose to call it a play
and display of the heart, after a label he had seen once
on a machine that recorded the echoes of his heart
when he had been tested at a hospital.

As Levanter gazed at the stark, ominous cliffs,
which reminded him of the walls of an ancient castle,
he slowly began to let himself unwind. He noticed a
mist rising above the reaches of the forests, beginning to
settle in one vast, flat shore over the width of the valley.

With a start, he scanned the terrace, afraid that he
might have let his attention wander for too long. Nothing had changed: all the same people were at the tables;
the three men he had come to watch still sat sipping
their white wine. The Deputy Minister of Internal Affairs from the Kingdom of Indostran seemed bored by
his two bodyguard skiing companions and was no
longer talking to them. Levanter had seen the Deputy
Minister look up toward the PicSoleil glacier several
times, monitoring the encroaching mist. He was known
to be an avid skier and was probably anxious to take a
final run before the weather changed. Soon, he leaned
down to buckle his ski boots. The bodyguards gulped
down their wine and, like their boss, attended to their
ski boots. The Deputy Minister summoned the waiter
and paid the check.

At this time of day, most skiers preferred to climb
no higher than the midstation. Levanter had noticed
that nearly all the gondolas of the final fourteen-minute
lift in the PicSoleil system had been departing empty.

The three men rose, zipped up their parkas, pulled
on their hats, and started toward the entrance to the
gondola station. They looked like three pudgy businessmen who had learned to ski late in life. In their country,
skiing had recently become fashionable. Everyone even
distantly attached to the Court traveled to the Alps in
winter. The higher-ups enjoyed the super-chic resorts.
But the Deputy Minister of Internal Affairs was not
liked by the foreign press, which blamed him for mass

arrests, tortures, and deaths, so he skied at the less popular ValPina, where he could remain inconspicuous.

Levanter got up and put on his large-frame sunglasses, drew his ski cap over his forehead, and walked across the terrace to take his skis from the rack. Carrying them in one hand and the poles in the other, he realized again how heavy the skis were, but he was sure no one else had noticed.

The Deputy Minister and his bodyguards passed through the turnstiles, flashing their one-week passes to the sleepy attendant. Levanter went through right behind them, holding his pass in front of his face. The PicSoleil gondolas, brightly painted, modern four-seat cabins, circulated at regular intervals on the steep cable. As one pulled close to the platform, the three men quickly tossed their skis into the outside racks. Levanter managed to slip his skis in too, but as he was about to enter the cabin, one of the bodyguards pushed him aside, as if by accident, and jumped in just as the gondola was moving out of reach. Levanter was not surprised; he knew they would not want a fourth passenger with them.

"Sorry," said the man, shutting the door. "Terribly sorry," he repeated through the half-lowered window as the gondola began its ascent.

"That's all right, no problem!" shouted Levanter cheerfully. "Just unload my skis at the top. I'll take the next gondola up!"

"Very good! Don't worry!" the bodyguard shouted back as the red cabin started to angle upward, its yellow lettering—Glacier PicSoleil Gondola 45— shining in the bright sun.

Waving up at the three passengers, Levanter turned as if to wait for the next gondola, but instead he left the platform through a side turnstile, removing his glasses and hat. He went out of the station and cut across the terrace to the start of the downhill run. He was sure no one had seen him. The Deputy Minister was here incognito, not on an official visit, and therefore no local secret-service agent would have been assigned to cover him. Levanter picked up a pair of skis he had left in another rack that morning and put them on.

He pushed himself off and started to descend. After two minutes, he stopped on a large slope where he had a good view of the gondolas of PicSoleil. In the distance he could see a group of skiers traversing the white plateau. But here he was alone. As he looked up toward PicSoleil, he saw three gondolas, in evenly spaced succession, too far away for him to read their numbers. He unzipped his parka and took out his compact binoculars. Now he was able to make out the lettering and spot Gondola 45, the sun bouncing off its windows, well on its way up.

Soon it would pass over a chasm more than a thousand feet deep. From another pocket Levanter pulled a transmitter and extended its antenna. The transmitter, no bigger than a cigarette pack, operated on two simple alkaline batteries. In a moment of anxiety, it occurred to him that he had forgotten to test the batteries before inserting them that morning.

He reassured himself that even if the equipment failed him this time, he would have a dozen chances to use the skis as he had planned. This was the advantage of being on his own: if the circumstances changed, new opportunities would arise.

As the gondola approached the stretch of cable suspended between the pylons on either side of the chasm, Levanter's thoughts raced to the man in the cabin. He had first heard of the Deputy Minister in the course of his work with Investors International. This was the man who had created the notorious PERSAUD, a special independent branch of the police in charge of Indostran's internal security. Trumped-up charges of "anti-Court activities," both current and retroactive, had been leveled against thousands of teachers, university professors, writers, artists, and enlightened clergy, who were sentenced without trial to spend years in PERSAUD prisons, penal colonies, and work camps. These prisoners, men and women, were not permitted to read or write or to receive letters. They were given no medical attention, and not even their families were allowed to visit them. To extract confessions and denunciations of others, they were beaten with belts with heavy buckles, burned with cigarettes, dragged behind cars and motorcycles, subjected to electric shocks, pushed into pits which they had been forced to dig and which were strewn with splintered glass. During interrogations male prisoners had their testicles prodded with the spiked tails of deep-sea fish; women detainees had their pubic hair singed with cigarette lighters and were then gang-raped. PERSAUD had ordered public executions of several intellectuals; the deaths of many others were never made public.

The previous winter, at an all-night party in a popular Alpine ski resort, Levanter had met several officials from the Court. Free of the religious restraints of the palace, the men were exuberantly dancing and drinking with dozens of beautiful young women. Everyone spoke openly, and it was here that Levanter learned about the Deputy Minister's annual skiing vacations in ValPina. During the party Levanter took several snapshots of the guests, who were delighted to pose for him with their evening's companions on their laps.

At another party a week later, Levanter showed them the contact proofs of the photographs. All the officials were anxious to have enlargements, and one member of the Court's Advisory Council offered to pay Levanter well for all the pictures of himself.

Levanter thought for a moment. "The only payment I want is for you to promise to release the intellectuals jailed by PERSAUD," he said half-jokingly.

"Why such an interest in intellectuals?" the dignitary asked jovially. "I was told you are the head of Investors International. What would an association of investors care about the release of some intellectuals?"

"Intellectuals are our best allies," Levanter explained. "They invest all their energy and resources in ideas that change man's condition. It's a long-range investment, which seldom pays off during their lifetime. That's why we want to support them."

Smiling, the dignitary took Levanter by the arm. "How about a small deal then?" he said softly. "For each color photograph of me with one of these beauties, I will secure the release of one intellectual."

Levanter thought the man was making fun of him. "Release?" he asked in disbelief.

The dignitary nodded, chuckling at Levanter's astonishment.

"But these people have been arrested by PERSAUD as enemies of the Court," Levanter said.

"So they have. But they have no influence. The rich don't fear them, workers mistrust them, peasants don't know about them."

"Yet they've been in prison for months, even years, deprived of contact with their families—"

The dignitary looked at Levanter amused. "What do you expect? Once they're arrested as enemies, they must be treated as such."

Levanter delivered five photographs with a list of prominent intellectuals who were known to have been in PERSAUD prisons and camps. The dignitary put the list aside and eagerly reached for the enlargements.

"What about our deal?" Levanter asked.

"Give me two weeks," the man said, without taking his eyes from the pictures.

In less than a month, five intellectuals were released and two of them who needed medical treatment not available in their country were allowed to immigrate to the United States. One, a middle-aged writer, came to Levanter. He was pale and emaciated; his jaw and nose had been broken.

The writer said he assumed that his sudden freedom was the result of a long campaign carried out on his behalf by writers and editors from P.E.N., members of the International League for Human Rights, Amnesty International, and other such powerful organizations. When Levanter told him what had actually brought about his release, the writer was visibly upset.

"That's humiliating," he said. "I thought that PERSAUD was torturing me for my beliefs, that they believed my ideas would spread to the masses."

"Does it make any difference why PERSAUD tortured you?" asked Levanter.

"It does," he answered. "I saw myself as a political prisoner. I endured my prison ordeal convinced that PERSAUD feared us more than we feared them. If it is true that they persecuted us merely because we are weak, maybe we are too weak to fight them. After all, what can a few intellectuals do? We have no means," he said.

"But we have," said Levanter. "We have the means because we have each other."

"But what can we do together that they will not answer with violence?"

"They use violence anyhow," Levanter insisted. "They need no provocation. Our only hope is to teach them to fear violence by letting them experience it."

The writer was pacing. "I have never been a violent man. I don't believe in violence. Violence does not advance the human condition. Ideas do."

"Ideas don't perish in prison cells," Levanter said. "People do."

Gondola 45 was directly over the chasm. Levanter wondered if the Deputy Minister and his bodyguards were feeling insecure as they looked down from the swaying cabin onto the mountainside of snow and ice opening into a deep pit of rocks and crevasses.

The sound of a faraway jet plane filled the valley, distracting him for a moment.

Levanter envisioned himself in a secret army blockhouse. He scans the panel of the central control unit. Suddenly, a small object appears on the radar scanner. The computerized group-intelligence system promptly identifies the object as enemy combat aircraft armed with long-range missiles, and orders its immediate destruction. The scanner indicates that the object is moving closer. He imagines a sleek vehicle thundering toward him on a mission of destruction, its pilot and crew reading the digits, setting the dials, moving the levers, selecting the final destinations of their missiles. Meanwhile, below, in the cities, towns, and villages designated as targets, unsuspecting men and women go about their lives as usual. The instrument panel indicates that the enemy plane can now be seen with the naked eye. His thumb makes contact with the surface of the missile button and rests there, ready to push. A backup intelligence-verifying computer again prints the order to destroy. There is not much time left.

The sound of the jet closed in above him, bringing him back to the present. His thumb on the transmitter button, Levanter trained his binoculars directly on the gondola and pressed the button.

The impulse from the transmitter spanned the tranquil valley and, faster than thought, reached the receivers of the detonating devices in the ski bindings. The gondola seemed to swell before it burst open. Bits of debris, metal walls, windows, chunks of bodies, and flecks of clothing and skis showered down into the chasm. But the main cable remained intact and the other gondolas hung motionless, their passengers safe. The spectacle was over; it might never have occurred.

Levanter thought of the effort he had expended collecting skis from various manufacturers to find the ones best suited for his purpose. He recalled transforming his apartment into a virtual ski and radio shop, familiarizing himself with transistorized gadgetry, dismantling and reconstructing an exhaustive array of walkietalkies, television and radio remote-control devices, miniature calculators, and Citizens Band radios. He remembered arranging his black-market purchase of the most reliable form of moldable nitroglycerine explosives, buying an amount that was not large enough to attract the notice of any law-enforcement agency but was surely sufficient to blow himself skyhigh. Finally, he recalled the tedious business of splicing open each ski, replacing its fiberglass innards with sandwiched sheets of explosives, installing the detonator and the transistorized receiver inside the bindings, then meticulously resealing both skis. Traveling in the plane with the skis as part of his luggage and claiming them at the airport in Europe—this too had been a worthwhile risk.

He felt his energy, time, and money had been well spent, but at the moment, all he wanted was to descend, to be back in ValPina, to feel the leisurely atmosphere of the resort, to mingle with the tourists crowding the sidewalks and shopping arcades, to watch the steady stream of cars from all over Europe.

He skied down, inspired and elated. He had no further use for his binoculars or the transmitter; he tossed them into a crevasse and heard them rebound against the rocks. He listened to his heart. Its beat was regular.

By the time he heard the first sketchy radio reports about the explosion that killed the Deputy Minister and his two bodyguards, Levanter was already feeling removed from the act, already feeling it was something he had done long ago.

He was elated about having finally helped the execution of justice. He thought of the anger that raged in him each time he read a newspaper account of Stalin's henchmen who lived unscathed in the safety of retirement, fearing nobody but old age. And he thought of the Nazis, how justice had waited a decade before meting out its impersonal revenge.

Dusk fell. He was driving toward Paris alone. His headlights ferreted out sleepy villages tucked in the snow, and he felt secure, snug in a world that allowed one to slide easily between memory and deed.

Shortly after Levanter had established himself in the investment business, he went to Paris to visit a laboratory that was working on new photographic emulsions. He was leaving a shop on the Left Bank one day when a man on a scooter cut ahead of him and stopped at the curb. The man took off his helmet and glanced at Levanter as he walked by. Then he turned and looked again. Levanter couldn't believe what he saw. But there was no mistake. They embraced.

"Rom!" shouted Levanter.

"Lev! I can't believe it," the man exclaimed in Russian. "How can this be?" Romarkin was laughing and weeping. "I heard you were somewhere in America, but I couldn't find out how to reach—"

"What about you?" Levanter interrupted. "I haven't seen you since our Moscow days twenty-five years ago! How did you get here?"

"Let's sit down," said Romarkin, still flushed. They went to the corner café, ordered wine, and toasted each other.

Romarkin opened his collar. "All these years, and you still speak fluent Russian," he said. "You haven't forgotten."

"Never mind that. How did you get here?" Levanter persisted.

Romarkin sipped his wine. "Before I answer," he said haltingly, "tell me something, Lev, and tell me honestly. Did you think, back then, that I was ill? Mentally ill?" Romarkin, suddenly looking anxious and intense, leaned across the table. "Remember, at the university, when I asked that question?"

"Of course I remember. How could I forget?" Levanter said. "But what happened to you after that?"

Romarkin was almost whispering. "I was shipped to Siberia. You know that. Three years of corrective labor. Then I was sent into the army. Luckily, I excelled in gymnastics, so they put me on the track-and-field team. I was good at the high jump. Very good. Last year, when the team visited France for a meet, I made my highest jump ever—right over the Iron Curtain. I asked for political asylum here, and they gave it to me. Since then I've been just another refugee." He took a big gulp of wine. "But I don't want to talk about the present. I have to know. You have to tell me, Lev."

"Tell you what?"

Romarkin tugged on his ear, as he used to do when they were studying together. Then he whispered, "Every morning, for the last twenty-five years, I have asked myself, as a monk asks a merciless God for enlightenment—what possessed me to raise my hand and ask that question about Stalin? Surely thousands of others in that auditorium wondered the same thing. Why was I the only one to ask it? Why?"

Levanter and Romarkin had worked together at the International Youth for Peace Festival, sponsored and organized by the government and the Party. Romarkin, the son of a proletarian family and a good public speaker with an engaging manner and an impeccable academic record, was ideally qualified to run a hospitality program for the several hundred West European intellectuals, artists, and political and union officials invited to the Festival. He promptly made Levanter his second-in-command.

After the opening ceremony, Romarkin and Levanter watched as an air-force marshal was escorted to his limousine. Just as he was about to enter the sedan, a student carrying a large camera with a flash attachment stepped out from behind the police cordon to photograph the marshal. Somehow, as he snapped the picture, the flash bulb shattered with a loud crack. In a blind reflex action, two of the marshal's security guards drew their guns and fired at the photographer. The student fell to the sidewalk. Blood poured from his neck and chest, seeping through his clothes, spattering his camera.

Without glancing at the body, the marshal and his aides jumped into the limousine and sped away. The terrified bystanders dispersed in panic. Security guards wrapped the dead man and the remnants of his camera in a blanket, dumped the body into the trunk of one of their cars, and quickly mopped up the small pool of blood on the pavement. In minutes they had all departed. Only Levanter and Romarkin remained. Levanter was trembling, Romarkin was pale and silent.

The Festival's organizers and the press corps and radio-television crews were given a wing in one of Moscow's largest hotels. Romarkin and Levanter shared an enormous suite on the sixteenth floor.

Early one evening, Romarkin asked Levanter to accompany him on an errand. He dismissed his assigned chauffeur and drove the official car through the poorly lit city streets, stopping in front of a large residential compound that housed several Festival delegations. Romarkin got out of the car and disappeared.

In a few minutes, he returned with a young, pretty Chinese woman. He opened the car door and she climbed into the front seat next to Levanter. Romarkin got behind the wheel again and addressed her in Russian. She smiled but obviously did not understand. Jokingly, Romarkin introduced her as Chairman Mao's Robot. When she heard him say "Chairman Mao" the young woman nodded and smiled again.

As they drove, Romarkin told Levanter that she had become separated from her group for a moment just inside the compound, and he had taken her arm and led her away. No one had seen them. He had quickly shown her his Festival identity card, which verified in six languages, including Chinese, that he was an official. The Robot followed him without any resistance, he said, because, like the rest of her comrades, she had never been taught to reason independently. She and everyone else in her delegation automatically obeyed authority. Romarkin assured Levanter that, as most of the delegates to the Festival were ordered by their superiors to mix with the delegates of other nationalities, the authorities expected some of them not to return to their quarters for the night.

At the hotel, they took an empty service elevator and went nonstop to floor sixteen. As soon as they entered the suite, Romarkin telephoned the hotel manager and told him that certain confidential Festival files were being stored in his suite and hotel personnel were not to enter for the remaining four days of the Festival unless summoned by him or Levanter.

Then, mockingly, Romarkin proposed a series of toasts to Chairman Mao. They all drank several large glasses of plain water in rapid succession. Romarkin and Levanter pretended that the water had made them drunk; the Robot dutifully pretended she was drunk as well. The three of them staggered to a small bedroom, down the short hall from Levanter's room.

Both Levanter and Romarkin started to make love to her, and the Robot did not resist. She seemed resigned, as if they—her superiors—had the right to do this to her, as if she had been transported here from her homeland to do what she was told, and to do it in the spirit of Mao that she had been ordered to promote while abroad. Throughout the night, she continued to submit obediently. No matter whether she was entered hurriedly, stroked harshly, caressed gently, or kissed passionately, passing from one pair of arms to the other, her face never lost its agreeable, complacent expression. She either lacked sensation or suppressed it—they could not tell which.

In the morning, the suite again became a busy Festival office. Phones rang constantly, the calls handled by three secretaries; prominent foreign visitors and officials continually stopped to collect passes for various activities; and in the corridor outside the suite Soviet and foreign reporters milled about, hoping to corner celebrities for interviews.

Romarkin, director of the whole operation, attentive and efficient, handsome in his official Festival suit, a model of the young activist, reigned in the main room. In the adjoining room, Levanter presided, attending to the foreign dignitaries' various needs, which ranged from providing a doctor for an ailing French film star, to sending flowers to a Hungarian soprano, to politely pointing out to the effete Arab poet that if word spread that he had spent the night with two British male delegates his reputation might be hurt.

The Robot remained in the bedroom, free to leave at any time, but apparently incapable of doing so without a command. From time to time, Romarkin casually strolled across the room, walked down the hall, and quietly entered the bedroom. Any office worker would assume that he was leaving through the rear service door to avoid reporters. When Romarkin came out to return to his desk, Levanter took his casual stroll to the bedroom.

What intrigued Romarkin and Levanter most was the Robot's lack of response. As they made love to her, they watched for signs of emotion or hints of feeling. But she was like a person in a trance, her body almost immobile, her face impenetrable. Not once during the days and nights she remained in the bedroom did she indicate that she objected to anything or that she wanted to leave. Always complacent, she ate whatever they brought her.

The last evening of the Festival, they slipped the Robot out of the hotel as inconspicuously as they had brought her in, sat her between them in the car, and drove to the Chinese delegates' compound. Suddenly she began to embrace and kiss both men, clinging to their chests, necks, thighs, crying and sobbing quietly like a hurt and disappointed child. They returned her kisses, tasting the salty tears that poured from the narrow corners of her eyes. Romarkin pulled himself free and stepped out of the car, holding the door open for her. The young woman took this for a command. All at once, she stopped crying and dried her tears. Like a disciplined soldier, she stepped from the car, bowed her head, and, without looking back, walked straight to the main entrance of the compound.

A few weeks after the Festival concluded, the Lomonosov University in Moscow had called a compulsory Party-sponsored meeting for all students as part of a national celebration to mark the publication of Stalin's latest book, a treatise on Marxism and linguistics. Romarkin and Levanter were sitting together near the middle of the university's largest auditorium, filled with thousands of students, professors, Party officials, and security officers. A member of the Central Committee was halfway through a grandiloquent speech, full of praise for Stalin's achievement. Stalin, he declared, had now laid the Party's philosophical foundation for ridding the country of reactionary linguists, who, until they were exposed by Stalin, were posing as true Marxist-Leninists. When the speaker finished his address, he received prolonged applause and a standing ovation.

During the question-and-answer period, carefully planted people in the audience, Party members as well as non-Party members who were considered trustworthy, asked seemingly spontaneous questions that allowed the speaker to restate some of his major arguments.

Levanter was bored. He surveyed the auditorium, trying to find in the sea of faces around him someone who looked as bored as he was. On his right, Romarkin sat looking intently at the officials on the dais.

Suddenly, in the midst of the public tribute to Stalin and to his book, Romarkin raised his hand high above his head. Levanter saw what was happening out of the corner of his eye and could not believe it. For the last three years he and his friend had been virtually inseparable. They shared a dormitory room, studied together, spent vacations together. But now Levanter wondered why Romarkin had not told him that he had been selected to ask a question. Had he surrendered the bonds of their friendship? Had he told Party officials about their escapades? He must have, because here he was, calm and imperturbable, his hand raised high as though in surrender, as rigid as the Robot, patiently waiting to be called on. Levanter panicked. Had the Party found a way to get through to Romarkin—and thus to him as well?

The speaker gestured toward Romarkin. "Yes, young Comrade, tell us what's on your mind. Go ahead!" he urged with exaggerated cordiality. "Speak up."

As Romarkin rose, Levanter sank deeper into his seat.

"I have read with great interest Comrade Stalin's treatise on Marxism and linguistics," Romarkin announced in a loud steady voice. "This very work," he said, "unmasked the ideological errors of our leading linguists, and has led to their expulsion from the Party and from university teaching positions. Yet until Comrade Stalin's book appeared last week, our Party considered these men to be eminent Marxists and authorities in the field of linguistics." He stopped, glanced around, then continued matter-of-factly. "Of course, in no way do I question the wisdom of the Party's decision. But no official biography of Comrade Stalin mentions that he was ever a scholar in the highly specialized field of linguistics. My question is: Would you, Comrade, tell us when and for how long Comrade Stalin studied linguistics?" Romarkin sat down, an engaging smile on his face.

A stillness fell over the audience. Levanter felt thousands of eyes on him and his friend. The speaker said nothing. He did not thank Romarkin for having spoken. He did not even look directly at him.

No one coughed, sneezed, whispered. The whole audience seemed to have kept its attention riveted on the dais; the people on the dais stared fearfully at the speaker.

"This is no time to dwell on what is obvious," he announced anxiously. "If, in his wisdom, Comrade Stalin has chosen to write on the subject of linguistics, he clearly has earned the right to do so. Any other questions?" He looked over the auditorium, shifting his weight from one foot to the other.

The smile still on his face, Romarkin sat bemused. He seemed to be unaware of what he had done. Afraid to think of what had happened, afraid to glance at his friend, Levanter could not move. Romarkin must have lost his mind.

The meeting ended. People rushed to the exits. Levanter was walking beside Romarkin, and everyone else drew away from them. Outside, as he and Romarkin were about to turn into a side street, they were suddenly stopped by a group of KGB agents. Romarkin was taken away in a car and Levanter was escorted back to the dormitory. There, one KGB agent searched their room while another questioned him. Levanter was asked about his family, about Romarkin, and about their mutual friends. He was ordered to identify faces in photographs and names in address books, letters, and lecture notes belonging to both of them. When the questioning was finished, the agent demanded that Levanter sign a statement labeling Romarkin a subversive.

"You're here to help us," the agent lectured Levanter. "But if you refuse to sign, you will rot for years in Siberia—in the dungeons—and you still won't save Romarkin. He was doomed the minute he raised his hand in that auditorium."

Levanter could not take his eyes from the agent's face. "I will never sign such a statement," he said. His own voice came to him as if from behind a thick curtain. "Never. But remember this: one day, in Siberia, I shall voluntarily admit that when I was at the university I was indeed a member of a conspiracy dedicated to wrecking the Party apparatus. I will produce facts and name names. And when I do, you—who will probably be a captain by then—will be accused of failing to obtain important information about the conspiracy from me during this investigation. You will be denounced for negligence. Perhaps even for being sympathetic to our cause."

The agent studied Levanter carefully. In his years of interrogations, he must have looked into the eyes of hundreds of people, tortured to the point of death, who would not break. Perhaps that is why he sensed Levanter's determination not to sign anything. The agent frowned, then tore up the unsigned statement. "You liar," he thundered, stamping toward the door. "If you so much as whisper—" He slammed the door behind him.

After the Romarkin incident, the university decided to put Levanter out of the way for a while. It was thus arranged for him to be drafted into the army for six months' service in a unit wholly composed of delinquent students.

At the camp, Levanter was ordered to report to the correctional unit's new commander, Captain Barbatov. A young sergeant escorted Levanter to the captain's office, announced him, saluted the squat figure behind the huge desk, then turned smartly on his heels and left the room, closing the door behind him. Barbatov did not acknowledge Levanter's presence. He merely opened a folder and began to examine its contents.

Levanter studied the captain, who seemed to be moving his lips slowly as he read. His head drooped over his chest, as if engaged in a losing battle with gravity. Above the right breast pocket of his well-tailored uniform were a row of ribbons and a battered Red Star.

Barbatov closed the file, pushed back his chair, and stood up. As he walked around the desk, Levanter noticed that he wore the high-topped boots and revolver of a cavalry officer, in flamboyant disregard of infantry rules. An army knife with an ornamental handle hung from his belt in paratrooper-commando fashion.

"It says in your dossier, Private Levanter," he said

good-naturedly, "that you were not a bad student and were even one of the organizers of the Youth Festival. But it also says that you befriended some very bad people." His bulging eyes glared at Levanter. "I have no education. I was sent to do combat with the Nazi vipers so that your kind could study in peace." Barbatov spoke with a pronounced lisp and paused often. "That's why your experience from the Festival can be very useful to me," he continued. "That's why I have decided to put you in my office." He sniffed, blew his nose, then leaned back against the wall. He looked at Levanter with a mocking grin.

"I'll be glad to be of service," said Levanter, snapping to attention.

Barbatov handed Levanter a document that had no name filled in but had already been signed by the regimental commander. "Type your name in the blank, and you will become my aide-de-camp," he said. "Keep this paper on you. It's your pass, and it frees you from all field exercises. Report for duty immediately."

Levanter examined the document. He folded it carefully and put it in his pocket.

His first official assignment was to prepare the complete training schedule for the unit, coordinating staff with available equipment and assigning field training areas. To make certain that he was indispensable to Barbatov, Levanter made the schedule in his own secret code and posted a giant visual reproduction of it over one whole wall in Barbatov's office.

The mass of numbers, symbols, and colored cardboard arrows impressed the captain enormously. "They'll never be able to accuse us of revealing our training plans to the enemy!" he exclaimed with pride.

The captain was barely literate. Whenever he had to read a dispatch or memorandum, he read aloud, laboriously sounding each word, syllable by syllable. Yet, Barbatov had an outstanding military record. He had fought throughout World War II and was one of the most decorated national heroes.

Recognizing Levanter's value, Barbatov chose to segregate him from the other inductees, assigning him a comfortable room connected to his own quarters, having his meals delivered from the officers' mess along with Barbatov's, and issuing special permission for him to use the regimental officers' facilities and to witness regimental troop maneuvers.

Levanter soon learned how to space out the paperwork over most of the morning. Toward midday, Barbatov would start drinking his vodka. Alcohol made him drowsy, then irritable, then drowsy again, and by midafternoon he stopped paying attention to what went on in his office.

As the new unit commander, Captain Barbatov was anxious to demonstrate that he could teach discipline and instill fear. Determined that the student inductees be spared no training hardship, he established a daily reprimand quota, requiring that at least three to five soldiers be censured every day.

Late each afternoon, when Barbatov was usually in a stupor, a recruit brought in the sick list and the unit reports. It was Levanter's duty to prepare the master roster of the day's reprimands and praises to be read before the regimental colors were struck that evening. He kept track of all the reprimand sheets so that he could be sure to remove the name of any student for whom further censure could mean transfer to a harsher correctional unit. He managed to fill the quota by inserting names of men who were no longer in the company, or were en route to a new location, or had recently been released from the army. Since Barbatov signed everything without reading it. Levanter's alterations were not discovered.

One day a week, when Barbatov's superior, the regimental commander, was absent from camp, Barbatov would visit the commander's secretary, the only woman on the base. He would stroll into her office and talk about the weather or tell her how pretty she looked that day, meanwhile sidling over to the commander's desk and stealing one or two blank passes, already signed but not yet stamped. Back in his own office, in full view of Levanter, he would slowly and painfully fill in his own name on a pass. Next, he would get a warm hard-boiled egg from the officers' mess, shell it, and roll it over a stamped army document, picking up enough ink from the regimental imprint to transfer the seal onto the blank pass. After dark, he would leave the camp and drive to the neighboring village to round up his peasant cronies for a night of carousing.

The mornings after his drinking bouts, Barbatov usually stumbled back an hour or two before reveille. Later, his eyes glazed from so little sleep, he would stagger into the office and down more vodka straight from the bottle. Sometimes he would sit on Levanter's desk and stare at him for as long as an hour.

"You think I'm an alcoholic numskull, don't you?" he asked one day.

"I think about my work," answered Levanter tonelessly.

"To you I am an uneducated peasant, stupid enough to get himself wounded fighting the Nazis, while you, the intellectual, slept at home."

Levanter looked up from his typewriter. "During the war I was too young to fight the Nazis," he said. "The only reason I'm alive today is that I kept running away from them."

"Running away, running away!" Barbatov shouted. "That's all you Jews did for centuries. Even when the Jews in the ghettos finally rebelled and fought the Nazis, they knew they couldn't win. They fought to bargain. You hear? Always to bargain." Barbatov leaned down, his sweaty forehead nearly touching Levanter's face.

"Those Jews were all slaughtered, Captain," Levanter explained patiently. He resumed his work on the papers in front of him.

"So they were. But even there in those ghettos, they traded, you hear, traded the gas chamber for a bullet, and death by a bullet was for them a better bargain. Again, the Jews got themselves a better bargain!"

Levanter raised his eyes from the lists. "I have to finish my work now, Captain," he said.

Suddenly Barbatov smiled and said in a snide voice, "I should know better than to argue with one like you, Levanter. Forgive an ignorant peasant." Then he went back to his quarters to sleep.

Two months after Levanter was assigned to his office, Captain Barbatov received a special regimental citation for the great improvement he had made in the performance and discipline of the correctional unit and for his precise enforcement of prescribed regulations. Another month passed. As the training program became tougher because of Barbatov's zeal, Levanter worked harder to soften the impact on the recruits, continuing to reduce the number of students reprimanded. But he worked in total secrecy.

Many of the students, jealous of Levanter's easy life and angered by his apparent complicity with the authorities, were hostile to him. They accused him of devising arduous training exercises while he himself did not take part in any of them. They blamed him for the deaths from overexertion of two students and for the unit's inadequate medical care and lack of recreational facilities.

Barbatov knew the students resented Levanter, and as he became more and more dependent on his aide-de-camp, he too became petulant and resentful. Often, when he was drunk, he would threaten to send Levanter back to the tent. Levanter did not take Barbatov's threats seriously; it was obvious to him that the captain could not run the program alone, and that Barbatov knew it.

One morning, Levanter was jolted awake before dawn by the sound of screeching tires. Seconds later, Barbatov barged in, wearing a helmet and a camouflage coat. A submachine gun dangled from his shoulder, and two heavy antitank grenades hung from his belt. Levanter rose from his bed as Barbatov marched around drunkenly, searching the room as if for missing evidence. Suddenly his eye fell on a dirty napkin lying on the floor. With a menacing glint in his eyes, he turned to Levanter.

"What is this? A restaurant? A hotel?" he screamed, gesturing toward the napkin, his face reddening with fury. "Clean up this mess. Now!" he bellowed. Levanter jumped forward and bent down to pick up the napkin, but Barbatov shoved him aside. "Not with your hand! Push it to the wall with your circumcised prick." His words were slurred, his voice thick with vodka. Pretending not to understand, Levanter stood at attention. "I said, clean up this garbage with your stub of a pecker!" Levanter did not move. Barbatov clenched and unclenched his hands. "Refusing to obey an order? Then I want you in full attack gear. On the double!"

Levanter dressed under Barbatov's scrutiny. There was hardly time for him to button his pants or lace his boots. He grabbed his rifle and pack, clipped on the spade, and sprang to attention.

"To the jeep," Barbatov commanded.

When they reached the training range, correctional-unit recruits were scattered all over the pitted terrain. Barbatov ordered all platoons to assemble along the obstacle course for a training demonstration. He shoved Levanter out of the jeep and kept him standing at attention while the troops gathered along the course. Barbatov stood up on his seat in the jeep.

"This is Private Levanter," he shouted into a bullhorn, pointing to the solitary figure. "Like all his people, he got himself a better bargain: he is in charge of planning your exercises, but you have to do them. You see, Levanter thinks he is too smart to do them himself. And because he is so smart," Barbatov said, drawing out the last word, his thick lips in a sneer, "Levanter will show you damn peasants how to do the exercises." He looked down at Levanter and yelled, "Ready?"

Levanter saluted. He made his mind go blank.

"Attack!" screamed Barbatov, jumping out of the jeep. Crouching low, Levanter started to run, rifle in hand. "Machine-gun fire!" barked Barbatov. Levanter somersaulted over the parapet into the wet, freshly turned soil of the nearest trench. His pack and spade slipped off, nearly tripping him, and he barely managed to pick them up before the next command came. "Attack!" Already panting, Levanter clambered over the top of the trench. Just as he had begun to crawl forward, smelling the new grass, he heard Barbatov shout, "Hit the dirt!" and he dropped back down into the mud, which spattered into his eyes and clung to his mouth. The rough strap of his new helmet cut into his chin, and he could feel his coat ripping. Barbatov ran alongside. "Tanks. Dig in!" Levanter pulled out his spade, but the blade was locked. The students lining the course hooted raucously, shouting insulting words of advice. Levanter began scooping up the lumpy soil with his hands. Again Barbatov screamed, "Attack!" Levanter staggered to his feet. He was covered with mud and dirt and was having trouble breathing as his throat filled with phlegm and pain seared his chest. He tried to hurdle a trench but missed and fell into the crater. He scrambled out and rolled over into the next one. His head was bleeding now, and as he plunged up against the breastwork his vision blurred. He was attempting to leap over another trench when his legs gave way and he pitched headfirst into the hole.

He came to slowly. In the distance he could hear the platoons marching away, the footsteps receding, the singing growing fainter. Filthy and aching all over, he found he was lying on Barbatov's coat. The captain knelt at his side, pouring coffee from a tin mug over his face, then wiping the mud off his forehead and cheeks with a handkerchief.

"There you are, silly boy," he muttered, his face creased with worry. "All brains but no muscle!" He grinned and urged Levanter to his feet, steering him toward the jeep. As he drove, he kept glancing apologetically at his passenger. In the barracks, he helped Levanter remove his gear. Then he went to his quarters and returned with several bottles of his best beer.

One evening the following week, Barbatov completed the counterfeiting of a pass, winked at Levanter, and drove off to the village. At midnight, Levanter went into the captain's room. As usual, Barbatov had not taken his service revolver or his Party card, and he had also left behind the large map of the forthcoming divisional maneuvers, marked SECRET.

Levanter rolled up the black window shade. To attract the military police, he turned on the light. In minutes, a jeep pulled up in front of the barracks, and two MPs dashed inside the quarters, calling Barbatov's name. Levanter showed them his papers and, with a straight face, explained that Captain Barbatov had gone into town for the evening. One of the MPs immediately phoned regimental headquarters and was informed that Barbatov had no authorization to leave the camp. The MPs confiscated the captain's revolver, his Party card, the divisional maneuvers map, and several blank passes they found. Then they locked and taped the door and left without another word.

The next morning Levanter was notified that Captain Barbatov was no longer in command of the correctional unit. Levanter was to assume the regular duties of a private. When he moved his gear to a tent, the other soldiers greeted him with contempt and ridicule, snickering at him because his protector had been caught reentering camp drunk, carrying a false pass, and was to be court-martialed.

Later that same day, a sergeant entered the tent, called Levanter's name, and ordered him to collect his gear. Levanter was sure his falsification of the rosters had been discovered and he was about to be arrested. Instead, he was driven to Barbatov's barracks and ordered to report inside.

A slender man stood looking out the window. Levanter announced his presence, and the officer turned to face him. He was a middle-aged major wearing a rumpled uniform. He acknowledged Levanter's salute with a curt nod; no expression showed on his lined face.

"I can't find any correctional-unit training-program files or codes—only this cabalistic chart," he said, gesturing toward the wall. "I am told that you worked closely with my predecessor, Captain Barbatov."

"I did, Major," replied Levanter. The officer waited. Levanter said no more.

"The program must go on," the major said. "You will provide me with the same assistance that you gave Captain Barbatov. Understand?"

"Yes, sir!" Levanter responded. "I will need a specific authorization assigning me to your service."

The major handed him a typewritten document. "I happen to have a blank transfer authorization, Private Levanter. It has already been signed by the regimental commander. You need only type your name in the empty space."

Levanter knew he had to leave the East, but he knew also that he would need a profession that could support him in the West, a profession with a universal language. While he was finishing at the university after his army service, Levanter enrolled in night courses at a school of photography. Before long, he had built his own darkroom and chemical laboratory.

In addition to his classes and darkroom work, he

spent hours every week in the school's library examining the catalogues and magazines that described advancements in photographic art and reproduced the work of well-known photographers. Levanter soon learned that photography by its very nature depended on imitating reality in an imaginative, subjective way, but that usually a photographer's technical style could easily be reproduced.

To counteract imitations of his artistic methods, Levanter began to evolve his own techniques and a style that could not be readily copied. He used a camera adapted to his experiments, and films and papers coated with either existing emulsions that he modified or emulsions he made himself.

Less than two years after he began the course, he was invited to exhibit his work at national and international salons of photography. His photographs were reproduced in art publications, won prizes and awards, and a one-man exhibit of his photographs was organized in the capital. He received offers to work for domestic and foreign manufacturers of photographic products and was invited to exhibit his photographs and to lecture abroad by several Western art societies. Convinced that his work would be the finest form of advertising for the export of domestic photographic products, the authorities granted Levanter a short-term passport for his trip to the West.

During his last week in the Soviet Union, he walked through fields in the farthest suburb of Moscow and noticed remnants of the frail fence that had surrounded the tents of the traveling state circus. Now, in winter, the circus was gone, and the fence and field were abandoned.

It was snowing. The whirling powder had whitewashed the outlines of the railing. Between flurries, the fence looked like a good subject for a black-and-white photograph. Around him, the air was growing blustery; the winds seemed to have chosen the field as their arena, tumbling over each other, raising clouds of snow and puffing them away. He had difficulty holding the camera steady.

A passer-by, hugging his coat, made his way along the wooden railing, which wound through the field like a frozen snake. Before the man vanished in the white squall, Levanter took the picture.

The cold and wind bit into him. Levanter thought that if he died here, his frostbitten body would not be discovered until spring came and the snows melted.

From far away came the sound of a motorcycle plowing through the drifts. Soon a burly state militia officer arrived, stopping his bike next to Levanter. The officer turned off the engine and removed his goggles.

"Your papers, please," he said in an even voice.

"What have I done?" asked Levanter.

The officer looked from Levanter's face to his camera. "A man just reported that he saw someone taking pictures of this field. Is that you?"

Levanter nodded.

"Then your papers, please." The officer extended his thickly gloved hand.

Without a word, Levanter took off his glove and reached under his coat. After a moment of digging through layers of sweaters, he produced his student I.D. card.

The officer glanced at the card, then silently put it in a leather bag hanging from his shoulder. He jerked his chin at Levanter's camera. "Open your camera, Comrade, and expose the film," he said.

"But why?" asked Levanter.

"Because of what you photographed," answered the officer patiently.

"I photographed this field," Levanter said, "the fence that crosses it, and an old man who walked past."

"What else?"

"What else is there, Comrade?" said Levanter. "There is nothing else. Here, take my camera. Whatever you see through the viewer is what I saw." He held out his camera, but the officer pushed it back to him.

"You are here, on one of the coldest days of the year, in the middle of a storm, just to take pictures of an empty field, a broken fence, and some old man passing by."

"I am!"

"That's a lie!" said the officer.

"It's the truth!" said Levanter.

"Tell the truth, or I'll arrest you!"

Levanter tried to sound patient. "I took a picture of an old man against the fence and the fence against the field. That's all."

The officer became very angry. "I won't listen to such crap anymore," he said. "I know you photographed this field." He paused. "But we both know that such a field, any field, could serve as a landing site—" He paused again, this time apparently for effect. "A landing site for, let's say, invading paratroopers. Is that what you photographed? Would a Soviet judge believe that you did not? Now, no more trickery. Take out the film!"

Levanter obeyed. Sheltering his camera from the snow with his coat, he opened it, pulling the entire roll off its spool and exposing it to the light. The corkscrew of film dangled from his hand. He let it go; in an instant it was carried off by the wind and disappeared in the snow.

Levanter returned to the field the following day. It was gray and cold. A man dragged himself along the fence, clutching his coat and, every few steps, tugging his hat lower. Seen through the viewfinder, the man's figure, the fence, and the field already appeared as a finished photo. Levanter took the picture.

As a student, shortly before he left Moscow for America, Levanter had gone to a private screening of two prewar Soviet films starring a lovely young actress. She was so beautiful that Levanter went to considerable trouble to find her. He eventually learned that the actress and her much older husband had escaped during the German occupation of Russia. Now, in New York, he was finally able to trace her through a Russian cultural foundation.

As soon as he located the number, Levanter telephoned and told the actress how impressed he had been by her films. He implored her to see him and was thrilled when she agreed.

They met several times for lunch or drinks or a stroll in the park. She was in her forties; over two decades had passed since he had seen her films, but he still found her breathtaking. Levanter was so inhibited by her grace and sexual appeal that he was unable to steer their relationship in any direction; he merely listened as she spoke her perfectly enunciated Russian. She recounted the episodes of her life, told him about her movie career and how it was abruptly curtailed by the war. She explained that she had never made another film and, ever since she had been in exile, first in France and then in America, she had worked as a model, often for low pay, to try to support her husband, whose deteriorating health had made him unemployable and now kept him housebound.

Walking beside her, Levanter fantasized their being together in his apartment. He is crouching before her. Slowly, he is lifting her skirt, gently separating her legs, and then licking her flesh through her underwear until she squirms. He starts to pull down her panties and, with his mouth upon her flesh, guides her toward the bed. Suddenly, in his fantasy, he hears the actress murmuring, "Tell me, what shall I do for you?"

But here his passion ran into an obstacle: the Russian language. Could Onegin possibly tell Tatyana that he wanted to eat her? Would Vronsky say to Anna Karenina, "I want you to suck me"? Could Levanter speak such thoughts in the language of Turgenev and Pasternak to this dignified, educated woman? He could not. In Russian, the language of his childhood and adolescence, he regressed to memories of parents and schoolteachers, to early emotions of shame, fear, and guilt. Only in English could he name the nature of his desires; his new language was the idiom of his manhood.

"You don't mind speaking Russian with me?" asked the actress as they walked through the park.

"Not at all," Levanter answered, glancing at the outlines of her thighs. "You speak it so melodiously." He raised his eyes to her breasts.

"My English is so crude, so imprecise," she said apologetically.

They walked in silence. Then, in a burst of courage that startled even him, Levanter invited her to his apartment.

"What for?"

Levanter caught his breath. "I have a collection of photographs I took in Russia," he said. "They're all mounted—too big and heavy to carry around. But I am certain you would appreciate them."

At the apartment, the actress sat on the narrow

convertible sofa. He perched on a chair facing her. On the floor between them lay the stack of photographs. Levanter handed them to her, one at a time. The actress studied each picture, occasionally asking him when and where it was taken, and then placed it on the cushion beside her, the growing pile diminishing Levanter's chances of casually sliding next to her.

He grew tense and uneasy, aware of every move he made. He couldn't figure out what to do. The convertible sofa was the only bed in his small apartment. Should he go over and take the pile of photographs away? Could he then ask the actress to stand up so he could remove the cushion she sat on, pull the handle to unfold the mattress, take out the pillows and blankets from under the backrest—and all for the purpose of performing an act that thus far had not even been named?

Levanter imagined himself nonchalantly approaching the sofa, leaning against it, just inches from the actress, and saying, "Why don't you get up for a moment." She turns to him, an inquiring look on her face. Then she smiles politely and says, "No thank you. I'm quite comfortable here."

Then what? He knew he could no more say simply, "I want to turn this sofa into a bed; I want to make love to you" than he could tell her what kind of love he wanted from her.

The more he searched for the appropriate Russian words and phrases, the more apprehensive he became. The mother tongue had turned into an uninvited chaperone, guarding his passion from getting out of hand. Yet he almost laughed out loud when he remembered that the word for convertible sofa in his native language was *"Amerykanka"*—translation: "American woman."

They sat quietly, from time to time glancing at each other, the actress snuggled in the corner of the couch, Levanter stiff and pensive on his chair. The actress was barricaded by the stack of photographs which she went through for a second time. She gave the last

one a long, attentive look. Then she got up. It was time
to go. Levanter helped her with her coat and, inhaling
her perfume, escorted her to the door. They exchanged
the banalities of a polite good-by. As she walked down
the stairs, he caught a glimpse of her hips. In a minute,
she was gone. He felt like a schoolboy who had pa-
thetically failed his first blind date.

It was when he was fifteen. Excellence in many
cultural and athletic activities of the Youth Movement
over two years had earned him a gold medal, an award
that entitled him to a full, state-paid summer vacation at
a Youth Movement camp.

Located deep in the country on the bank of a river
and surrounded by dense forest, the camp gave teen-
agers a respite from the cities so recently ravaged by
war. As he was boarding the train, Levanter's suitcase
fell onto the tracks and sprang open. Seized by embarrassment and terrified that the train was about to depart, he hesitated about trying to retrieve any of his belongings. Unexpectedly, one of the boys from the YM
contingent lowered himself under the train and, picking
up the suitcase, threw it and most of its contents to Levanter. The boy barely managed to crawl out and climb
back into the carriage before the train jerked and
started to move.

During the five-hour journey, Levanter and Oscar,
the boy who had rescued his things, became friends. Oscar was a year older than Levanter and about four
inches taller. If Levanter could have magically changed
his appearance, he would have wanted to look exactly
like Oscar: sandy hair, pale blue eyes, chiseled features.
He was pleased that he was assigned to the same
twenty-bed bunkhouse as his new friend.

The YM camp, one of the largest in the country,
accommodated over two thousand boys, with several

hundred teen-age girls at the adjacent girls' camp. The two camps shared the river front and often held joint events.

One day Levanter and Oscar strolled past a tall, good-looking girl with blond hair pulled back in a single braid. Oscar remarked that she could be an ideal blind date, and if he encountered her walking alone in the city at night, he would break her eye. Breaking the eye was what he called rape, he explained. Noting Levanter's surprise, he admitted that he had been raping girls and women for three or four years, and by now had raped several dozen. Twice within the past year he had been picked up by police as a rape suspect but was released both times because the victims could not identify him positively. He had worked out a fail-safe way to break the eye, he said, and credited himself with inventing a hold to keep the victim at his mercy: the twist, he dubbed it. Thanks to the twist, not one of his victims had ever managed to see his face—that was why he called them blind dates.

Along with these bits of terminology, Oscar had developed a whole sex vocabulary. A female's head was a melon, her mouth a lock, hands were grabbers, the back a sun deck, breasts points, nipples contacts, and her belly a plate; her legs were sticks, the groin the cut, and her buttocks pillows, divided by the narrows.

First he would grip her hair from behind, so she couldn't turn around, and trip her. Then, with his fingers, he would squeeze and turn the contacts and pull on them; when she seemed unable to withstand the pain anymore, he would release the contacts but almost simultaneously enter her cut. At this point, she would usually submit without further resistance.

Oscar had also worked out a certain philosophy: sex was a spring that nature kept permanently wound, and man's obligation to himself was to unwind it as often as possible. Rape was a mere short cut to the unwinding; it was also a sport that required expertise.

Since the sex act required physical arousal of the male, and not of the female, nature had arranged for males to break the eye of females.

Levanter asked Oscar to show him some of his eye-breaking tricks when they were alone in their bunkhouse. Oscar told him to cross the room. Levanter got up from his bed and started walking. Suddenly a strong hand gripped the back of his hair, immobilizing his head; a knee pressed into his back. In an instant, he was tripped onto the floor, face down; in another instant, Oscar wedged himself between Levanter's legs. A flattened frog, unable to move, Levanter was helpless.

"That's the twist," Oscar announced with pride.

Oscar showed Levanter a diary he had kept of his past blind dates. For each encounter, he had noted the victim's characteristics, the place where he had first seen her, where he had attacked her, whether she was a virgin, and where he had finally left her. And he kept a list of prospective blind dates, two or three likely candidates, whose schedules and whereabouts he had already established. He was also an expert on the natural environment: he knew the best places to accost a female, where to drag her, where to play with her, and how to get away after he was finished with her. He talked about rape with the ease of a barber describing how to give a good haircut.

Often, Oscar said, he could assess the nature of a blind date by the way she carried herself on the street—he could guess whether she was timid and fearful, hysterical and resistant, strong-willed or submissive, and he would restrain her accordingly.

If he had to stifle her screams, he explained, he would hold her lock until she lost her breath; if he needed to immobilize her, he would penetrate the narrows instead of the cut and keep her pinned down; when he required a longer time for his arousal and climax, or if she seemed too powerful or too resistant, he would tie her grabbers behind her back, bind her sticks, and stuff a handkerchief in her lock.

Oscar admitted that there was one disadvantage to his method: he took all his blind dates from behind. As he was unwilling to risk being identified, he had never kissed one on the lock and could enjoy their faces only when stalking them, only from afar. Even if he succeeded in blindfolding one, he said, he would still be afraid to kiss her on the lock for fear of being bitten on the lip or cheek and, thus branded, being recognizable to the police. Furthermore, in one of his recurring dreams, he confessed, he was giving a blind date a deep kiss, his tongue flicking back and forth inside her lock, when she suddenly clamped her teeth down and, like an epileptic having a fit, bit off his tongue, spitting the spongy scrap straight into his face. Blood gushed from his mouth and he could see the severed tongue tumbling down his chest. Thanks to this dream, he said, he had perfected the twist.

To notice a blind date, to follow her unseen, nurturing his thoughts of what he would do with her, teasing his desire as if it were a dog about to be unleashed, then, in one spontaneous moment, to break her eye— this was for Oscar the essence of his blind dating. And blind dating—along with other occasional acts of daring, like crawling under a train seconds before it started moving—was all that interested him in life.

At coeducational events, Oscar would point out a girl he found attractive. The girl, responding to what she took for a sign of his interest, would smile at him and he would smile back at her as if he were simply too shy to approach her. In a low voice, he pondered the girl's reaction when, in the woods or on a street, behind a bench in the park or in a niche in a basement, he would trap her and command her to obey him. He described in great detail what he would do to her when he had ripped her clothes off and subdued her again and again, until he was exhausted.

At first Levanter had listened to Oscar with mixed fear and curiosity, eager to know more about his friend's adventures. But after a while, when Oscar went into his erotic speculations, Levanter grew sexually aroused, always thinking of the blond girl with the long braid.

As Levanter and Oscar were seen together more and more often, one of the counselors who knew Levanter from the city and was particularly fond of him warned him about Oscar. Oscar's YM membership had been suspended twice for misconduct, the counselor said; he had been in trouble with the law, and he was known to be emotionally unstable. Levanter listened attentively, agreed to be less dependent on his friend, but immediately put the whole conversation out of his mind, and went right back to Oscar and their imagined blind dating.

Oscar told Levanter that he had found a short cut through the forest to the girls' camp and that it was an ideal place for blind dating. The forest was dark, the foliage above would mute any screams, and the mosses underfoot offered nice soft padding. He could stalk his blind date even before twilight, safely break her eye, and return to camp unnoticed in time for supper.

Once the two boys bicycled along the short cut. Oscar stopped midway and they dragged their bikes out of view and hid in the underbrush. From behind the dense bushes, they watched an occasional camper go by. When they saw a girl, Oscar started to outline how he would reach for her hair, shove her into the woods, and force her to kneel. He would tear off her clothes, then grasp her pillows, and for a moment hold her, all tense, with his groin pressed hard against her until she began to writhe and thrash under him, and then he would spread her apart even more and pump into her with all his force, one hand over her lock, smothering her scream, the other holding her sun deck as she bucked back and forth, in pain and fear.

Levanter was captivated. What his friend envisaged was to him an adventure, a thrilling game of hide-and-seek. The girl would be hurt, but Levanter tended to agree with Oscar, considering the bruises and scratches of the forced entry as the only sources of her pain. He rationalized that a virgin making love for the first time, even willingly, had to suffer some pain. Defloration was an act of violence. Thus, he reasoned, it approximated rape. He argued with himself that, in the manner of an ordinary virgin being deflowered, the blind date would not be visibly crippled or mutilated and might even become aroused.

The distance between talking about a rape and actually performing one still seemed enormous to Levanter. He argued with Oscar that, unlike a city, a vacation camp could not assure one of anonymity. But Oscar dismissed his caution as naive. Fear is the same everywhere, he said, and everyone is blinded with panic when jumped from behind, no matter where, no matter when.

Oscar stopped taking Levanter to the path. Levanter began to suspect that Oscar was annoyed by his apprehension and didn't want him around anymore.

One morning, browsing in the sports shop that serviced the two camps, Levanter saw the blond girl with the long braid. He was too shy to approach her, even to attempt to strike up a conversation; all the chats he had rehearsed in his mind became useless the moment he was near her. Carefully Levanter edged to the counter. He heard a salesman tell her to return at five o'clock to collect the table-tennis nets that she had brought in for repair. The girl left the shop. Levanter followed her discreetly until she entered the forest short cut. Suddenly, he knew what he was going to do.

After lunch, Levanter feigned a headache and was sent to his bunk. He remained there, under the covers, eyes closed, until the last of the boys had come in to change for the afternoon swim. Then he slipped out through the rear exit and picked up a bike left there by a counselor who had gone to town and was not expected to return until the next day. Levanter pedaled around the camp and soon was in the forest.

Halfway through the short cut, he veered into the bushes and stopped. He hid the bike near the place Oscar had evaluated as the best spot for a blind date and sat behind the large bush, waiting. He checked his watch: four-thirty.

It was quiet in the forest. The sun had barely begun to set. It still brightened the highest trees, keeping the birds away, but below, where Levanter waited, twilight descended.

A uniformed YM janitor pedaled his bike along the path. He puffed and panted, trying to ride over the roots that swelled out from little patches of sand or moss. Finally, he disappeared from sight. Levanter found himself almost hoping the girl would not show up.

Then he saw her. She walked fast, with a firm stride, as if training for a parade. Her long single braid swayed from side to side.

He felt neutral, neither aroused nor afraid. He expected his body to act when the time came but could not think about it now. The braid was all he concentrated on. The girl was a few feet away. She passed the mark he had fixed for striking.

As he was about to sprint toward her, he remembered another of Oscar's rules: once you start running toward your blind date, run as fast as you can; the sooner you grip her, the smaller the chance that she will have time to hear your footsteps and turn around to see you. To the police, once you grip her she has been assaulted, so you might as well continue and make the best of it.

He started to his feet, then lunged forward. In an instant he had the braid and, using all his strength, held the girl's head from moving. She screamed, but when he put his other arm around her neck and tightened it as a threat that he could choke her, her voice faded completely. His arm tilting her head up to the sky, his knee pushing into her thighs, Levanter steered her off the path and into the bushes. Only when he had her behind the thicket, safely away from the path, did he catch his breath. The girl was pleading with him to let her go. Terrified that she detected a weakness in him, Levanter panicked and shook her by the hair. She stopped begging and sobbed quietly. Levanter looked down at her slender neck, then lower, at her back, where her dress was soaked with perspiration.

Slowly he removed his arm from under her chin while increasing the pull on the braid. The girl made no sound. Then, with his free hand he ripped her dress and, as she began to moan and whine, he pulled her panties down around her feet. Following Oscar's lessons, he tripped her, and, as she stumbled, he kicked her panties aside and guided her body by the braid, lowering her to the ground. Completing the twist, he fell upon her. She was now immobilized, her face pushed into the leaves and moss, her breath coming in staccato gulps. With one hand, Levanter pulled down his pants and placed himself between her legs. When he felt his flesh against hers, he slid his hand beneath the torn dress, found her breast, and began pinching the nipple. He licked her neck, his tongue gathering the droplets of sweat that surfaced like sap on her skin.

He was becoming aroused. He reassured himself that as long as he maintained his grip on her there was no danger she would ever know who he was. He was safe. Dusk continued to fall. In the dense bushes of the hollow, he was as safe as the little lizards that had scurried away when he pushed the girl through the thicket.

He began to think about her. He recalled how she had stood in the shop, smiling, talking, glancing around, unaware of what she meant to him. And he remembered seeing her once on the riverbank, with a tall, handsome boy, a YM swimming champion; every time the boy had inclined his head toward her, her face had lit up with such admiration and joy that Levanter had been filled with envy and had to look away. If she were a thing, he thought, one day he could own her.

He began to think about her body as he had thought of her all those times; he could remember the filtered rays of sun upon her corn-silk hair. The images seemed remote, yet the girl was now under him. He was preparing to sink into her with all the force of nature's spring unwinding.

He was fully aroused. Gently, he kissed her neck. Listening to her sobs, he moved his hand down, stroking her, pushing aside the moss and leaves that stuck to her. Her body eased a bit, and when he detected that, in one smooth motion he planted his flesh in her, guiding it with his hand until it was firmly in place, deep and hard, breaking through a delicate inner barrier that seemed no thicker than a leaf. She screamed, and he thought that, without having spoken a single word to her, he had just become her first lover. The thought quickened his movement. She tensed and lay whimpering. He did not want to rush, reminding himself that as long as he was behind and inside her, pinning her down with his weight, she could not see him, and he could do as he wished for as long as he wished. But, like bark pried off a tree, his thought separated from his body; and he stiffened, ready to scream, his hand pulling her hair harder, almost against his own will. Then, his entire body seemed to let go, suddenly free of the inner pull. He collapsed, but the physical release did not bring about the release of his need. He became conscious of time and glanced at his watch: only a few minutes had passed. The girl moaned under him. He became tender, kissing the soft skin on the nape of her neck, sniffing its fluffy hair, tasting the salty sweat, his fingers lightly stroking her temples. He rested.

Then a wave of excitement came again. He felt more in command this time, less at the mercy of his flesh. She seemed to sense that her attacker was not through with her and began pleading with him to let her go. He pushed her face deeper into the earth, and when she gasped and coughed, he entered her again, more forcefully, changing the angle of pressure, feeling her resistance and steadily breaking it. When, at one moment, she tensed and he slipped out, she started to thrash. He grew impatient and angry; he spread her flat. She let out a high-pitched scream and strained to pull away from him. He remembered another of Oscar's lessons; he slowly moved his legs, first one, then the other, until they were over her shoulders and he was sitting upon her with all his weight. As his feet forced her face harder into the ground, he thrust into her once more, but not where he had entered her the first time; her moans turned into a piercing shriek. There was something unnatural about the sound. He imagined an inner spring had snapped inside her, and even though he thought of withdrawing, he once more succumbed to his own need. His body grew taut and he pushed into her with all his might, no longer able to withdraw. He felt his neck tensing, his fingers involuntarily digging into her skin. Soon it was over; he was drained.

As she moaned, her body splayed under him like a grotesque puppet with its limbs dangling; all he wanted was to see her face. Her body alone could not tell him what he wanted to know. Only on her face would he be able to read what she felt.

Both his body and his mind were empty. Slowly he lifted himself from her, reflecting that his blind date was not over yet. He kept her pinned down with one hand, and with the other used her torn dress to wipe the blood off his groin, thighs, and hands. He stuffed the panties into her mouth, then ripped strips of fabric from her dress and bound them loosely around her feet and hands so it would take her some time to get free. He remembered to tie one strip over her eyes so she could not see him as he left.

He was finished now and ready to get away. It was almost dark and he was not afraid. He dressed slowly, as if to convince himself that he was in no danger, then jumped onto the bike and rode back toward camp, ready to slip into the bushes if anyone approached from the opposite direction. He replaced the bike and quickly entered the bunkhouse through the back door. No one was there. He crawled into his bed and pretended to be asleep. The smell of her lingered on his hand. His memory randomly protracted or compressed images of her in the forest; he was astonished that he could recall so much without having made any effort to remember.

Soon the other boys returned. He opened his eyes and told him his headache was almost gone. He took a shower, but even when he was dry, the scent of her flesh persisted on his body.

Oscar came in. Levanter was at first tempted to tell his friend about his blind date. But he was feeling possessive about the girl and didn't want to share the details of his encounter with her. Instead, Levanter complained about his headache and the lost afternoon.

In the middle of the night, everyone in the bunkhouse was awakened by a sudden commotion. All the lights were turned on and, as Levanter and the other boys watched, two uniformed policemen, accompanied by the camp director and two camp counselors, marched in and took Oscar and all his belongings away with them. The lights were turned off, but Levanter could not sleep.

Even before morning roll call, the whole camp seemed to have heard of Oscar's arrest. As Levanter was known to be Oscar's closest friend, he was besieged with questions. Levanter shrugged and said that he too was astonished by the arrest.

After the routine morning ceremonies, the camp director, looking quite angry, addressed the two thousand boys lined up before him. He announced in a stern voice that the previous afternoon a vicious sexual attack on a girl camper had been committed and that police authorities had already arrested the perpetrator. It was a boy who had confessed to similar crimes in the past: Oscar.

Levanter felt overcome by a horror he had never experienced before. He realized for the first time how irreversible was the process that had already claimed the girl and Oscar. He stood paralyzed by panic. He knew only one way to end it.

The director had finished and was ready to give the signal to dismiss the campers. Levanter stepped out of line.

"Sir," he called. He felt his knees begin to buckle under him and summoned all his strength to stand straight, before the whole camp. In the past, he had been called forward to receive praise. Now he was stepping forth to turn himself in.

He felt numb again, as he had before he sprang upon his blind date. He could no more step back into line than he could undo the rape. He waited.

The director recognized him instantly. "There is Levanter, our gold medalist," he announced, his voice turning cheerful. "What is it, my friend?"

Levanter's mouth was dry. His tongue moved sluggishly as he started to speak. "I raped that girl, Oscar didn't," he heard his own voice say. "I did it alone."

A frightful silence fell. Levanter heard the wind snap the flag around his pole.

The director looked at him baffled. "We appreciate your motive for making this statement, Levanter, because we know Oscar has been your friend," he said firmly. "But we know Oscar is the only culprit." He was about to end the roll call.

"As I'm making this statement officially, sir," Levanter interrupted, his voice now clear, "I insist that my admission be formally entered in the record of the investigation."

"Let it be in the record, then," the director said indulgently. "Come to my office in an hour."

After roll call, the boys surrounded Levanter.

"You couldn't have raped her," said one of Levanter's bunkhouse mates. "You were sick and slept the whole afternoon. I saw you!" he exclaimed. "We all saw you in bed," added another, and two or three nodded in agreement. "Maybe you dreamed about raping a girl," said one boy, and others laughed. "There's not much any of us can do for Oscar now," one of them said with a snicker.

Levanter did not know what to say. "What if you're all wrong?" he finally asked. "What if I did do it?"

"But I saw you sleeping" another boy yelled. "And I saw you going to the shower after you woke up, just before supper," shouted another.

At the director's office, he was introduced to a young police lieutenant, who patted Levanter on the shoulder and directed him to a chair.

"There's no use, Levanter, no use at all in what you're trying to do," he said. "When the local police summoned us last night, we already had our suspicions. Then, early this morning, faced with the evidence, your friend Oscar admitted that he has raped many girls before, though, for some reason, he still denies that he raped this one." He paused and looked hard at Levanter. "Could it be, Levanter, that he asked you in advance to take the blame for it?"

Levanter did not respond.

The lieutenant continued in an even voice. "What's more, we found his diary, in which he describes, in his own handwriting, dozens of his past assaults. These rapes match the police files. What more can we ask for?"

The director handed the lieutenant a sheet with Levanter's statement. The lieutenant glanced at it, then, to indicate that he refused to accept it, gently pushed it across the table to Levanter.

"Oscar might have raped other girls," said Levanter. "But I raped the one yesterday. I can identify the girl and the exact spot where I did it."

The lieutenant appraised him thoughtfully. "Of course you can," he said. "Oscar might have pointed her out to you. He might even have showed you his raping grounds."

"I can provide all the details of how I did it," said Levanter insistently. "I can show you exactly what I did to make this girl—"

"Of course you can," the lieutenant cut him off softly. "But you don't have to. You see—" He paused. "We know all this already. There's no doubt that the poor girl who was raped yesterday was attacked by the same man who raped a dozen others in our town. In each case he used the same tricks—grabbing the victim's hair from behind and wounding her in the same perverted way." The lieutenant spoke in an even, controlled voice.

Levanter leaned on his hand and breathed in the girl's scent that still lingered under his nails. "But I can give you a precise recollection of what went on in the forest," he argued. "Minute by minute. Where I stopped her, how I shoved her. What and how I touched. I can tell it all, and you can ask her to verify my account."

The lieutenant gave him another thoughtful look. "Let's leave this girl alone, Levanter. She's suffered enough; she's still in the hospital and, as a friend of the man who raped her, you're the last person in the world she would want to hear from." He looked at the director. "They say she's going to need surgery, you know," the lieutenant said quietly.

The director nodded. "I'm sure Levanter realizes that his claim, however honorable his motives, is an attempt to obstruct justice," he said. Without allowing Levanter to say anything further, he got up. The lieutenant and Levanter followed. The director took Levanter by the arm and gently led him to the door. He embraced him at the threshold. "You're a good man, Levanter, a good YM medalist, too. But there's a limit to friendship. I'm glad you won't be seeing Oscar for a while. He's going to get at least three years for this case alone."

The following spring, Levanter attended his school's annual citywide dance. Each time the band took a break, Levanter and his friends gathered in a knot. One time, a group of students from another high school joined them, and introductions started. When Levanter turned to one pleasant-looking girl and said his name, another girl, a tall blonde with short hair, who had been looking the other way, wheeled around, quickly, as if startled. Levanter looked at her. For a moment he had the feeling he had seen her before, but he couldn't place her.

As the others paired off to dance, the blond girl spoke to him.

"So you are George Levanter?" she said, looking at him curiously.

"Sorry to disappoint you," Levanter joked. "Yes, I am."

They started to walk away from the dance floor. As they moved toward the side door of the gymnasium, he could hear the tapping of her high-heeled shoes on the polished floor.

"I was told you were a friend of someone I met once," she said.

"Someone you met once?"

"Someone I met only once," she corrected.

"Who is it?"

They had left the gymnasium and began to walk more slowly in the corridor outside. It was empty, lit only by a few bare bulbs.

"A boy." She said it without feeling.

"And you say he was my friend?"

"I said you were a friend of his, not the other way around."

Levanter was confused. "What's his name?"

They reached the end of the corridor and stood next to the large window, looking out at the schoolyard. A solitary lamp lit the basketball backboard; the net swung in the breeze.

"Will you promise never to repeat what I'm about to tell you?" she asked. She turned around and leaned back against the window, facing Levanter.

"I promise," said Levanter. He could barely see her features.

"The boy's name was Oscar. He raped me last summer," she said flatly.

Levanter felt the blood rush to his face. In seconds he was covered with sweat. He stepped backward, uncertain of what to do or say. Now he recognized her. But the braid was gone. She was more shapely, more womanly. He wanted to see her eyes, but they were obscured in the shadows.

"The police told me Oscar had a friend named Levanter, who claimed to have done it," she said. "I've never understood why you would claim that."

Levanter did not say anything.

She kept on. "Of course, since several boys in the dormitory saw you asleep that afternoon, you knew all along nobody would believe you. You had nothing to lose." She paused, offering Levanter time to speak.

He said nothing.

"Still, why would anyone want to pose as a rapist?" She tried again to make him respond.

"Would it really matter to you now whether it was Oscar or somebody else who hurt you then?" he asked.

She shrugged. "I've never doubted it was Oscar. He raped girls before, you know. No one saw his face, true, but he did the same things to them as he did to me. You were his friend, he probably told you."

83

Levanter detected some anger in her voice. "Do you really want to talk about it?" he asked.

"Not about it. About him."

"All right," said Levanter. "I met Oscar by chance on my way to camp. Once we became friends, he told me he had raped girls before we'd met. But I never saw him doing it, and I was never sure he was telling the truth." Levanter felt the heat emanating from her body.

"Ironically, I remember seeing you at camp, but not Oscar," she said.

"Do you really remember seeing me?" Levanter asked. He was more at ease now.

"Yes, I saw you two or three times. The last time was at the sports shop—actually, that was the day it happened, my last day at camp." She sounded plaintive. "You were picking up sunglasses or postcards or something. I stared at you: you looked lost."

"And I saw you and stared at you many times," said Levanter. "I recall everything about you. You see, I followed you every chance I got."

"Pity you weren't following me that day. You might have prevented him from—" she stopped.

Levanter no longer felt intimidated. He moved closer to her. As he spoke, he looked out at the empty yard. "In my thoughts I called you Nameless."

"That's kind of romantic," she said, "but now you can call me by my real name—"

"I know your name," Levanter interrupted her quickly. He did not want to hear her say it. "I inquired about you the first time I saw you at camp. But you'll always be Nameless to me." He had straightened up, away from her, and stood staring at his feet.

"Why didn't you ever talk to me?" she said softly. "Other boys did."

Levanter did not look up. "I know," he said. "But I was too frightened. I saw you with a tall, good-looking guy, that swimming champ. You laughed at everything he said, and he looked at you as if he owned you. I was jealous. I would have given anything to be as close to you as he was." When he raised his head, he could just make out that she was smiling.

"I remember him," she said. "He was funny. But I only talked to him a few times."

"I watched you every time the two camps were together," Levanter said. "When Oscar talked about raping girls, I would imagine myself doing it to you. I know that's a terrible thought, but it's the truth."

She listened in silence.

"You see, Nameless, I was in love with you. Maybe I still am." He did not move. He felt his pulse beating in his temples.

She did what he could not bring himself to do. She moved close enough for their faces to touch, but Levanter was reluctant to put his hands on her. They could see each other's eyes. A cold shiver ran through him. She reached up and folded her hands behind his neck. Tentatively, he ran one hand lightly over her back, sliding it down her silk blouse, feeling the brassiere, then the panties under her tight skirt. The hand lingered there for a moment, then he brought it up to rest gently at the back of her neck.

With his other hand, he raised her chin until her eyes caught the dim light from outside. He looked at her for a long time, trying to memorize her face as he had memorized the rest of her.

Slowly, Levanter pulled back.

"Are you afraid of hurting me?" She hesitated. "Because of what he did to me?"

"I am afraid of losing you, Nameless. Of losing you again," said Levanter.

"Don't be afraid," she whispeerd. "You won't lose me unless you want to."

He saw Nameless every day, right after school. He waited impatiently, afraid that she would not show up, until he saw her jump off the streetcar as it slowed at the corner.

They went to the public library and sat together at one of the large tables doing their homework. Each evening, as they stood across the street from her home, about to part, Levanter already began to fear, even while he was still with her, that she might not want to see him again. Perhaps during the night, pondering the events of the day, she would come across some hidden truth about him.

Yet he made no effort to bind her to him. Under various pretexts he avoided introducing her to his parents, and postponed meeting hers. She had told him he was her first boyfriend; he argued that meeting him might make her parents unnecessarily apprehensive about their only child.

Levanter had not kissed her and avoided every opportunity to make love with her. He remained genuinely shy, fearful that he would do something that would make her leave him.

Summer came. On the first hot weekend the two of them rode their bicycles out of town. Nameless said she was tired, and they stopped at a lake in a nearby forest and lay down on the still, grassy shore.

"It's so peaceful here," she said once she had caught her breath. "So private, so safe."

Levanter looked into her face. He marveled at the perfect symmetry of her features.

She studied him, her eyes moving from his lips to his eyes, then back to his lips. She reached toward him.

In an instant of panic, he sat up.

She rolled over and rested her head on his thigh. He felt reassured and ran his fingers lightly over her back. He looked down and saw the nape of her neck. It was white and frail, barely covered with delicate, thin fuzz. Tenderly, he framed her head between his hands, kissing the spot and licking the little drops of perspiration. Involuntarily, in their own remembrance of the past, his fingers started to stroke her temples.

Nameless sprang up with such force that he was thrown backward.

"What happened?" Levanter scrambled to his feet, confused.

Her face, so wholesome and calm just seconds before, was now disfigured with rage.

"It was you. Now I know it. It was you!" she screamed, covering her face with her hands.

Levanter turned away from her. Behind him, he heard her climbing onto her bicycle. When he dared to look around, Nameless was far away, pedaling as fast as she could. He found himself wishing she were a thing; then one day he could own her.

Levanter never telephoned the Russian actress again. She presented a dilemma that he could not solve. For years, he ceased to be aware that the language buried under his American experience was still strong enough to trigger an unexpected emotion.

The language itself kept surfacing at the most unlikely moments. One morning, as he was walking to a meeting at a New York hotel, Levanter passed an old woman and overheard her mumbling to herself in Russian as she plodded slowly down the street. He turned to get a better look at her.

Peering through her old-fashioned bifocals, she noticed his curious stare. "Look at this stupid one!" she said out loud. "Staring, as if he'd never seen an old woman before!"

Addressing her politely in Russian, Levanter said, "Forgive me, Madame, I did not mean to stare at you. I merely heard you speaking Russian. This is America. People don't understand you."

"How do you know they don't? You understand

me!" she retorted angrily, then tottered away, murmuring to herself, "Another smart one, ready to speak for everybody."

Levanter was invited to teach a course in investment and had to rent a place to live in Princeton.

"We've found a marvelous house for you," the real estate agent announced cheerfully. "Right next to Khrushchev's daughter!"

"Khrushchev's daughter?" Levanter asked. "Who?" He thought for an instant. "You must mean Stalin's daughter."

"Khrushchev's daughter, Stalin's daughter, what's the difference?" The man shrugged.

Levanter was overwhelmed by the extraordinary quirk of fate. He knew that Svetlana Alliluyeva had come to America and that she lived in Princeton. But he had never imagined how it would feel to be near her. Apprehensive, he agreed to rent the house.

Weeks later, when some American friends actually invited Levanter to meet Svetlana Alliluyeva, he still found it difficult to accept the knowledge that she was the daughter of Stalin. He studied her surreptitiously, silently repeating to himself that this woman was indeed Stalin's daughter. The thought of her proximity to Stalin paralyzed him. Even though he knew he was responding irrationally, he could not bring himself to speak Russian.

From the start, Levanter addressed her in English, apologizing for being out of practice with the language of his parents. In the months that followed, they met several times. Their conversation ranged from events in recent European history and the Soviet Union's role in shaping the world today to a letter from one of the many readers of her books. But the two of them never exchanged a word in Russian. Her name alone, even over the telephone, was enough to call up visions of his Moscow past, and for him she became a direct link to the awesome power that Joseph Stalin had wielded. Levanter had to remind himself again and again that he was a lecturer in Princeton now, not a student in Moscow, and that he was talking with a woman who was just another neighbor and only happened to be the daughter of Stalin.

Later, in Paris, Levanter told Romarkin about his acquaintanceship with Svetlana Alliluyeva, and his friend was overwhelmed.

"Can you imagine?" he thundered at Levanter. "Can you imagine meeting her in Moscow when her father was still alive? Suppose in the late forties you had come to one of those university social events. You noticed an average-looking woman. And when you asked, 'Who is that woman?' you were told, 'That is Svetlana, the daughter of Joseph Stalin!' Can you imagine how great your astonishment would have been then?"

Levanter showed him a few photographs of Svetlana Alliluyeva. Picking up the snapshots reverently, as if he were handling fragile and irreplaceable heirlooms, Romarkin carefully spread them out on the café table and studied each one. "It can't be," he whispered. "The daughter of Stalin an American. It can't be." He shook his head. "If within a quarter of a century you or I can go through life under Stalin and then go halfway around the world and meet his daughter as an ordinary next-door neighbor, well, I guess that means anything can happen."

Levanter could no more part with his language than he could forget about his cultural heritage, as he was often reminded.

One of his European professors, who had just immigrated and knew very little English, asked him to dinner at his apartment. When Levanter arrived, he found the professor in the kitchen. The air was filled with the pungent scent of spices, herbs, and freshly cooked meat. The professor, impressed with the variety of American foodstuffs, was surrounded by fresh vegetables and an assortment of open jars and bottles. He told Levanter he was preparing a special Ruthenian beef goulash.

As they chatted in Russian, Levanter noticed several empty cans, each with a picture of a dog's head on the label. He edged over to the counter and looked more closely. The cans, clearly marked DOG FOOD, seemed to have just been opened.

"Where is the dog?" Levanter asked.

"What dog?" The professor was stirring the goulash, inhaling the aroma.

"Don't you have a dog here?"

"Heaven forbid!" exclaimed the professor. "Animals are a nuisance. What gave you that idea?"

"Americans love dogs. I thought you had gotten yourself one."

"I will never be that much an American!"

Nonchalantly, Levanter looked around the kitchen. "What meat do you use for such a succulent goulash?" he asked guardedly.

His host beamed. "Beef, my friend, only canned beef," he said, gesturing with his chin at the cans.

"Canned beef? Fascinating! But why canned?" asked Levanter.

"Better quality. Tastier and tenderer."

"Why this particular brand?" asked Levanter, pointing to the empty cans.

"I was in the supermarket, and when I saw the picture of the smiling dog, just like in the old country, I knew it was the choicest American canned beef!" The professor nudged him with his elbow. "Don't you remember our 'Smiling Dog' brand beef? You've been away too long."

As they sat down to eat, the professor breathed in the scent of the goulash, an expression of bliss on his face. During the meal, he praised the high quality and tenderness of American meat, assuring Levanter that it was superior even to the "Smiling Dog" beef he remembered so fondly. Levanter said he was not hungry that evening and accepted only one small helping.

Another European immigrant, a respected poet, invited Levanter to a reception at his home following the wedding of his son, a graduate student at Yale. The bride, a Yale coed, was from an old banking family, and the guest list of two hundred was composed predominantly of "natives," as the poet called them—the New England relatives and friends of the bride's family.

During the reception many of the guests admired an antique, cast-iron, muzzle-loading mortar cannon, about the size of an office desk, mounted on a platform in the center of the living room. At one point, the poet urged the guests to gather more closely around the cannon and, in a voice heavy with emotion that exaggerated his accent, explained that the cannon had been built for his ancestors in the second half of the seventeenth century, for only one purpose: to be fired in celebration of every wedding in the family. The last time it had been used was when the poet himself was married, just before the start of World War II, and the cannon was the sole family heirloom that had been salvaged after the war. He and his wife had recently arranged to have it shipped to them from Europe. And now, he said, to celebrate the marriage of his son the old cannon was to be fired again, for the first time on American soil. As the curious guests formed a circle around the cannon, the poet assured them that he had loaded it with a blank charge. He then grouped his wife, the bride and groom, and the bride's parents behind the cannon. The wedding photographer readied his camera.

A single spotlight shone on the cannon's shiny muzzle, angled upward, over the guests' heads! The band played the national anthem, then the anthem of the poet's homeland. The poet and his wife embraced, weeping. Many of the guests were moved by the pomp and the outburst of feelings, but most fidgeted, waiting for the finale, eager to get back to partying. The band stopped. With a shaking hand, the poet lit the long wooden match. He stretched his other arm around the newlyweds. Everyone was silent as the flame touched the fuse.

There was a sudden flash. A powerful blast shook the room, the cannon jumped, and dense smoke billowed from its barrel.

From the other side of the room, a woman shrieked, "My God, I'm hit!" Everyone turned calmly in the direction of the voice, apparently assuming that it was all part of the slavic ritual. Near the wall, a white-haired matron stumbled, then fell to the floor. She was covered with blood and her gown was ripped open, revealing strips of skin hanging from her thighs. The guests, now in an uproar, gathered around her. She fainted.

Leaning over the victim, Levanter realized that her wounds must be superficial, as they were caused only by the wads of cotton and shredded denim that the poet had used as a blank charge.

But the poet panicked at the sight of the blood. He rushed to the phone to call for an ambulance. Levanter followed, explaining to him that, as a firearm was involved, he had to call the police. His fingers trembling, the poet dialed the police emergency number.

The police operator answered quickly and asked for his name and address.

So nervous that he mispronounced the words, the poet finally managed to spell it all out in a quavering voice. Then the operator asked him what had happened.

He stammered. "A woman shot."

Levanter heard the operator ask, "Shot by whom?"

"By a cannon," said the poet, barely audible.

"By what?" the operator asked.

"A cannon," repeated the poet.

"Please spell that," said the operator, evidently uncertain that he had understood.

"C-a-n-n-o-n."

"Cannon?" the operator repeated.

"A cannon," said the poet.

"How many others injured or killed?" asked the operator matter-of-factly.

"One woman wounded." The poet moaned.

"Property damage?"

"None." He sighed.

"What kind of cannon?"

"One of a kind. An antique."

"Is this a museum?" asked the police operator.

"A private home."

"A cannon in a private home?"

"Yes. A family cannon," the poet whimpered.

"Who fired the cannon?" asked the operator.

"I fired it," said the poet, lowering his voice.

"Your profession?"

"Poet."

"Poet? But what do you really do?"

"I write poetry."

"Ambulance is on the way," announced the operator.

Only when he was with Romarkin did Levanter feel that the language and heritage of his past were not out of place in his new life. Their reminiscences seemed to justify the break both of them had had to make with the very past that held them together.

Whenever Levanter was in Paris, the two old friends spent countless hours talking. One evening when the café they were in was about to close, Levanter and Romarkin went next door to a small nightclub, where business was just beginning. Only a few tables were occupied, and a handful of solitary drinkers lounged at the bar. The waiters hurried around officiously, checking and adjusting the cloths and settings. A couple of prostitutes strolled back and forth between the cloakroom and the tiny lobby, keeping an eye on the entrance. Four musicians, presumably unwilling to start playing for so few customers, clustered around the piano, listlessly tuning their instruments, while the maître d' fiddled with the spotlights.

Levanter asked for a quiet table, and he and Romarkin were led to the remotest corner of the room, diagonally across from the bar.

As soon as the waiter brought the champagne that was the price of admission, Levanter and Romarkin settled back comfortably.

"Tell me, Lev," said Romarkin, "have you found that people are good in the West? Are they better than where you and I came from?"

The club was beginning to fill up; a boisterous party took the five front tables. The band started to play, and two couples got up to dance.

"I have found people to be good everywhere," Levanter answered. "They turn bad only when they fall for little bits of power tossed to them by the state or by a political party, by a union or a company, or a wealthy mate. They forget that their power is nothing more than a temporary camouflage of mortality."

One of the prostitutes, who had been eyeing Levanter and Romarkin from the moment they arrived, came over to their table. She sat down, tucking in her blouse to accentuate her breasts, and smiled at Romarkin.

He smiled back, and the waiter immediately brought her a glass and filled it with their champagne. The woman raised her glass to both men and quickly drained it.

Levanter ignored her and leaned toward Romarkin to continue their conversation in Russian. The woman listened for a few minutes, then interrupted them.

"You speak a beautiful language. What is it?" she asked in French.

"It's Eskimo," Levanter replied. He turned back to Romarkin, hoping she understood that her services were of no interest to them.

She laughed. "Eskimo? Come on, don't be silly. What are you?"

Levanter made himself look angry. "I resent your laughter and attitude, Mademoiselle," he said. "We are Eskimo, and we are proud of it."

The woman continued to giggle. "But, Monsieur, Eskimos look like this," she said, pulling back the skin on her temples and squinting. "Like frozen Chinese! But you—" She stopped, as if to search her memory. "You two could be Italian or perhaps Greek. But not Eskimo."

"Mademoiselle," Levanter said harshly, "we Eskimos are a proud race, and we are no more 'frozen Chinese' than the French are 'marinated Italians' or the Swedes 'mummified Germans.' " In a final attempt to send her away without insulting her, Levanter spoke to her in a confidential tone. "You see, my friend here and I are in Paris to secure your government's aid in our revolutionary struggle to free ourselves from American and Canadian colonialism. We have just met with your Minister of Foreign Affairs." She was no longer laughing. "So now, Mademoiselle, we must go back to discussing our business undisturbed."

The woman flushed. "Please forgive me, Monsieur," she pleaded. "I'm ignorant about Eskimos because I don't have much education. But I'm not against Eskimos or anybody. In my line of work I can't afford to be prejudiced." She stood up and, without even straightening her skirt, quickly slipped away.

A little while later, a resounding drum roll interrupted them again. The proprietor of the club hurried onto the stage. He had opened his doors at the end of World War II, he announced, and since then his club had welcomed many distinguished and exotic guests. But tonight was truly special. For the first time ever, he said, he had the privilege of welcoming two real Eskimos, distinguished representatives of their esteemed nation. He spread his arms and solemnly bowed toward Levanter and Romarkin. The spotlight was turned from the stage onto their table. Everyone—the loners at the bar, the prostitutes and the waiters, the handholding couples at the tables—turned to see the two Eskimos and started to applaud fervently. The band struck up the "Marseillaise."

Levanter hunched down in his chair, his head lowered. Romarkin, however, seemed to enjoy the sudden attention. He rose and extended his hands toward the clapping crowd.

The proprietor called for silence and, all smiles, addressed Romarkin. "One of our charming hostesses had the pleasure to hear you speak your beautiful Eskimo language," he said. "For the rest of us who have not had the privilege, may I prevail upon you to say something to us in Eskimo—a poem, a phrase, a word, anything?" The guests began to applaud again.

Romarkin bowed to the audience. Levanter suddenly felt he was back in that auditorium in Moscow. He tugged on Romarkin's jacket, trying to force his friend to sit down. He was too late.

As though about to deliver a prepared speech from a dais, Romarkin puffed up his chest, then, in a loud, clear voice he began to swear in Russian. It was the juciest vocabulary of obscenities Levanter had heard since his Barbatov army days. Romarkin finished with a theatrical flourish that drew enthusiastic applause from his listeners. But not from all of them.

Two burly men at the bar did not join in. When Romarkin started his harangue, they had straightened as if prodded by red-hot pokers. When he finished, they angrily smashed their glasses on the floor and began to yell at Romarkin in Russian. They could tell by his obscene Soviet lingo, they shouted, that he was one of Stalin's bully boys. But this was France, they screamed, storming toward Romarkin through the clutter of tables, and he had no right to assault them with his filthy tongue just because they were old Russian émigrés and he was, no doubt, a Soviet agent posing as a tourist. Incensed, raging and ranting, they pushed chairs and people aside in their mad scramble to reach him.

The proprietor seemed unable to move. The waiters stood by helplessly, perplexed to see other Eskimos in their club and baffled that one Eskimo's remarks should have offended his countrymen.

Levanter and Romarkin barricaded themselves behind two tables, hurling glasses and bottles at their attackers and defending themselves with chairs. Soon the police arrived. Levanter quickly assured the proprietor that if he and Romarkin were not arrested he would immediately pay for the damaged property. Pleading with the police to release Levanter and his friend, the proprietor explained that Eskimos, like the French, were often known to clash over their political views.

The day after his friend's nightclub speech, Levanter went to see Jacques Monod, the French biologist and philosopher, whom he had first met when Monod was on a research trip in the United States. Levanter recounted the story of Romarkin, beginning in Moscow.

"Even now, in France," Monod said, "your friend Romarkin doesn't dare to admit that blind chance and nothing else is responsible for each random event of his life. Instead, he is searching for a religion that, like Marxism, will assure him that man's destiny is spelled out in the central plot of life. Meanwhile, believing in the existence of an orderly, predetermined life scheme, Romarkin by-passes the drama of each unique instance of his own existence. Yet, to accept a notion of destiny, he might as well believe in astrology, or palm reading, or pulp novels, all of which pretend that one's future is already set and needs only to be lived out.

As Monod reached for a cup of tea, Levanter noticed a slight tremor in his hand.

"Are you not well?" asked Levanter.

"I haven't been for some time," said Monod. He managed to restrain the trembling long enough to pick up the teacup.

"What is it?" Levanter asked.

Monod named the condition. "It was diagnosed at the onset, a few months ago," he said, sipping his tea.

Levanter was stunned. Monod, who had contributed so much to the world's knowledge of how the living cell manufactures the substance of life, was being deprived of this very substance; he had a disease for which there was no known treatment.

He was only sixty-six years old. He looked healthy and was continuing to conduct his research, attend scientific conferences, and on weekends sail his boat and drive his sports car. Looking at him now, Levanter found it inconceivable that Jacques Monod would soon die.

Levanter struggled to remain calm. "Is anything being done?"

"Increasingly frequent blood transfusions." Monod dismissed the subject. He mentioned that he would be leaving for Cannes and suggested that Levanter go there too so they could spend some time together.

"Won't you find the trip rather tiring just for the weekend?" Levanter asked.

"I'm not going just for the weekend," Monod replied.

"But the transfusions? Can they be done there?" asked Levanter. Monod said nothing. Levanter felt his throat constrict. "Why won't you remain in Paris? All the life-support equipment is here."

Monod looked at him steadfastly. "To be hooked

up to life through a machine?" he asked abruptly. "The flame isn't worth the candle."

At any given time in history, Levanter's father once claimed, civilization is the result of sheer chance plus a thousand or two exceptional men and women of ideas and action, most of whom know or have heard of each other. If you were one of them and wished to become acquainted with any other, you needed no more than two or three consecutive introductions. Levanter had discovered that, regardless of the field in which they excelled, all these men and women were, at least at some time in their lives, small investors, people who risked their personal energy and means to achieve certain unpredictable ends.

One day, after a meeting at a large New York publishing house, Levanter stopped by unannounced to see a friend who was an editor there. She was going over a set of galley proofs with an imposing, gray-haired man, whom she introduced to Levanter. It was Charles Lindbergh, the aviator. To Levanter, Lindbergh was heroic but tragic: a man who achieved international fame, only to become, as a result of the media's obsession with a crime against his family, one of the world's most hounded public figures. Levanter apologized for interrupting and turned to leave.

Lindbergh said, "Please stay. We're almost finished."

Levanter and Lindbergh left at the same time. It was a clear fall day, and Lindbergh proposed they walk for a few blocks. As he steered Levanter up Fifth Avenue, he affected a slight stoop and tugged the brim of his hat down over his face. Levanter surmised that this public posture had become second nature to Lindbergh after years of trying to avoid recognition.

"I know you flew over Eastern Europe before the war," Levanter said. "A few years later, during the war, when I was six, I was separated from my family and wandered alone through the same villages you saw from your plane."

Lindbergh recalled his flight very well. He was on his way to visit the Soviet Union, flying his plane over the Ruthenian flatlands, the narrow rivers, lakes, and marshes that seemed never to end. He remembered the small villages and how from above they had appeared like islands in the midst of swamps, the poor peasant huts with roofs of thatched rye and wheat, the haystacks scattered about.

Levanter said that when the flight of *The Spirit of St. Louis* bridged the two continents, Levanter's family had considered Lindbergh one of the century's greatest heroes. But later, when Lindbergh received the Order of the German Eagle from Goering, its citation signed by Adolf Hitler, Lindbergh had dealt a frightful blow to their faith in human wisdom. Later, Levanter's parents were distressed and baffled by Lindbergh's participation in the America First movement, which was dedicated to keeping the United States out of the war.

"When the war was over," Levanter said, "my parents felt that we had survived because America finally entered and helped to win the war. And they felt that the rest of our family—sixty of them—had died because America First was a great influence in keeping America out of the war for so long."

They walked for a while without speaking. Then, almost as an afterthought, Lindbergh said that when he went to Germany and the Soviet Union in the thirties, he perceived his visits as good-will missions, just as his flight had been. He had sensed, he explained, that the Germans, who were themselves obsessed with ethnic origins, were relieved that Lindbergh bore them no ill will because the convicted kidnapper of his baby was of German origin. The Soviets, on the other hand, he said, invited him to inspect their aviation industry in the hope that he would praise it. When he did not, their propaganda soon labeled him a fascist.

At the entrance to Central Park, a short woman in a mink jacket approached them, displaying lipstick-smeared teeth behind a gushing smile. Lindbergh cringed and began to back away, but it was Levanter the woman was after.

"I know you. I've seen you on TV!" she exclaimed in a high-pitched voice.

Levanter, who only occasionally appeared on television on behalf of Investors International, turned away. He took Lindbergh's arm and started to walk on, but the woman dogged their steps.

"Haven't I seen you on TV?" she demanded.

"You must be confusing me with someone else," said Levanter emphatically.

Disappointed, she walked away.

About a year later, Levanter was traveling in Switzerland and visited Lindbergh at his chalet there. Lindbergh invited him and his friends for a meal at a nearby inn.

During dinner, Levanter suddenly realized that he had forgotten his attaché case under a chair in the lobby of his hotel. In the case were not only his passport, credit cards, and money but also the only copy of the unpublished results of a pilot study that he had spent the past months compiling. He was afraid that if he called the hotel, the person sent to look for it might steal the case, simply claiming that it hadn't been there. Yet the longer he waited, the greater was the likelihood that he would lose it. Nervous and uncertain about what to do, he stopped eating and fidgeted in his chair.

Lindbergh leaned toward him and asked quietly, "What's wrong?" Levanter told him about the attaché case and how worried he was about the manuscript in it.

"Come, I'll drive you to the hotel right now," Lindbergh said.

"But your dinner—"

"I don't need to finish. Let's go."

As they drove, Lindbergh praised his small automobile as a marvel of German engineering. With only simple reconditioning of the engine, he said, his car had gone well over a hundred thousand miles.

Levanter said he had been surprised to find so many expressions of positive interest in the Germany of the Third Reich in Lindbergh's book. Lindbergh explained that, compared to other countries he had visited before the war, Germany seemed to him to strive for a more efficiently organized means of production and had achieved admirable technological progress in aeronautics. He thought of the German state as an airplane and of its racial hatred, persecution, and aggression in the early thirties, as a temporary flight abberation caused by the pilot's misreading of the plane's control panel. Later, he realized he was wrong, and this was one of the many lessons he had derived from life. Mass atrocities, he said, like acts of individual heroism, often appear unthinkable before they occur.

"And inevitable only after," said Levanter.

"What is your manuscript about?" Lindbergh asked.

"A study of individuals," Levanter explained, "who through chance accidents have been propelled into national prominence and become important investors."

From the black shroud of sky, a snowstorm was spreading a white mantle over the earth. Lindbergh's small car plowed slowly against the icy wind. He drove with steady hands, looking unwaveringly ahead. The car, engulfed in a blanket of moving snow, was like an airplane lost to everyone but its pilot, steadily pushing through the clouds, ice, and wind.

They found the attaché case, untouched, under the chair in the hotel lobby. They started back. The storm had passed, and the night was cold, the sky clear. Unexpectedly, Lindbergh stopped the car and turned off the engine. He got out, motioning Levanter to follow him. From above came the sound of a jet plane, its drone growing more and more persistent as it moved closer. Lindbergh listened. When the plane's flickering lights came clearly into sight, he pointed toward it.

"Another 747, right above us!" he exclaimed. "One of the safest planes ever built!" He looked up at the sky, listening to the sound of the jet engines reverberating in the air long after the plane disappeared into the darkness.

It was Levanter's fifteenth Christmas in his new country. He hailed a cab. The driver, an older man, was voluble and friendly and they struck up a conversation. The man mentioned that he had come to the United States from Eastern Europe after World War II. He named the town he was from.

"That's the very town where some of my relatives once lived," Levanter said.

The driver was clearly delighted. "Can you remember their address?" he asked.

Levanter named the street.

"Small world!" exclaimed the driver. "My brother and I owned a grocery right in the neighborhood. It was a tiny street, with only three private houses. I delivered groceries to all of them."

"Then you knew number nine?" asked Levanter.

They were stopped at a traffic light. The driver turned around. "I sure did. Nine—the last house on the left. It was like a villa. A couple lived there, an old professor and his young wife, a pianist. They had a boy who was sick in the head." He glanced at Levanter in the rearview mirror. "Were those your relatives?"

"Yes," said Levanter. "Why do you say their boy was crazy?"

The driver pondered for a while. "I saw him myself. He couldn't speak. Never smiled or laughed. Just kept staring at you. Their own maid was afraid of him. She told me he would sneak out alone at night and stay away until morning, then sleep during the day. A real spook." The light changed and he drove on.

"After the war a lot of children couldn't speak," said Levanter, "or smile or laugh or play in the daylight."

The driver shook his head. "This one was not like other kids," he said. "I saw him. He was crazy. No doubt about it."

"As I remember him," Levanter said, "the kid was quite normal."

For a few moments the driver was silent, concentrating on the traffic, and Levanter thought he had dropped the subject.

"Believe me, he was crazy," said the driver as he pulled up at Levanter's destination. "But that's almost thirty years ago. You couldn't have been more than a kid yourself," he continued, taking another look at Levanter.

"Perhaps I was too young to know this kid when you knew him," said Levanter as he paid the fare. "But when we got older, I came to know him better. He was no crazier than you or I."

"What do you mean?" asked the driver.

"That story's for another ride," said Levanter, leaving the cab.

Levanter often reflected that his European upbringing was probably responsible for his tendency to pay far more attention to forms, questionnaires, letterheads, and rubber stamps than most native-born Americans. And he never sent an envelope without extra touches—self-adhesive mail stickers: FOR INTERNAL USE ONLY, RUSH, HANDLE WITH CARE, UNCLASSIFIED, SPECIAL ATTENTION—which he knew would attract attention and distinguish his letters from all other mail. An American business friend told him that any time one of Levanter's envelopes arrived, his secretary was certain that the letter should not wait a minute longer and delivered it to her boss immediately, even if it meant dispatching it to his home by messenger.

One day Levanter ran into one of his current correspondents, a friend who had spent the summer at his family's home in the South. He seemed a bit uneasy when he saw Levanter but agreed to join him for a drink.

"I keep marveling at the care you give your mail," he said after a moment. "Your letters really create a great stir."

Levanter looked at him quizzically.

His friend went on. "All those colorful labels stuck on each envelope," he said. "Even the mailman was intimidated. A couple of times he made separate trips to bring your letters, as if they were special delivery, even though all the stickers said was EXPEDITE or VERY URGENT or CONFIDENTIAL."

Levanter felt like a prankster praised for playing a practical joke on a superior.

"But some of your letters—I mean stickers— caused a major event in my family," the man murmured.

"An event?"

"That's all I can call it. You see, one of my sisters has been an epileptic since childhood," he said. "She's in her forties now. Because of her illness, she never married and never worked away from the house. We all, the whole family, have always taken care of her."

Levanter squirmed.

"She's the one who collects the mail every day," the friend went on. "A few months ago, she picked up your letter with a sticker proclaiming EPILEPSY— UNDERSTANDING IS HALF THE TREATMENT. She disregarded it at first, she said, but your next letter arrived with another slogan: HELP EPILEPTICS LIVE AND WORK IN DIGNITY."

Embarrassed, Levanter listened in silence.

"Where do you get such stickers and stamps?" his friend asked.

"I got those from a foundation that I occasionally contribute to," said Levanter lamely.

"I see," the man said. "In any case, by then my sister was convinced that I had put you up to sticking all those messages on your mail to prod her into getting a job. When a letter arrived with EMPLOY EPILEPTICS, she ran away from home, leaving a note that she had taken the hint and did not want to be a burden to the family anymore. It took us and the authorities several weeks to trace her. We found her in pretty bad shape, but she's back home now."

"It never occurred to me—" Levanter stammered.

The other man shook his head. "It had never occurred to us either that she was so sensitive about her condition. No film or TV play about epileptics had ever upset her; she never took them personally. Yet she really took off over that EMPLOY EPILEPTICS sticker. Amazing what the printed word can do!"

Like many other Europeans living in America, Levanter was awed by the effect the size of the country and its large population could have on one's sense of freedom and enterprise.

An acquaintance of his, an elderly man from Belgrade who had settled in Minneapolis, was full of stories about émigré investors.

"For instance, take this fellow from Galicia," he said to Levanter one day. "Came to this country a poor immigrant. No English, no profession to speak of, no relatives. Works nights sweeping floors, and learns the language by day.

"One day, just for fun, he places an ad in two newspapers, one on the West Coast and one in the East: TICKLE HER FANCY—THREE ORIGINAL TICKLERS FOR A DOLLAR ONLY. He lists a post-office box. If he gets any answers, he figures he'll send every customer three ordinary goose feathers for their buck. After all, where he comes from men have other things to worry about than tickling the fancy of their women.

"In a few days, the post office calls him to say he has received several thousand letters. He picks up his mail and starts opening the letters. Out pour orders from all over the country. Some with one dollar, some with several dollars. Before he knows it, he is investing in the mail-order business. He buys thousands of goose feathers, envelopes, and postal stamps, hires three sweet young things to help him fill the orders. He places more newspaper ads in papers throughout the nation, hires more employees.

"In the first few weeks he makes over sixty thousand dollars. But this is a large country, and a lot of people are willing to part with a mere dollar to tickle the fancy, or whatever else is ticklish, of their beloved. The orders keep coming. Today that guy is a millionaire. Over the mantelpiece in his Malibu Beach house hangs a plaque—a solid-gold relief of three goose feathers!"

After a few glasses of wine, the man admitted to Levanter that he had been forced to leave Yugoslavia when the whole capital seemed to know of his eccentric sexual proclivity. "How many people like me are there in the world?" he asked.

Levanter shrugged.

The man answered himself. "A fraction of a fraction of one percent," he said. "In a small country like Yugoslavia, that's no more than a dozen people at most. They hide like animals, even from each other. But in America, a country of two hundred twenty million," he continued, "a fraction of a fraction of one percent runs into tens of thousands. Here, people with my preference, like people with various political views, are free to advertise, to communicate with each other, and even to congregate in public places. When I learned about it, I felt like a left-handed person discovering a whole town of left-handers."

He reached into his desk drawer and brought out a thick book.

"Our most recent directory," he said, handing it to Levanter. "It lists thousands of people who like the same thing I like: names and professions, addresses, telephone numbers, even photographs of some of them. In fact, it seems that in America there are more men and women with my taste than there are inhabitants in the whole city of Belgrade. Imagine that! There I was a freak. Here I am one of the multitude. Nothing to be ashamed of anymore."

A few years after Levanter's arrival in America, a New York-based booking agent for conventions mentioned that he had just arranged a three-day meeting of the newly formed Alliance of Small Americans. Like the better-known Little People of America, it was an organization made up of unusually short men and women, both midgets and dwarfs.

Small Americans, the agent said, tried to avoid convening in big cities. In subways and buses, their faces were pushed into other people's thighs, bellies, and bottoms. Most public telephones were hung too high for them to reach. In general, dwarfs or midgets in trouble were afraid to ask for help, because most people of average height assumed they were also mentally handicapped. It was not uncommon for little people to be sexually abused and molested by those who saw them as mere children, though they were endowed with the minds and appetites of adults.

The meeting had been booked in the Midwest, in a place called Impton. The agent told Levanter that when he went there to inspect the facilities and to reserve rooms in hotels and motels for the conventioneers, none of the managers had ever heard of the Alliance of Small Americans. Thus, when he requested only hand-held microphones for the assemblies and asked for the lowest tables and chairs, the managers assumed that Small Americans were Boy Scouts and Girl Scouts. The agent laughed as he told Levanter that he had done nothing to disabuse them.

"I'd like to be there in Impton," he said chuckling, "to see all their faces when these assorted dwarfs and midgets start descending upon them."

Curious about how such things went in his adopted country, Levanter landed at the airport that serviced Impton and two other neighboring townships, rented a car, and drove to the center of town. He went straight to the Taft, the largest hotel, which advertised itself as "unconventionally superconventional," and took a room.

The desk clerk handed him a guest registration card. Levanter looked up at the huge banner suspended from the ceiling: THE TAFT WELCOMES ALLIANCE OF SMALL AMERICANS: THE SCOUTS OF TODAY, THE LEADERS OF TOMORROW.

"Who are these Small Americans?" Levanter asked the clerk while filling in the card.

"Just boys and girls from all over the country. A Scouts' convention, you know," said the clerk.

"How many are coming?"

"A few hundred. Some might arrive tonight, the rest tomorrow." He glanced at Levanter inquisitively. "You here on business?"

Levanter smiled. "Looking for business."

"It's all the same, isn't it?" The man returned the smile.

After dinner at the hotel, Levanter strolled over to the registration desk and leaned against the far end. A number of people were milling about the lobby: a couple with five children waiting for their luggage so they could depart, two businessmen who had just arrived, and several elderly men and women of the sort always found in the lobbies of respectable hotels, sitting, drowsing, reading, or just idly watching each other and the people who pass through.

Suddenly, a tiny man came through the revolving door. He was less than three feet tall, fat and pursy, his head nearly as big as his torso, his arms so short that the wrists seemed to grow out of his elbows. He approached the desk and, in a squeaky voice, asked the clerk to send a bellhop out to collect the luggage he had left outside with his wife. He then reached up, took a registration card, and, using his knee for support, began filling it in, writing with his left hand.

"Did you see what I just saw?" the clerk whispered to Levanter when the short man walked away.

"It's a big country," said Levanter. "A lot of left-handed people."

The clerk looked puzzled. "Left-handed? A lefty is one thing, a freak is another. Why, this fellow is shorter than my six-year-old kid."

"Will your kid grow any taller?" asked Levanter.

"That isn't funny, Mister," said the clerk.

Just then the little man returned, accompanied by a fat woman, an inch or two taller than he. She had a round face, double chin, full bosom, and plump thighs bulging out of tight shorts.

Everyone in the room stared at the newcomers. The departing family clustered together, the five kids peeking out from behind their parents, mocking the waddle of the little couple. A few senior citizens who had dozed off in easy chairs woke up and, adjusting their glasses, blinked at the spectacle. The two businessmen stood dumbfounded, dangling their room keys.

The couple went up to the desk. Standing on tiptoe, they called out their names and asked for their room. The man said the reservations for the conventioneers had been made for the whole group, but he and his wife had arrived early.

"What convention?" asked the clerk.

The little man proudly pointed to the identification tag on his lapel. "Small Americans! What else?" he said.

"Are your kids the delegates?" the clerk asked.

"We don't have any children," said the woman.

"We are the delegates," the man said emphatically.

The clerk glanced toward the cashier at the other end of the desk. But she deliberately looked in the other direction.

"So you are!" the clerk said at last. "It just didn't click right away that some grownups would be accompanying the kids," he said cheerfully.

"Not 'grownups'!" the small man corrected him with a smile. "Adults!"

"I didn't mean it that way! Adults, of course!" Sheepishly the clerk handed the room key to the bellhop.

The little couple went to the elevator, followed by the bellhop, who could not restrain his snickering.

Levanter was still standing next to the desk.

"In this line of work you have to expect anything," said the clerk, rubbing his forehead. "How was I to know that these two worked with the Scouts? Adults, indeed!" he chortled.

"It's a big country!" Levanter said once more.

The clerk had just settled down behind his desk when the revolving door spun around again. Three little women and four tiny men came through and advanced toward the desk. The clerk, engrossed in his work, did not see them.

"You have some more guests," said Levanter.

The clerk stood up. When he saw the group, an expression of utter disbelief crossed his face. Openmouthed, the cashier stared at the midgets. Everyone in the lobby turned toward the registration desk.

The new arrivals were barely as tall as the desk. All wore convention identification tags.

"Are you all delegates to the Scout convention?" the desk clerk asked, nodding toward the banner over the entrance.

"Do you mean to the Small Americans convention?" asked one woman.

"Yes, that's the one."

"We are. What do Scouts have to do with it?" asked one of the men.

"It's their convention, that's what," answered the clerk, handing the group registration cards.

"If you mean the Alliance of Small Americans, then it is ours," another man said. "Scouts have nothing to do with it."

"I don't believe there are very many Scouts in the Alliance," one of the women added.

"What do you mean there aren't many Scouts?" The clerk was now on the verge of panic. "We've prepared the whole place for them. Why, we even installed additional bunks in a number of rooms so that many of the kids could be together! Look at that!" Once again he gestured toward the banner.

"It's your banner, not ours," said one man.

"Maybe the Scouts are having a convention at the same time," said one of the women.

The clerk did not answer. By now he seemed to have grasped the hotel's misunderstanding.

Word that the little people had come spread to other parts of the hotel. Soon cooks in white hats, waitresses in aprons, and patrons with napkins tucked under their chins crowded into the lobby to get a good look. As the new guests marched off to the elevator through the throng of spectators, two hotel technicians, trying to be inconspicuous, started to take down the banner.

Levanter walked over to the bar across the street. A waiter from the hotel came rushing in. Laughing so

freak this town out," she said. "What are
e?"

r told her about the New York booking
w he had decided to visit Impton because
ntion. He couldn't tell whether Jolene be-

a scared town," she said. "Recently, for
sick guy was beating and raping women
The newspaper warned that he was on the
rls kept right on hitchhiking and kept right
to this guy's car. I heard a radio interview
the ones who was raped. She said it was her
se she had hitchhiked, and now she was
less paranoid about it." Her voice rose.
elieve it? Here's a girl who was raped and
she blames herself for it and says she's
less paranoid. That's Impton for you."
what is it for you?" asked Levanter.
ometown," she said with a shrug. "I was
he only child of Anglo-Saxon parents. Very
d Scottish stock! Descendant of a proud
l embalmers, auto technicians, wholesalers,
ssors, and low-rank military." She lit a ciga-
ed deeply, then, in the same self-deprecating
tone, asked, "The rest of the picture?"
ter nodded encouragement.

Snapshots from Jolene's album. Woman-
ns in grade school, age twelve. Jolene loses
ty to a high school varsity basketball player,
oses his. More dates. Click. Jolene discovers
n. Click. High school. Meets Greg, law stu-
al rich boy. Click. Going steady and bedding
h Greg. Click. No orgasms with Greg. Click.
lone. Click. College athletes discover that Jo-
out. Click. She gets into their games for free;
to her games for free. Click. Jolene trips on
rass and airplane glue and prescription cough

hard he could barely speak, he tried to tell everyone
what he had seen.

"What's going on?" Levanter asked.

The waiter's shoulders were shaking. "Would you
believe there's a busload of freaks over there?"

"It's a big country," said Levanter offhandedly.

The waiter ignored his remark. "Would you believe they're all little pigmy people no taller than that?"
he went on, bringing his hand to the level of the bar-
stool.

By now all the patrons had left the bar for the
Taft. Levanter decided to take a drive through town.

It was only nine o'clock but the main street was
already almost deserted. A few teen-agers drove by, the
finish on their polished cars reflecting brightly lit shop
windows, the roar of their supercharged engines competing with blasts of music or chatter from their Citizen
Band radios.

Levanter passed the town hall, two department
stores, a bowling alley and a shooting gallery, the post
office, two drugstores, three banks, a shopping mall, the
police station, and the bus and railroad terminals.
Within fifteen minutes, he had crossed downtown Impton twice.

He stopped for gas on the outskirts of town. The
station attendant peered closely at Levanter, then at the
car, as he filled the tank.

"The wheels are local, but you're not," he said
with a friendly smile as he wiped the windshield.

"I'm not," Levanter said.

"By-passing Impton?"

"Passing through. For a day or two."

"You'll never guess who stopped here for gas ten
minutes ago," said the man, leaning through the window.

"How about some midgets?" said Levanter, looking up at the sky.

"I'll be darned!" he exclaimed. "How did you know?"

"It had to be someone you don't see very often," said Levanter.

"Good thinking!" the attendant agreed. "I almost flipped when they drove up. Like in a circus: Seven Dwarfs in one small car. Bet I don't see a sight like that again for the next twenty years!"

"Don't bet on it," Levanter said as he paid for the gas. "You might see some more small miracles before the night's over."

"That'll be the day!" The man was chuckling as Levanter pulled away.

Back at the hotel, Levanter found a small table in a far corner of the crowded, noisy bar. He ordered a drink and settled back to observe the scene. The Taft bar was the best in town, and most of the patrons, all prosperous-looking, seemed to be locals who knew one another.

A group of Small Americans—five men and three women—appeared at the door. The room immediately became quiet. Everyone turned to look. Several couples at the back of the room stood up, straining to get a view of the little people, who did not seem to mind the attention. They moved to the center of the room, and one of them, a man with a flattened nose and exaggerated chest, asked a startled waiter to seat them, but not on the high barstools. The waiter led the group to two side tables, which, with some effort, they helped him push together. Seated there in a bunch, with their round faces, bulging necks, fatty arms, and stubby hands and fingers, they could have served as models for a human still-life theme—a bowl of plums, doughnuts, and bonbons.

The hum of voices started up again. But the Small Americans remained the focus of attention. Many of the patrons could not ta[...] terest in the sedate co[...]

Only one person[...] the bar, seemed unaffe[...] Americans. She had [...] then had resumed talk[...]

A brunette, with [...] and long legs, she app[...] Every time she laughe[...] bles drew their eyes a[...] and glanced furtively a[...] tle people got up to go, [...] panions were among t[...] seemed tired and a bit [...] much to each other. Th[...] face was one of bored[...] empty room. When sh[...] showed a flicker of i[...] watched, she picked up h[...] bit unsteady, smiling as if [...] Levanter could offer her [...] table, her back to the bar. [...]

"Please don't mind [...] speech a little slurred. "[...] know me. I want to get rid [...]

Levanter smiled. Th[...] good-by to the two men sh[...] watched them walk out.

"I'm Jolene. One of In[...] case you haven't noticed," s[...]

"I've noticed. I'm Geor[...]

"Do you mind if I hav[...] she asked.

"With me or alone?" he [...]

She laughed. "With you [...] then sat quietly for a few m[...] Lilliputians?"

Levanter nodded.

"They'[...] you doing he[...]

Levant[...] agent and h[...] of the conv[...] lieved him.

"This i[...] example, a [...] hitchhikers.[...] loose, but g[...] on getting i[...] with one of [...] fault becau[...] trying to b[...]

"Can you [...] beaten, ye[...] trying to b[...]

"And [...]

"My [...] born here, [...] distinguish[...] line of loc[...] food proce[...] rette, inha[...] but jocula[...]

Leva[...]

"O.K[...] hood beg[...] her virgin[...] who also [...] the orgas[...] dent. Loo[...] steady wi[...] Orgasms [...] lene puts [...] they get [...] acid and [...]

syrup. Click. Greg and Jolene marry. Click. House in the best part of town, a gift from Greg's parents, who pray for grandchildren. Click. Greg successful as a lawyer. Click. Jolene and Greg give a lot of parties to show off their split-level house. Click. They split up. Click. Jolene alone. Click. Jolene at the Taft with yet another stranger. Click. End of album of unique snapshots of an ordinary life. A sweet old-fashioned girl, a perfect subject for any lens to fondle. Do you have a movie camera, Mr. Levanter?" she asked, teasing.

He didn't answer.

She put out the cigarette she had just lit.

Bluntly, Levanter suggested they go upstairs to his room. Without a word, she stood up. As they walked through the bar, Levanter felt the bartender and waiters watching their exit. Crossing the lobby, they passed one of the hotel guards, who recognized Jolene and bowed to her but pretended not to see Levanter.

"It's not often that people here notice anything," said Jolene as they waited for the elevator. "Last week, a fourteen-year-old kid who had driven a car only once before stole an airport bus from downtown. He drove straight to the arrivals terminal, picked up a full load of passengers, collected their fares, and headed back to town, dropping passengers off at stops along the way. Then, somewhere on the highway, he sideswiped a truck. The truck started to chase him and the kid jumped out of the moving bus. Luckily, the truck driver pulled in front of the bus and after a small crash made it stop. Only then did the passengers realize something was wrong. So much for our observant townsfolk!" She laughed.

"Still, they seem to know you here," said Levanter, feeling a bit uneasy.

"My hometown, remember?"

"And you don't mind that they know what you're doing?"

"What do I care what they think? They don't pay my bills." Holding her head high, she looked around the lobby defiantly, but there were no more witnesses.

When they entered his room, she quickly took off her dress and slip. Next, she kicked off her shoes. Then, lying back on the bed and lifting her hips, she hooked her thumbs under the top of her pantyhose and smoothly slid them off. Underneath was a G-string. She sat up, piled her hair on top of her head, then let it fall over her shoulders.

Levanter undressed in the bathroom. When he came back in his robe, she was still wearing her brassiere and G-string.

Jolene asked for a drink. He poured one for each of them, then sat on the sofa across from the bed and watched as she slowly sipped hers.

She noticed Levanter eyeing her bra and G-string. "It's called a grope suit. They're easy to get anywhere in the country—in sex boutiques in big cities or by mail order in small ones." She stared up at the ceiling. "The patch in front is covered with human hair. The main feature is the rubber rod inside. It stimulates you every time you move. The bra too. Each cup has a snug hollow on each side that massages your nipple and little rubber things all over that gently rub your breast. A lovely sensation."

She paused, waiting for Levanter's reaction. When he did not respond, she kept on talking.

"Whenever I visited Greg in his office, his partners would usually drop in to say hello. While we were talking, I'd look them straight in the eye and then, right there, I would just move or bend slightly or press deeper into my chair, and I would come, over and over again. The best part was the fun of seeing if I could control the expression on my face so no one would know what was going on inside me." Her gaze lingered on the threadbare rug at the side of the bed.

"When I was a little girl, I'd play with myself, but

never in front of anyone. Now I do it with people watching me, and they never know what I'm doing."

She sat quite still. They could hear a faint buzz of voices from the hotel corridor. Levanter refilled her glass.

"I began wearing my grope suit everywhere," she continued. "Even under my bathing suit. I wore it to go shopping, to dinners with my in-laws, to picnics and cocktail parties. At these posh affairs, I would often find myself talking politely about this or that with Impton's finest. Then, out of the corner of my eye I'd see this type giving me an obliging smile—you know, one of those guys who's so proud of his hairy chest, the kind who pretends to take life and women as they come. I'd encourage him by smiling back. And as he was walking over to introduce himself, I'd turn toward him, and the rubbing of the rod and the bra would arouse me like crazy. I'd be all heated up and come even before I could tell him I was married. And the jerk would never know how well I was doing without him."

Levanter listened without stirring.

"I once wore my secret to church," she said. "Even there, with Greg and his family, I could not resist the temptation. But every time I knelt, I felt a little damned when that drive took hold of me."

She finished her drink and put the glass down.

"And I'm wearing my secret tonight, Mr. Levanter. Are you willing to compete with it?"

Without waiting for an answer, she unhooked her brassiere and took it off. After a slight delay, she removed the G-string. She did not display her costume, but as she stood up, naked, and carried it across the room on her way to the bathroom, Levanter could see that her description was accurate.

When she came back into the room, Levanter was ready for her. Without warning, he grabbed her by the waist and forced her down onto the floor. She did not resist. For a moment, he lay still on top of her, feeling her cool skin. Then he pinned her down, wedging his legs between hers, spreading her wide apart. He flung her arms over her head with one hand and held her wrists still until she was flat and taut. To make certain she was pinioned, he first trailed his other hand idly over her body, then cupped and pulled at her flesh until she squirmed. She couldn't free herself from his hold.

He sank into her suddenly. She strained and twisted, but he rammed into her, battering her with all his weight, smacking her loins, each butt tearing the tender tissues of her flesh, pounding her back against the floor. She began to scream. Levanter covered her lips with his, stifling her sounds. He exhaled his breath into her mouth, pressing her throat with his hand; throttled, her excitement accelerated, swelling the veins in her face and neck.

Starved for air, she ripped her hands free, clenching and unclenching them convulsively as if trying to grasp the air itself. A shudder rippled through her. Levanter removed his mouth from hers, and, like a hysterical child on the verge of both laughter and tears, she screamed, trying to wrest herself away from the weight of his body. She opened her mouth, struggling for breath, and in her exertion arched her body, gasping. Then she went limp and fainted. Levanter's pulse raced, his lungs strained for air, and his eyes blurred. For a moment, everything went black.

When she came to, she wearily ran her hands through her disheveled hair. Her expression was soft, and she looked as if she were trying to smile. She traced her fingers listlessly over her body, gently cupping her breasts, raising her knees. Drops of perspiration glistened on her belly. She reached for him, and drew him close to her.

After a few moments, she squatted with her back to his outstretched body. Her feet were between his thighs, her hands pressing on his knees. She started swaying and her buttocks grazed and stroked his flesh until he could stand it no longer and wanted to pull free of her. Then she slid back over him, until her damp flesh was over his face. He could hardly breathe. As she leaned forward, her breasts rubbed against his belly, her hair fell over his thighs. He felt her mouth around his flesh; like a rampant growth, she sucked the strength out of him. Suddenly conscious of his parched mouth and intense thirst, and no longer willing to fight her, he gave in to the tension that swelled within him.

They woke up late the next morning. She was bruised and moved with difficulty. They went downstairs. The hotel lobby was swarming with Small Americans. A new banner, STAND TALL AND BE COUNTED, announced the opening of the convention.

They drove through town in her open convertible. Levanter noticed several passers-by staring at the two of them with obvious hostility. He asked Jolene what angered them, and she said it was simply the unthinking reaction of the townspeople who had known her for a long time and were unaccustomed to seeing her openly consorting with a stranger.

She took Levanter to lunch at the Impton Inn, the best restaurant in town. The hostess who escorted them to their table was polite to Jolene but curt with Levanter.

While they were eating, a group of well-dressed men and women arrived and were seated at a table nearby. One of the men, pale and stern-looking, glanced around, and when his eyes fell on Jolene his jaw tightened. He looked searchingly at Levanter.

"Who is he?" asked Levanter.

"That's Greg," she answered, unperturbed. "My click-click Greg. Remember?"

"And the others?" Levanter asked.

She turned to look at them again. "Friends, acquaintances."

"What do they do?"

"They're all in business."

Levanter looked puzzled. "I thought you told me Greg was a lawyer?"

She played with her salad before she answered. "He gave up law when his father died and he inherited the family business. Now Greg is head of Impton Consolidated, one of the largest companies in the state."

"You were the wife of a very important man," said Levanter, all at once aware of how little she had actually told him about herself.

"I was," said Jolene. "That's why you're being stared at. This is a company town. The company practically owns the town, and Greg owns the company. Now that I've left Greg, everyone thinks there's no longer a place for me here. They think they can disown me. And they certainly don't want you!" She laughed, reaching for his hand and squeezing it in full view of the people at the other table.

Levanter was comforted by the thought that he could fly back to New York as soon as he wished.

"When did you leave Greg?" he asked.

"A few months ago."

"Is the separation legal?"

She let go of his hand. "It may not be legal, but it sure is clear-cut, as far as this town is concerned."

"But technically you're still married to Greg, aren't you?" Levanter persisted.

"Only technically. So what?" She looked at him with a defiant expression.

"Wouldn't you be better off leaving Impton?" Levanter asked.

"There was a time when I simply wanted to run away," she said, "to start a new life. But, like so many others before me, I discovered that in this country we belong to our families, our families do not belong to us. Only newcomers, like you, know how to change their lives overnight, how to develop new interests, take up different professions, generate fresh emotions."

Levanter made no comment. She looked at him with an ironic smile.

"I read in a magazine that the average American housewife doesn't run away until she's past thirty-five, has been married for at least fifteen years, and has one or two kids. And, quite likely, within a year she is traced by detectives solely because, in her new surroundings, she betrays herself by wearing the same hairdo, clothes, jewelry, and make-up. What's more, she is likely to date a man who physically and professionally resembles the one she ran away from." She took a few bites of her lunch. "I have devised a system for running away while remaining at home," she said. "I find strangers, as I found you." She paused. "But something significant happened to me last night."

"What do you mean?" he asked.

"For years, I've been hiding in my private maze, cut off and isolated. I didn't even know who I was anymore," Jolene said with a nervous smile. "All the men I've been with before you have been from around here. They're as local as I am, and I knew the standards they judged me by—those are my standards too, after all. With you I should feel apprehension, since I don't know what your standards are. But I don't feel cautious at all. I am not afraid to say or do anything that might displease you, as I have been with other men. I'm myself—it's the ultimate risk."

"I'm planning to leave tomorrow," Levanter said. She was silent.

Before they finished their meal, two Small Americans appeared in the doorway of the restaurant, lingering a moment on the threshold before they wandered uncertainly into the room. Again, as in the bar the night before, everyone looked at them and the voices in the room dropped to soft whispers. The hostess beckoned them haughtily to follow her and placed them in the farthest corner. As Levanter glanced about the room, he observed that in the Impton Inn today it was he, not the midgets, who got all the attention.

After lunch, Jolene went home to rest. Levanter walked along the main street. He stopped in front of the window of a large general store, startled by the array of handguns, rifles, shotguns, ammunition, and holsters. Then he realized that the sale of guns was legal in the state, and no permit was required to own a weapon. Only a visitor would be startled by such a display. He entered the store, walking past magazine racks, shelves of personal-hygiene products, and the pharmaceuticals counter, straight to the gun department.

A young man had just bought a rifle and two boxes of ammunition. The salesman placed two more boxes beside his purchase. "That's on the house," he said, as he wrote up the order. The customer paid, picked up his package, and left.

The salesman turned to Levanter, smiling. "What can I do for you?"

Levanter studied the pistols and revolvers in the glass case.

The salesman looked down at them also. "These are just a few samples of what we carry," he said. "Tell me what kind of gun you own, and I'll tell you what others you might still need."

"I don't own a gun," said Levanter.

The salesman looked surprised. "Do you want something for defense or for a hobby?" he asked.

"Defense as a hobby," said Levanter, smiling.

"Nowadays, the only hobby a man needs," the salesman agreed. He reached into the case and pulled out a revolver. "How about a mini-derringer? A real five-shot beaut. Easy to load, easy to shoot, easy to conceal."

Levanter contemplated the revolver. With it, one's creativity at the moment of danger was reduced to the crude squeezing of the trigger. He shook his head.

The salesman leaned over the counter and said in a confidential tone, "Did you know that an awful lot of violence is committed against strangers? Last year, over one third of those killed did not know their assailants." He put the mini-derringer back in the case. "What line of business are you in?"

"Investing," said Levanter.

"Travel a lot?"

Levanter nodded.

"Then how about this Bulldog forty-four?" He pulled out another revolver. "An ideal featherweight, easy-to-hide gun. The best investment you can make these days."

Levanter pretended to be unconvinced.

The salesman tried another tack. "Are you married or single?" he asked.

"Single. No children."

"Where do you spend most of your time, city or country?"

"Big cities."

The salesman pulled out two longer pistols. "One of these might do. The fifteen-shot Parabellum. Custom-made for mixed neighborhoods, you might say, if you know what I mean!" He winked. "But for sure speed, here's a true beast," he said, passing another handgun to Levanter. "A real savage!" he said. "Eleven shots in a single second! As they say, it aims to please, it pleases to aim." He looked proud of his wit.

The gun felt cold and smooth in Levanter's hand.

"The other day a man comes in," the salesman said. "He's a black, a neat dresser, and speaks with an accent. So I think he's one of those darky diplomats who do business with Impton Consolidated for one of those safari-land countries where the blacks kill each other like flies."

Levanter did not comment.

The salesman went right ahead. "So I lay out the best guns I handle: Browning, Beretta, Smith and Wesson, Winchester, Colt, Charter Arms, you name it! He picks up a Mossberg twenty-gauge shotgun and pats it and feels it like a girl, and he aims it at the street like a toy. So I say, 'Sir, I'll give you the best deal in town if you want a few hundred of these for your people!' And he smiles real sweetly at me and says, 'My people would sure love to use them every day!' So I ask, 'What country are you from, sir?' And he gives me this scary look and says, 'Harlem, New York!' " The salesman chuckled, his heavy belly bouncing up and down.

Apologizing for not being able to make up his mind, Levanter put down the handgun. The salesman was close to giving up. It was a rare customer who did not find a gun that pleased him, he said. He put his elbow on the counter and ran his fingers through his hair. Suddenly he looked up at Levanter as if seeing him in a new light. "Say, do you mind if I ask you a personal question?" he asked.

"Shoot!"

The salesman failed to noticed Levanter's little joke. He kept on. "Do you go out with a lot of women?"

Levanter nodded.

The salesman recoiled. "Mostly with other men's wives, I take it," he said, a disapproving look on his face. "It was you this morning in Jolene's car, wasn't it?"

"It was," said Levanter.

"I knew it. I thought you looked familiar when you walked in here. Don't you cross Greg that way again," he whispered.

"What if I do?" asked Levanter with a smile.

The salesman backed away from the counter. "Let me give it to you straight: if you do, you don't need a gun—you need a tank." He turned to another customer who had just come to the counter.

Levanter walked back to the Taft. As he was about to enter the revolving door, he was stopped by a solid-looking police officer, tall, with closely cropped gray hair. Wearing a well-fitting uniform, puffing gracefully on his pipe, he introduced himself courteously as the Chief of Police. He recognized Levanter, he explained with a polite smile, from a description given him by one of his deputies. He suggested that Levanter accompany him to the police station to discuss what he termed "a delicate matter." Levanter got into the police car.

At the station house, the Chief led Levanter into a small office and shut the door. They were alone. The Chief gestured Levanter to a chair and sat down opposite him.

"You could have refused to come here with me, Mr. Levanter," he said, "but you're reasonable and so you did not. Now I hope you will listen to me and continue to be reasonable." He placed one hand on his belt and stroked his holster with the other.

Levanter slowly shook his head. "If you are about to tell me I ought to get out of Impton," he said, "I can spare you the trouble. I've already made plans to return to New York tomorrow."

The Chief nodded sympathetically. He pulled his chair closer to Levanter's. "Now why do you think I want you out of town?" he asked.

"Because of Jolene."

The Chief got up and walked to the window. He stared out at the street for several seconds, then spun around and made a sweeping motion with his hands, as though brushing away Levanter's remark. "The truth is," he said, stressing each word, "that I want you to stay in Impton. About a month will do."

"Why on earth would I stay in Impton for a month?" asked Levanter.

The Chief picked up his pipe and tapped the bowl. "Because you're needed here, George, that's why."

"Needed by whom?"

The Chief plucked at the creases in his trousers,

then looked at Levanter mildly, as if to placate him for what he was going to say. "Let me begin by saying you're needed by me, needed by Greg, and needed by the folks of this town."

"I still intend to leave tomorrow," Levanter said sternly.

The Chief thought for a moment, then said, "And I've got the means to make sure you don't slip away when my back is turned." A faint smile crossed his face. "Under county regulations, members of the police force are allowed to moonlight in uniform during off-duty hours and can hold security jobs for private employers. You know, like guards for nightclubs or apartment houses, banks, and so on. As for me"—he pushed out his chest and drew in his belly—"I moonlight by hiring out off-duty police as security guards for all branches of Impton Consolidated. They wear their regular police uniforms and carry their service guns. It gives the boys a nice extra income and cuts down on the temptation for graft! And so," he said with a grin, "I hope I can persuade you not to leave Impton."

"A real guns-for-hire setup," said Levanter. "Would any one of these guys act if he saw his generous employer doing something wrong? Has anybody in this town or in the state ever complained about conflict of interest?" he asked.

"Would you like to be the first to try?" the Chief asked sarcastically. Then, his voice becoming slightly sharper, he said, "In any case, Greg wants an uncontested divorce from Jolene. She's nothing but a whore. She refused to give him a divorce and thought she could force him into a financial settlement by openly carrying on with out-of-towners every weekend. But her blackmail hasn't worked. Not only that. Because of her filthy behavior she has lost any right she might have had to their daughter."

"Jolene didn't tell me she and Greg had a child," Levanter said.

"They have the sweetest little girl in town. There are probably a lot of things Jolene didn't tell you, George. But when she picked you up, even she didn't know she had picked up the one lover who was going to be her undoing."

Levanter squirmed. "How am I so different from all the others?"

"You're the first real stranger, and an alien too: no business or political connections, no family, no church, no community around here to claim you. You don't even have a decent reason to be in Impton."

"You've certainly done your homework, Chief. How did you find out all this?"

The Chief shrugged, giving Levanter a disarming smile. "On the telephone," he said, pleased with himself. "I started with the car rental. You gave some references there. I followed those leads and ended up talking with that ass of a booking agent, the one who gave us all those human miniatures instead of the real kids we were expecting." He paused, as if deciding whether to tell Levanter the rest. Then he continued, "And just before you and I met, my deputy radioed me that you were about to buy yourself a handgun but couldn't find one to your liking." He pointed to the gun riding in his holster. "Customized Magnum Blackhawk. Six-and-a-half-inch barrel. Hundred-and-fifty-yard range! Six seconds to reload," he boasted. "Last year it sure helped me to win the State Police Combat Championships!"

Levanter glanced at the gun. "Would you use it to prevent me from leaving Impton?" he asked.

"Glad you asked," the Chief snapped. With one of the keys on his large ring, he unlocked a drawer in the desk. He pulled out the drawer, placing it on top of the desk, right in front of Levanter. In it, Levanter saw a pistol equipped with a silencer, a snub-nosed revolver, a Swiss army knife, a drinking glass, and several empty drug vials.

The Chief moved closer to Levanter, towering over him. "A teacher at the Police Academy who spoke with an accent a bit like yours," he said, "once explained to us that in this nation people in fifty states are governed by over a million different laws, and they defend themselves against these laws with over a hundred million guns." Looking attentively at Levanter, he paused. "And so it is only our Constitution and our television that bind us together." He grinned jovially. "With the exception, of course, of aliens and criminals, who are first bound together by the FBI that finger printed them all."

Like a card player about to make his final bid, he grew serious. "You are an alien, George, a member of that special clan of the fingerprinted. I would like you now to pick up all the objects you see in this drawer, one at a time, and then put them back!" He pushed the drawer closer to Levanter.

Levanter felt assailed by the uncalled-for threat. "What if I refuse?" he asked.

"You know the odds. I'll make sure you pick them up anyway." The Chief laughed softly, patting his holster again.

Reluctantly, Levanter picked up and replaced the articles, one by one. When he finished, the Chief carefully wrapped them in paper, replaced the drawer, and locked it. He looked hard at Levanter. "I reckon you'll make a perfect witness for Greg," he said, nodding. "With you and your accent on the stand, that bitch, that used-up piece of trash, won't have a chance in court."

He opened the door for Levanter. "Right before might," he said, smiling.

Driving back to the Taft, the Chief turned to look at Levanter. "So many trailer parks around here"—he spoke slowly and distinctly—"there's always some crime being committed by hoods we don't know, felons from out of town." He went on in a confident tone. "If you leave this town before I tell you to, any one of the gismos you just fingerprinted will be found near the scene of a crime: a nice proof that you committed it during your stay here. Even a fancy lawyer from New York can't help you here. So you see, George, I have stuck you to the cross without nails!"

Evidently pleased with this conclusion, he drove without speaking for a few minutes. Then he turned again to his passenger. "Last year, one of those American Nazi Party lunatics went on trial here for beating up a decent man of the Jewish faith who was attending a convention. Well, the judge and the lawyers reckoned that with a Nazi against a Jew, with all the public knowledge of what the Nazis did to the Jews, they didn't have a prayer of finding an unbiased jury!" He gave a hearty laugh. "I'll tell you, they couldn't have been more wrong! Not one of the twenty or so folks they asked about Nazis and Jews during the Second World War could tell what exactly went wrong between them! The only people in these parts who hate Nazis are the ones who put Nazis and Communists in the same bag. Now you"—he paused—"you went to a Communist university down there, in Moscow. You were a Communist, weren't you?"

"In a Communist country, all the universities are Communist. But I was not," said Levanter.

The Chief listened absent-mindedly, then continued. "Imagine yourself on trial. Let's say, for murder. A jury here would no more believe what you say about why you came all the way to Impton than they would believe that you were not a Communist, or that you were 'fingerprinted' by Impton's Chief of Police!" He chuckled.

Levanter shrugged and took a small mirror from his jacket pocket.

"What are you doing? What's that?" he asked.

"It's a mirror," said Levanter, displaying it in his hand. "A polished glass backed by silver coating to form images by the reflection of rays of light. Also known as a looking glass."

"I know what a mirror is!" the Chief cut in.

"But you just asked what it was!"

The Chief was annoyed. "Why do you carry a mirror?"

"To see myself. I can't think of any better way." As the Chief watched him scornfully, Levanter looked at himself in the mirror and combed his hair.

"I don't like to see you do that to yourself," said the Chief, grimacing. "Just keep in mind that at Jolene's trial you'll testify as a ladies' man, not a men's."

They arrived at the hotel, and Levanter stepped out of the car. The Chief gave him a long, searching look.

"Now you behave yourself, George, you hear! You don't, and I'll find you a bride right here," he shouted as he pulled away from the curb. "Then you'll never leave Impton!"

Bored and restless during his unexpectedly prolonged stay in Impton, Levanter would flip through the local newspaper for interesting items. There was a famous research laboratory just outside of town, and one day, Levanter spotted a reference to the man in charge, a scientist he had met with Jacques Monod a few years before. He decided to take a ride out. The scientist remembered him and was delighted to have the opportunity to show the complex of laboratories to a vistor. When most of his staff had left for the day, he took Levanter on a tour of the research facilities.

Levanter had been educated in the humanities and had little background in science. Even though his host tried to avoid technical terminology, to Levanter his explanations of various instruments and installations sounded like pure science fiction.

"This," said the scientist, pointing through a window at a giant structure, "contains a linear accelerator.

The energy used just to turn it on would dim all the lights of a city as large as Chicago."

"What would happen if such a mechanism blew up?" asked Levanter.

Mildly amused, the scientist waved his hand. "For a layman, there is, of course, a certain degree of strangeness in all this," he said, "but I can assure you it's all as safe as a baby's cradle."

They entered another lab. "This is an ultra-centrifuge rotor," he said. "The rotor is balanced on a flexible wire. If the wire should snap, the rotor would spin off like a projectile—with enough force to go through a thick wall of concrete."

Again Levanter asked, "What are the chances of such an accident?"

The scientist dismissed his fears. "Practically zero," he said.

Levanter was shown a number of scientific achievements: tanks that stored liquid nitrogen at minus one hundred and ninety degrees; an electron microscope through which one could view the atoms in a speck of gold; rows of rooms with walls covered with absolute virus filters; an instrument capable of slicing matter into sections thinner than wavelengths of visible light; and many other scientific marvels the uses of which he did not understand.

Then he took Levanter to his own microbiology laboratory, where he handed him a white lab coat to put on. They went through two sets of heavy doors, separated by an empty vestibule, and entered a large room.

"This is the core of our research on immunology and cell culture," he said. He switched on the lights. Every side of the room was filled with stacked cages full of mice.

As Levanter looked around, he saw a mouse run across the floor to hide under a stack of cages. The scientist did not see the animal.

"The temperature of this room is automatically

monitored," he said. "To prevent even the slightest indirect contact between mice in various test groups, the air, spread in linear sheets, is replaced in the room one hundred and sixty times an hour. That's why"—he smiled—"you can't smell mice in here. Yet there are two thousand of them, in more than a hundred cages."

Levanter shook his head in amazement.

The scientist went on. "We inject each group of mice with a particular serum," he explained. "The crucial element is keeping the mice in every cage totally separate from all the others. That's why the air doesn't mix in here; why it flows vertically, in sheets."

"Could a mouse escape from a cage?" Levanter asked casually.

The scientist smiled. "These cages are specially designed to make it impossible," he said. "As you see"—he drew Levanter over to the cages—"the cage grillwork is so narrow that not even the smallest mouse could possibly squeeze through."

"But couldn't a mouse escape when it is being put in or taken out of its cage for inoculations?" asked Levanter.

"Not a chance! The mice are handled one at a time by a member of our staff trained especially for the task." He seemed to be amused by Levanter's skepticism.

Levanter bent down as if to tie his shoelace. Under the stack of cages he could see the small white mouse, its nostrils twitching, its whiskers quivering. He straightened up. "Assuming the impossible," Levanter persisted, "what would happen if, let's say, one mouse managed to escape and to move about the room unnoticed for a while?"

"Assuming the impossible," the scientist said, humoring his visitor, "the mouse would probably sniff and touch other mice through the grillwork, thereby contaminating all of them. Since our research is based on collecting tissues from mice in strictly separated test groups, this would render the entire project invalid. That's why it's unthinkable." Clearly considering the matter closed, he reached for the light switch, ready to leave the room.

Levanter stopped him gently. "What if I told you," he said slowly, "that when we entered this room I actually saw a mouse running across the floor?"

The scientist looked at him. "I'd know that you were suffering from a momentary illusion."

"And if I insist I saw a mouse?"

"That you are a victim of hallucination!"

"If I swear I saw it?"

"That you are paranoid!" He laughed.

"How certain are you that at this very moment a mouse is not loose in this room?" Levanter persisted.

The scientist turned to Levanter as if to open a formal debate. "Absolutely certain. I know how this lab is run. This stage of our research has been specifically devised to avoid such slip-ups. Only the most reliable and responsible scientists handle the mice, and their research—in immunology, cell culture, and fractionation, for example—depends on what originates here, on accurately injecting the mice in one test group with serum, and on careful control against mishap. We are meticulous and vigilant in this lab." He scrutinized Levanter's face. "Are you convinced now?"

Levanter was not about to give up. "Still and all, what is the probability of finding an escaped mouse in this room now?" he asked with a grin.

"It's zero," said the scientist. "After all, a mouse is not an atom," he added. "Here, where we're accustomed to dealing with the tiniest particles of matter, a mouse would loom larger than an elephant."

"Would you stake your life against such a possibility?"

"I certainly would."

"And this laboratory?"

"Certainly."

Levanter got down on his knees and looked under the stack of cages. The mouse still crouched there, staring at him. He reached toward it, and the mouse ran straight out into the middle of the room. There, encountering the scientist, it backed a foot away from him.

Motionless, the scientist and the animal stared at each other. The blood drained from the man's face, his eyes went blank. The mouse sniffed and strained, then, as both men remained still, scurried across the room and hid once again under the cages. A long moment passed. The scientist regained control of himself and pressed an alarm button. A young research assistant rushed into the room.

The scientist could barely control his rage. "There's a mouse loose in this room!" he snapped.

The young man was incredulous. "That's just not possible, sir!" he said.

"I saw it! It's hiding under the cages!" exclaimed the scientist.

"It's an illusion!" said the assistant mildly. "You know as well as I do that no mouse could ever escape."

"I tell you I saw it!" the scientist repeated with emphasis.

Clearly unconvinced, the young man nonetheless apparently wanted to accommodate his superior. "I once thought I saw a mouse too," he said.

The scientist was on the verge of losing his temper. As he stepped toward the cages, the mouse ran out, scampered across the room, and hid under the cages on the opposite side.

Flushed and stricken, the young man stared at the floor. "I don't understand how—it just couldn't—" he mumbled.

Without a word, the scientist left the room. Levanter followed.

"Well, worse things happen," said the scientist when they were outside. "Oil tankers break in half. Jumbo jets collide. Flu vaccines paralyze. General competence and individual responsibility are on the decline, you know."

Thinking aloud, the scientist went on. "Now all the mice will have to be replaced, and everything based on the data we supplied to other research centers must be declared invalid. So will most of the findings we released for presentation at scientific congresses, seminars, and other conferences. A wipe-out."

Levanter couldn't think of anything to say to him.

"A human error," the scientist said, "and we'll probably never know whose. Still, Impton Consolidated will continue to pay the bills." He seemed suddenly cheered by the thought. "What luck that you offered to stay and be a witness for Greg at his unfortunate divorce trial."

Both sides of the busy New York street were filled with cars, so Levanter had to double-park. But before he could turn off the engine, a police squad car came along on the other side of the street and pulled up across from him. A sergeant rolled down the window and leaned out. "No double-parking. Move!" he shouted.

"I can't," Levanter called back.

The sergeant stepped out of his car and crossed over, hands on his hips. "What do you mean 'can't'? You just move!"

Levanter took his wallet from his back pocket. He opened it and slowly removed his driver's license and a laminated card. The card identified him as a member of the American Council for Global Security, Washington, D.C. The Council was a small educational society which regularly polled its members for their views on such issues as the television networks' fairness in their coverage of American military strength and reported the results in its monthly mimeographed newsletter. Membership in the Council was open to the general public for an annual fee of five dollars, which included the newsletter subscription and a membership card. Levanter had joined as soon as he returned home from Impton.

He handed the sergeant his driver's license and, purposely hesitating, the membership card. "You guys do your job, we do ours," he said indifferently. The sergeant glanced at the license, and then examined the membership card. Levanter watched him study the Council's symbol: an American eagle, clutching the globe, with the credo PEACE THROUGH VIGILANCE above it, bracketed by two military insignia stars.

Just as Levanter had hoped, the sergeant, sharing the confusion caused by a series of public disclosures about the White House, the CIA, and the FBI, assumed that the Council was yet another of the government's elitist intelligence units and that Levanter was one of its agents. He scanned the surrounding buildings, then bent closer to Levanter. "Stalking them right here?" he whispered, furrowing his brow in an expression of complicity.

"As you see," Levanter assured him.

Without further question, the sergeant returned the license and card. "Are they really in this crummy block?" He shook his head in disbelief.

"They are everywhere. But so are we," whispered Levanter, winking.

"Right you are." The sergeant saluted, returned to his car, and, waving at Levanter, drove away.

Levanter turned off his engine. He picked up two bundles of shirts from the rear seat and carried them into the laundry. As Levanter placed the bundles on the counter, the Chinese shopkeeper reached for them. Levanter stopped him.

"The shirts in this pile are just to be washed," he said. "Only the ones in the other pile are to be starched. Please be careful not to mix them up."

The muscles in the face of the Chinese tightened. He grabbed both mounds of shirts and threw them together into one linen bag. Without a word, he handed Levanter a receipt.

Levanter took the ticket from him and carefully placed it in his wallet. "Too bad you're disregarding my instructions," he continued in an even, calm voice. "I'll pick them up tomorrow, and I hope there'll be no mistake." He leaned slightly toward the man in exaggerated politeness. The man turned around, picked up the bag, and, almost running, disappeared into the back room.

When Levanter came back the next day to collect his shirts, the Chinese took his ticket without looking at him or saying anything. He handed Levanter two packages and turned away. Levanter put down an envelope he was carrying and tore open both packages. Almost immediately he saw that one of two shirts of identical fabric had been starched. Summoning the shopkeeper, he pointed to the starched shirt. "I warned you not to mix up my shirts," he said firmly. "And now look what you've done!"

The man was breathing fast, but still stood immobile, looking away from Levanter.

"Even a child could see that these two shirts are made of the same delicate fabric, which must not be starched. But you couldn't see it and used starch on one. Now that shirt is damaged. Do you expect to charge me for such inferior work?"

The Chinese became apoplectic; the veins swelled in his forehead, his eyes bulged in their sockets. He backed away from the counter and started to stamp on the floor, hitting his thighs with his clenched fists. He gasped, apparently searching for English words, but instead ranted something in Chinese.

"It seems you have forgotten not only how to launder shirts and how to speak English," said Levanter coolly, "but also how to behave like a true Chinese." He began to gather up his shirts.

The man stepped forward again, close to the counter. He had found his English. "I can forget America," he said. "I can forget English. I can forget you and your shirts. But you—you—" He seemed to be planning a decisive verbal attack. "You," he repeated slowly, pointing at Levanter, "you cannot forget what you do not know." As if proud of his logic, he laughed hysterically. "You cannot forget China because you have never been there," he repeated. "The Chinese people are very proud. They would never let your kind in," he declared triumphantly. He leaned against the counter. "Now go out of my Chinese store."

"I am about to leave," said Levanter calmly. "But I knew your thoughts in advance, so look what I have brought to show you." He reached for his envelope and drew out an eight-by-ten black-and-white glossy press photograph of himself surrounded by Chinese officials, standing under a large poster of Mao Tse-tung in front of Peking's Great Hall of the People.

The man took the picture, glanced at it, then brought it closer to his eyes. His teeth clenched, he tore the photograph into tiny scraps and, screaming incoherently in English and Chinese, scattered the pieces like confetti around the shop. A black worker came running from the back room. When she saw her boss jumping around in a rage, her mouth dropped open. The Chinese was throwing the last scraps of the photo when he noticed her. Suddenly he sat down, quivering, his face in his hands, quietly sobbing. Levanter left his payment on the counter, picked up his shirts, and walked out.

Returning home from a late dinner with friends, Levanter spotted an attractive prostitute standing in a knot of six Japanese men with attaché cases in their hands and cameras around their necks. The woman was taller than all the men and her voice easily carried to Levanter, who stopped a few feet away from the group.

"A screw's a screw," she was saying, sounding annoyed and impatient. "And if all you guys are with me in one room, you pay once for the room, but six times for me. Get it?"

In subdued, heavily accented voices, the men argued that since she had to undress and dress only once, they wouldn't take as much of her time as six separate men.

"A screw's a screw," repeated the woman. "Six screws is six screws. Take it or leave it."

But the Japanese men continued to bargain. She would save on taxi fares to and from her hotel, one reasoned.

"Six screws is six times the money. That's how I count," she said. She began to lose her temper. "I've had enough of your kind anyway."

A disagreement broke out among the men. Looking away from them, the woman saw Levanter.

"Are you with them?" she shouted accusingly at him. Levanter assured her he wasn't. She turned her back on the Japanese and came to him. "Are you going out?" she asked in a stern but inviting tone. She was young and fresh-looking, with a roguish air and expressive eyes.

"I'm already out," said Levanter. "Don't you want to know if I'm going in?"

She laughed, tossing her long, shiny hair. "Do you or don't you want company?"

"Not company," said Levanter. "You."

She told him her price. "There's this place two minutes from here." She named a midtown tourist hotel, took Levanter by the arm, and walked beside him, matching his long stride.

As soon as they entered the brightly lit hotel room, she took his jacket and felt in all the pockets. Then she patted his pants pockets. Evidently confident that Levanter carried neither a weapon nor a detective's badge, she began to stroke his hips more gently. Levanter handed her the money.

"I can tell you don't mind the light," she said as she bolted the door. "Some guys don't want to see what they do."

She stood in the center of the room, spread her legs, and began to undress, examining herself in the large mirror across from the bed. Conscious of every gesture, she removed each article of clothing in a deliberate fashion until she was naked. As her gaze wandered over the mirror, her hands trailed down her belly, her fingers alternating with the palm of her hand in making long curved strokes, squeezing and kneading her flesh, then gliding back over her body. She extended her arm toward Levanter and pulled him beside her. As he watched the two of them in the mirror, she rubbed and pressed her body against his, flinging her arms around him, licking his neck all the way up to his ear while she unbuttoned his shirt and loosened his belt.

As his hands stroked her thighs, Levanter saw her eyes in the mirror. Her gaze seemed to be directed beyond the reflection in the mirror; he began to wonder whether she was performing for the benefit of someone else, whether he and the woman were being watched from the other side of the mirror.

Levanter caressed the woman with one hand; with the other he reached behind him and picked up an ashtray. Then, in a single motion, he pushed her aside and swung his arm as if to hurl the ashtray at the mirror.

From behind the mirror came the muffled crash of an overturned chair and the sound of scrambling, of someone rushing away.

Levanter sped out of the room into the corridor and forced open the door to the next room. He discovered that he was right. A movie camera, mounted on a tripod, was aimed at the back of the mirror, and he could see the woman dressing hastily in the room he had just left.

All at once, two middle-aged men rushed forward and placed themselves between Levanter and the camera.

"I want this film exposed right now," said Levanter calmly.

"Listen, you good-for-nothing creep!" one shouted, stepping toward Levanter with clenched fists, as the other edged behind Levanter to cut him off from the door.

Levanter did not move. He reached for his wallet, took out his American Council for Global Security membership card, and pushed it under the nose of the man who had just shouted at him. "Take a look at this," he said.

The man took the card, scrutinized it carefully, then cautiously handed it to the other. Neither said anything as they returned the card to Levanter. They were clearly no longer in a fighting mood. In the next room the woman finished dressing, grabbed her bag, and, without a backward glance, ran out.

"I'm here on assignment," said Levanter, putting the card back into his wallet. "And there are others like me in the hotel at this moment. Now," he said in the most officious tone he could muster, "you have a choice: either you expose the film or we expose you."

The men looked at each other. Without a word, one opened the camera and pulled out the cartridge. "My gift to the Feds," he said, handing the film to Levanter.

The other one grinned at Levanter. "Why didn't you wait a bit longer and enjoy yourself with the chick?" he asked. "How often do you get to play in a porno flick?"

Ronsard-Thibaudet Samael, President of the African Republic of Lotan, was a world-renowned essayist and the author of numerous works on the nature of language. Investors International had decided to honor him with its prestigious Humanitarian Award.

Levanter, one of the organizers of the event, went to the New York hotel where President Samael's entourage was staying. He had an appointment with the State Department official serving as Samael's adviser during his visit and was given a careful security check by three United States Secret Service agents both before entering the elevator and as he stepped out of it.

A tall, red-haired woman, with full breasts and unusually white skin, was waiting for Levanter at the door. Levanter mentally nicknamed her Oklahoma: a lot of everything but no detail to speak of. She introduced herself as President Samael's adviser. Inside, she pointed to the papers spread all over her sofa, desk, and table, explaining that these were the detailed security plans for the Investors International dinner. President Samael was to be honored as a thinker and humanitarian. But since many Afro-Americans in the United States were fanatically opposed to his administration's domestic reforms and foreign policies, his visit had turned into a political event, necessitating elaborate security measures. The State Department adviser was the liaison for the various federal and city agencies involved.

Levanter looked over the list of notables invited to the dinner; then he and Oklahoma started working on the final seating plan.

There was a knock at the door, but Oklahoma made no move to answer it. Assuming that she expected him to respond, Levanter went to the door and opened it.

He faced a handsome, slender man whose dense silver hair contrasted with the black skin of his youthful face. The man was naked except for a pair of unusually narrow briefs. Such a tight, sparse garment, Levanter thought with amusement, could go a long way toward sustaining the notion of black virility. A freshly starched white shirt hung by its collar from the man's forefinger.

The man did not express any surprise at encountering a stranger at her door. Stepping past Levanter without speaking, he entered the room and went straight to the woman. He embraced her and whispered something in her ear. Levanter, ill at ease, remained at the door and looked away. But the man left as quickly as he had arrived, passing Levanter on his way out, still dangling his shirt. Levanter turned back into the room. Oklahoma, flushed, made no comment, and the two of them went on with their work as if nothing had happened.

A few minutes later there was another knock at the door. This time Levanter ignored it, and the woman went to answer. The same man entered. He was wearing a tailored dark blue suit, starched white shirt, fashionable wide tie, and shiny, pointy-toed shoes. Levanter, who had seen many photographs of President Samael, although he had never met him in person, recognized the man instantly and rose to greet him.

Oklahoma led him over to Levanter and introduced them. President Samael extended his hand and Levanter shook it. The President stepped back, looked at him, then turned to Oklahoma. With a straight face, he said, "Mr. Levanter and I have met once before, but it was some time ago and we have both changed." Addressing Levanter, he said, "You, Mr. Levanter, might even have forgotten our first meeting!"

"Indeed, Mr. President," said Levanter with an equally solemn expression, "it was, after all, so long ago."

Samael smiled. Assuring Levanter that he was looking forward to the dinner, he kissed Oklahoma on her cheek and left.

As Levanter and Oklahoma settled down to work again, Levanter remarked that President Samael was a very charming man.

The adviser raised her head and nodded. "A fine gentleman," she said. After a moment, she added solemnly, "And always smartly dressed."

In Tunisia on behalf of Investors International, Levanter attended a gala, where he was introduced to an Arab diplomat, a former Interpol official. A handsome man with dark, intense eyes, the Arab carried himself with an air of detachment. He offered to take Levanter for a ride in his new, custom-built Italian sports car.

They drove slowly through the crowded suburbs of Tunis, then moved onto an open highway, past giant billboards displaying life-sized portraits of the country's president, and turned off at a dirt road.

Passing through peasant villages, the diplomat honked the horn to clear a passage through the crowds of half-naked men, women, and children who crawled out of their huts to stare at the car. The long gleaming hood kept brushing against villagers who failed to jump out of the way in time. In one village, a camel stubbornly blocked the road, and the diplomat was forced to stop. A crowd of onlookers pressed closer to the sleek machine.

An old beggar, his hand outstretched, hobbled over to the car on Levanter's side. His chest was covered with dirt and sores, his trousers were in shreds, his feet bare. One eye was barely visible in a pool of oozing pus. He wore a wreath of fresh lemon-blossoms over his matted gray hair. He brought his face close to the window and fixed his good eye on Levanter. When Levanter made no move to open the window, the beggar began to twitch and placed his gnarled hands on the glass, his crooked fingers crawling over it like leeches.

Levanter reached into his pocket for some coins and pressed the window control button on his door, lowering the glass. A hot steaming odor filled the car. Levanter offered the money to the beggar, who jerked his hands off, refusing to take it. The diplomat started to press the button to close the window, but Levanter restrained him.

The beggar put his head next to Levanter's. Spittle drooled from his toothless mouth and a dry rattle came from his throat. Finally, in halting French, he managed to say, "Do you—do you know Cecil Beaton?" He watched Levanter in suspense, waiting for an answer. Levanter nodded; a smile crossed the man's face. "When I was young, Cecil Beaton knew me well. He photographed me. He said I was the most beautiful boy he had ever met." His sighted eye blinked; he watched Levanter's face as if expecting some response.

Just then the camel moved off the road. Obviously annoyed, the diplomat sent the window the rest of the way up and stepped on the gas. As the car took off, the rear fender grazed the beggar, and he fell to the ground.

Back at Levanter's residence, the diplomat politely escorted Levanter to the door. "Have you had a chance to visit the new baths in Hammamet?" he asked.

Levanter replied that he hadn't.

"You must." The diplomat placed his hand on Levanter's. "There you can enjoy some of the most stunning creatures nature has devised," he said, lowering his voice. "Young, so very young. And how beautiful!" He smacked his lips in appreciation. "I'll be glad to take you there," he added in a whisper, his fingers pressing Levanter's wrist.

"That's most kind of you," said Levanter. "Where do these girls come from?"

The diplomat looked at him with unabashed amazement. "Girls?" he said, chuckling and patting Levanter's forearm. "Who mentioned girls?" He glanced at Levanter as if seeing him for the first time. "My dear George, you are a fetishist, aren't you?" He was still laughing as he left, calling out, "I guess I'll see you when we're both back in New York."

A New York hostess invited Levanter to a party at which the United States Secretary of State and a Soviet poet whom Levanter had known at the university in Moscow were also to be guests.

At one point in the evening, Levanter saw the poet

talking with the Secretary of State and removing his wristwatch. He moved closer and overheard the poet urging the Secretary to do the same. Exchanging watches, the poet explained, was a Russian custom carried out in the spirit of friendship: one man's watch times his friendship for another. Aware that other guests were watching him, the Secretary, always the consummate negotiator, removed his Tissot and reluctantly gave it to the Poet, accepting the poet's Pobyeda in return.

When Levanter returned home from the party, he had hardly walked in the door before the phone rang. It was the Arab diplomat, who was one of the guests, calling on behalf of the hostess. He told Levanter that the wife of the Secretary of State had just called the hostess to say her husband wanted to renegotiate the wristwatch exchange. The hostess did not feel she knew the Soviet poet well enough and had asked if Levanter could tactfully persuade the poet to take back his generous gesture of friendship. The relative monetary values were apparently not at issue, the hostess assured the diplomat, although the Tissot was vintage and expensive and the mass-produced Pobyeda was cheap and new. The reason the Secretary wanted to retrieve his own watch was that it had been given to him during his youth in Germany, and there was a lot of sentiment attached to it.

The next morning, Levanter picked up the Pobyeda and went to see the poet to collect the Tissot. When he explained his mission, the poet went into a rage. He shouted that during his poetry reading tour in the United States he had traded many Soviet-made Pobyedas for the watches of some very distinguished Americans, many of them Harvard colleagues of the Secretary of State, and no one had ever reneged on the exchange. As evidence, he brought out an impressive collection of Rolexes, Omegas, Pulsars, and Seikos. He plucked the Tissot from the collection and handed it to Levanter.

"Who does he think he is?" the poet ranted in Russian. "Just because he was born in Germany and speaks with a German accent, he doesn't have to behave like a German!" He shouted that *"pobyeda"* might translate as "victory," but it certainly did not mean the victory of pettiness over friendship.

The Arab diplomat was relieved and grateful. "This was a delicate incident," he said, "and I knew I could count on you to handle that poet." He paused. "Although, by coincidence, I learned that the Secretary of State just bought his Tissot on a recent junket to Geneva."

At another time, Levanter was invited to a small dinner party at the New York home of an American businessman and his wife. The guest of honor was Madame Ramoz, wife of the President of the Republic of Deltazur, a small, underdeveloped country of many islands that depended on tourism and American economic and military assistance. Madame Ramoz often represented her husband abroad, and it was said that at home she commanded greater power than all the other government figures put together.

Madame Ramoz arrived in the company of several heavily armed bodyguards, who waited outside the apartment during the party, and an aide, a handsome colonel of the Palace Guards, who placed himself discreetly inside.

She was strikingly elegant, and Levanter was pleased to be seated beside her at dinner. Madame Ramoz explained that she had come to New York on behalf of her husband, the President, to address a Press Club luncheon the following day.

American newspapers had been publishing articles and editorials highly critical of the President, she said, reporting that on the pretext of fighting Communist rebels he had established martial law and that he was suppressing political opposition to his dictatorial rule through merciless arrests. As the economy of her country depended on American investments and its safety on American military aid, Madame Ramoz admitted one of the main purposes of her visit to the States was to present the truth and to counteract what she termed the antagonistic, Communist-inspired, liberal attacks on her husband, who had made the Republic of Deltazur a bastion of democracy and freedom.

Madame Ramoz spoke coolly, charmingly, and Levanter found himself staring at her. She was one of the most beautiful Eurasian women he had ever seen.

When she finished her polite discourse, Levanter said he was certain that because of American concern over the political situation in her country, the audience at the luncheon would be listening to her speech most attentively. Madame Ramoz told him that she had taken precautions against being misquoted or misrepresented by preparing her speech in advance and providing copies for distribution before she spoke. He said he regretted that he was not a member of the Press Club, and asked how he could obtain a copy of her speech.

After dinner, Madame Ramoz casually handed Levanter a copy of her prepared text. As she went off to talk with some of the other guests, Levanter quickly read the speech. He waited until Madame Ramoz returned to where he was sitting.

"Is this the final text of your speech?" he asked her.

"Yes," she replied with confidence. "Why do you ask?"

"I'm afraid there's a serious error in it."

"An error? What sort of error?"

"One that might cause you, Madame, and your husband a great deal of embarrassment," Levanter said quietly. "However, the error can easily be corrected."

Madame Ramoz looked at him with anxious curiosity. "Tell me about it," she said.

"If I point out the error to you, Madame, will you, in good faith, tell me if you intend to correct it?"

She looked at him intently. "Of course I will."

"Then," Levanter continued, "if, thanks to me, you recognize and rectify this error, will you do something for me in return?"

Madame Ramoz gave him a reproachful look. "That depends on what you want me to do."

Levanter watched her eyes as he spoke. "Through my role in Investors International," he said, "I have learned that two prominent reporters for an opposition newspaper in your country have been in prison for months without trial, on vague charges of subversion."

She did not react.

"There was some evidence of torture," he went on, "of resettling their families. If I save you from an error in your speech, will you intervene on their behalf?"

Madame Ramoz looked away, toward the handsome colonel, who stood across the room watching. Then her gaze moved back to Levanter. "I am merely the wife of the President, Mr. Levanter, but I promise to use whatever limited influence I have on the Ministry of the Interior. Now tell me about this error."

Levanter opened the speech to a page with a bent corner and indicated a passage he had marked with pencil. He moved closer to Madame Ramoz so she could read it with him.

" 'And so my husband, the President,' " he read, " 'took upon himself the arduous task of hatchet man to his country.' " He paused. "As it stands now," he said softly, "this passage suggests that President Ramoz became a vicious killer."

Madame Ramoz stiffened. Leaning over Levanter's arm, she examined the text closely.

"Surely you didn't mean that," said Levanter.

"What you undoubtedly meant was that Mr. President took upon himself the task of trailblazer for his people."

"But of course," exclaimed Madame Ramoz. "Everyone who has known and loved him through all these difficult years knows that! The speech was originally written in our language," she said. "The error must have been made when it was translated into English. I will make the correction. Thank you for your assistance to me and the President."

"Then I have been of some help, after all?"

"Yes, you have," she said. "Now, who are these two supposedly innocent reporters?"

Levanter scribbled the names on the back of his calling card and handed the card to Madame Ramoz, who took it and held her hand out. The colonel strode over from across the room and, bowing, took the card from her.

The two reporters were released from prison soon after Madame Ramoz's return to her country. Presumably under instructions from their government, they notified Investors International that all charges against them had been dropped and they were reunited with their families. A subsequent inquiry by Investors International confirmed that they were free.

Levanter had nearly forgotten about the incident when one day, some months later, a middle-aged, poorly dressed, Eurasian-looking woman stopped him as he was leaving the Investors International headquarters.

"Are you George Levanter?" she asked, shaking.

"I am."

The short woman edged closer. Her hair was matted and smelled of grease. "If I could, I would kill you," she stammered, her face pale and her movements jittery. "I swear I would," she whispered.

Levanter was startled. "Why? What have I done to you?"

"You have put my brother in prison," she

snapped. "He was tortured." Her face twitched and she started to cry.

"You're wrong," said Levanter. "I have never put anyone in prison."

The woman grabbed his arm. "But you work for that bitch, the wife of that hangman Ramoz."

"Madame Ramoz?"

The woman spat up at him. Her saliva dribbled down his chin, but Levanter did not move.

"You're wrong," he said slowly. "Utterly wrong. I merely pleaded with Madame Ramoz to set two men free. Nothing else, I assure you."

The woman looked up at him. "My brother was a translator. Now he's imprisoned for sabotage, kept in a 'safe house,' the government interrogation center. They put him on 'cushions of air'—his feet on one bed, his head on another, his body suspended in midair. And whenever he dropped, they gave him *'falanga'*—beating on the soles of the feet. The person who wrote to me about him learned from someone in the Palace Guards that it was George Levanter, from Investors International, who denounced my brother to the Ramoz woman at a party in New York."

Levanter was driving from Switzerland to France. He passed the Swiss border guards and entered no man's land: a quarter-mile stretch of highway separating the two borders. It was there that he saw a young woman standing next to a car, its hood open, its emergency lights flashing. She wore a tapered T-shirt with FOXY LADY printed in large block letters across the front and back. He pulled up beside her and asked whether she needed any help. She said she was waiting for a mechanic and needed only someone to wait with her.

She told him she was from the Middle East but had gone to school in the States and now lived in New York. Levanter remarked that anyone would assume she was an American. She wore skin-tight jeans and had thick black hair, evenly cut to shoulder length. Her make-up had been applied with such skill and care that her complexion appeared quite natural even in the glaring sunlight. Her T-shirt displayed a smooth neck and large breasts. She had a slim waist, gently rounded hips without a fold of fat, and long, slender legs with small, narrow feet; and she carried herself with grace. Everything about her appearance was sensual and provocative. On both sides of no man's land, customs inspectors and border guards were eyeing her with delight.

As Levanter chatted with Foxy Lady, the Swiss mechanic finally arrived. He took one look at the car's engine and announced that he could not fix it on the spot. He hitched it up to tow it to his garage in the small border town. Levanter turned his car around and, accompanied by the friendly cheers of the border guards, followed with Foxy Lady in his car.

He invited her to have lunch with him while she waited for her car. As they ate, she mentioned that she had just come from a Swiss clinic. The second time the clinic came up in their conversation, Levanter asked her why she had been there. At first she hesitated; then she said she had just undergone surgery for the removal of a tumor in her uterus. Her lids shyly lowered to half cover her eyes as she explained that, even though the tumor was not maglignant and the doctors had discharged her, her sexual activities would have to be restricted for some time. Levanter found her frankness enticing.

The mechanic was unable to repair the car before the garage closed. Levanter assured Foxy Lady that his business in Paris could wait and offered to keep her company. They took adjoining rooms in a motel. That evening they were the only dinner guests in the motel's restaurant, and the manager, a hospitable, elderly Swiss woman, treated them to a rare white wine. This wine, the woman explained, was made of grapes from the vineyards high in the glacial region of the Alps. The vines had been planted centuries ago by religious sects that had settled among the inaccessible peaks to escape persecution. She offered the glacier wine, she said, in honor of the beauty of Foxy Lady. She stared at her, repeating again and again that many chic people passed through this border area, yet she had never seen such a beautiful woman. Foxy Lady appeared to be excited by the compliments. Her cheeks were flushed. When she looked at Levanter, her lips quivered. As the woman spoke, Foxy Lady nudged Levanter under the table with her foot. Gently, she pushed his legs apart and he felt her toes on his calves. After dinner he and Foxy Lady retired to their rooms.

Later, Levanter knocked on her door to say good night, expecting to find her ready for bed. Instead, she was dressed, her make-up fresh and immaculate. He assumed that she wanted to go out again. But when he said that the motel bar was still open, she said she wanted them to stay in her room to get to know each other better. She surveyed herself in the mirror and hastily adjusted her clothes. She looked at Levanter with her expressive, shiny eyes; then she came to him and very softly began to stroke his hair. She kissed him, nibbling his neck, her tongue plunging into his ear. She pressed her breasts against him, then quickly unbuttoned his shirt and started to kiss his chest, her tongue caressing his nipples, her hands loosening the belt of his trousers. Levanter was aroused but he pulled away, afraid he might hurt her. She pouted. He explained that he was concerned about her operation.

Without a word, she began to undress, scattering her clothes and sandals around the floor with abandon. Her breasts were full and firm with small aureoles and short nipples. As if to tease him, she paused before removing her panties. Then she slipped them off and moved toward Levanter, exposing her flesh and a pad of white gauze, the final remnant of her visit to the clinic. She lay down on the bed and reached for him.

In her lovemaking that night, she was very inventive, eager to compensate for the part of her body that still had to remain dormant.

They returned to New York together. Foxy Lady adored dancing. Each time she entered a new nightclub or disco, she told Levanter, she felt as if she were on a high diving board, about to take her first jump before a crowd of spectators. Since Levanter did not dance well, he took it upon himself to introduce Foxy Lady to the best dancer in the place. She would always select the table that gave her the best view of the floor and offered others the best view of her. Then she and Levanter would screen the dancing couples, looking for a partner who could keep up with her frenetic energy without trying to upstage her. When the two of them had agreed on which man qualified as a candidate, Levanter took Foxy Lady to the floor. There, in the first few steps, they would veer toward the unsuspecting couple, making certain that the candidate could get a good look at Foxy Lady. Once he began to stare at her, Foxy Lady knew she had him. Feigning clumsiness, she would bump into the man and his partner. Levanter always promptly aplogized, but in the process made sure to introduce himself and Foxy Lady, casually remarking that, after his mishap, he was through dancing for the night. Amicably, he proposed to Foxy Lady that if she wanted to dance, she would have to find herself another partner. He would chat with the couple until they volunteered to join him and Foxy Lady at their table. Soon the candidate would ask Foxy Lady to dance. Within minutes, she and her new partner were the center of attention.

After each high-diving-board evening, Levanter and Foxy Lady returned to their hotel suite. For Foxy Lady the night had not yet ended. In the nightclub she had once again proved to Levanter that the world was in love with her; now she needed proof from him that he was completely hooked on her. Still elated, she would reach for the glacier wine to which she had become almost addicted and which he had taken great trouble to procure for her. She quickly bathed, and came to Levanter radiant. She would stand before him, slowly exposing her body, which she knew mesmerized him. It was a perfect, sculptured body zealously cared for each day by experts, its hairless skin glowing without a blemish, its muscles tightened and toned by the experienced hands of trained masseurs. Sustaining Levanter's arousal, guiding him up and down through the peaks of frenzy, was to Foxy Lady a final tribute to her own beauty.

Every time Levanter returned from a short business trip out of town, Foxy Lady would tell him, with her accustomed candor, what she had done in his absence. As if to remind him of her desirability to others, she related in great detail descriptions of evenings spent in male company while he was away. There were other times, she said, when she wanted to be among women, who found her as beautiful and desirable as men did. For many, she became their first female lover.

Foxy Lady would spin out the stories of her encounters one after another and Levanter would listen, trying not to feel threatened by her erotic exploits with others. He recognized that this was the stuff of her life: she was just as beautiful for everyone else as she was for him. To appreciate her beauty did not require special taste or unusual insight. Thus, his own desire for her appeared to him as ordinary as the desire of another man, who might at any time replace him. Levanter could no more ponder what her loss would mean to him than he could imagine ever possessing her entirely. He could think of her current lover as a rival, he could be jealous of two or three of her intimate friends, but how could he be envious of that stranger whom Foxy Lady had not yet met? He knew that in the constellation of her erotic adventures he was one of many stars.

For her, dancing and sex were her only means of making contact with other people, just as caring for her body and her appearance constituted her only sense of herself. To be seen, to please and dazzle with her looks were her only motives. She hated any activity that required being alone; but she would rather not go out at all than go out and not be noticed and admired. When she saw someone's eyes resting upon her, she seemed to come to life as if she were being touched by the eager hands of her lover.

Because Foxy Lady saw herself as the source of

Levanter's desire, she willingly gave herself to him; she submitted to pain, if inflicting pain was what he needed to make him feel he finally possessed her. But as soon as he was about to give in to the release of his own excitement, she regained control over him; then it was she who was the instrument of his satiation and he who was her slave.

He felt possessive of her beauty; still her sexuality was ambiguous to him. He could not pin down exactly what she wanted from their lovemaking, yet she seemed to understand everything he wanted. Whereas other woman had at times responded as if his urgings were odd, she accepted his needs as if they were to be expected. She seemed to be proud of her ability to bring out all his secret lusts and longings. In a sensual vigil over his flesh, she monitored every detail of his release, anxious to know the duration and intensity of each spasm.

In an effort to understand Foxy Lady, he began taking pictures of her, trying to capture her expressions, her gestures, her smiles. As the stack of prints grew, he would look at them, one after another, secretly hoping to discover in her looks what it was that both held and disturbed him. But just as the photographs failed to reveal her to him, they offered no insight into his compulsion.

He started to photograph her on transparencies. The slides would rotate in the projector and, as images of Foxy Lady flashed on his portable screen, he felt as if the beauty they conveyed was coming from someplace in his brain, imprinted by an artist who chose to remain unidentified.

He had known her for only a relatively short time, and whenever he mentioned his concerns about her sexuality, Foxy Lady answered that the tumor surgery had traumatized her body, upset her menstrual rhythm, and threatened to make her barren. Her body had not yet healed, and she had to have weekly examinations and injections. Midway between medical appointments, she grew depressed and unsure of herself; after the injections, she was euphoric and confident.

He had no reason to think that she fabricated the stories of her adventures, but he did suspect that what she knew about her own sexual life was incomplete, and perhaps unconsciously falsified. He had also developed a conviction that she was not truthful about the nature of her orgasms with him, that, at times, she claimed to have had them when she had not. He took this to be the aftermath of her operation; to him, she still remained sealed by gauze, and he kept wanting more of her. The time they spent together seemed to expand his life, the time away from her to shrink it. Foxy Lady became his habit.

Levanter returned from one of his trips two days earlier than he had planned. It was late; Foxy Lady was not in their suite. He felt restless and went to the hotel lobby to buy the next day's morning paper. On the off chance that he could find Foxy Lady, he asked the doorman whether he had seen her leave that evening. The doorman told him that, as it was raining and there were no cabs, the young lady had left in the hotel limousine about two hours earlier. Levanter said he was supposed to join her but had lost the address of the place where they were to meet and asked for the same car. The hotel driver took him straight to the club where, he said, he had dropped the young lady.

Levanter had never been to that club. He opened the door and was scrutinized by a young, tough-looking bouncer. As he went through the crowded entrance hall on his way to the cloakroom, Levanter was greeted by a young woman in a short leather skirt with tight laces along the sides. Her eyebrows were plucked to fine lines and she pushed out her chest to show off the shapely breasts beneath her flimsy chiffon blouse.

"I know you," she said in a low, well-modulated

voice. "I saw you once at a disco. You were with my friend."

"Your friend?" asked Levanter.

She nodded. "You were dancing with her that night and a couple bumped into you two on the dance floor. My friend told me you call her Foxy Lady. She's here tonight, you know."

"I know," said Levanter. "I've come to join her."

He checked his coat and started walking along the corridor to the rooms that opened in the rear. The young woman strutted beside him on her high heels, clearly determined to keep him company.

"She told me how the two of you met in Europe," she whispered. "Between two countries. Very romantic. Like in an old Garbo movie." The woman was so close he could smell her heavy perfume, and she brushed against him with her hips. "You were her first man, you know."

"Her first man? Couldn't be!" Levanter exclaimed.

"Yes. Her first man after the change!"

"After what?"

"You know after what. Her operation."

"You mean her tumor surgery?"

The girl squeezed his arm. She laughed, covering her mouth with her delicate hand. "That's a good one. I like what you call it: 'her tumor'!" She batted her long eyelashes, flipping her hair off her cheeks and shoulders.

Levanter was annoyed. "And what do you call it?" he asked.

She just laughed. She took his hand and, guiding it, she pressed it under her skirt, pushing hard until she was sure he felt what she wanted him to feel. "I'll call it whatever you want to call it, lover," she said in a throaty whisper. "Soon I'm going to have my 'tumor' removed too, you know! Why don't you look me up sometime?"

Levanter pulled his hand out from under the skirt and walked toward the sound of dance music. In an instant, the entire length of his relationship with Foxy Lady coursed through his mind; his infatuation with her physical beauty did not bother him, but for some reason he felt ashamed of what he had done with her in their lovemaking. He couldn't help imagining how she thought of him. Levanter was no longer simply the lover of a beautiful and mysterious woman. Rather, he was a sexually spoiled partner demanding easy gratification from another man, a man who had all along understood his needs so well and satisfied him so easily. Levanter looked around. Many of the women were beautiful, though none was as striking as Foxy Lady. Now that he knew who they all were, he felt cheated.

Foxy Lady was dancing. When she saw Levanter, she stopped abruptly and pushed away from her partner, a tall, muscular man. Out of breath, her hair mussed, she ran to Levanter, kissed him, and took him aside.

"How did you find me?" Foxy Lady asked him in a hushed voice.

"The hotel driver brought me here."

"I saw you talking to my friend."

"Yes. She told me you were friends."

She sensed his mood. "So she told you. Now you know," she said.

"Yes, I know," said Levanter, "about your 'tumor.'"

"It won't make any difference, will it? We will stay together, won't we?" she asked, looking at him anxiously.

"We won't," said Levanter. "I must leave you."

Foxy Lady pleaded. "You haven't given me enough of a chance. I don't even know myself yet. In a week my gauze will be removed," she said. "You won't be able to tell the difference between me and any other woman." She paused. "I'll be the only woman you've ever known who gets her orgasm entirely from inside," she joked.

"I was hooked on the mystery of you," he said. "And now it has been solved."

"But I haven't cheated you. No woman could have served you better than I have—you didn't want me to have a baby."

She looked at him attentively, then gently steered him to another corridor. Muted voices came from above a staircase. She stopped him before they reached it.

"As a child, I knew nature had made a mistake," she said. "I felt I was beginning to look like a girl and to be driven by needs I did not understand. By the time I was twelve, I would spend at least a few minutes each day in front of my mirror dressing up in girls' clothes or putting on make-up or a wig. I wondered about altering my sex. But in a Moslem country women are owned like animals." She laughed bitterly. "It's bad enough to be born a female. It's utterly unthinkable for a sane male ever to change into one."

Foxy Lady led Levanter over to a bench and urged him to sit down beside her. She took a deep breath.

"My family," she began, "was one of the richest and most influential in our country, and my father was a distinguished diplomat. As his only son, I was my father's pride, and the sole successor to his wealth." She thought a moment, then spoke in a detached voice. "When I was about sixteen, my father became alarmed as he realized I was losing my masculinity, so he summoned a team of French doctors, who spent weeks injecting me with male hormones. But Allah was not to be bested."

Levanter touched her hand, thinking how delicate and feminine it looked. She kept on as if nothing could stop her tale now that she had finally begun it.

"Despite these treatments, my breasts grew, as my body seemed to be insisting I was a woman. I felt there was no one I could turn to. My mother had died when I was small, and I had never felt close to either the young woman my father married soon after or their two daughters. Thus, I was really surprised when my stepmother came to my aid. Only later did I realize why she did it."

Levanter looked at her questioningly.

"I was still the only legitimate successor to my father's wealth," Foxy Lady explained. "She had not borne my father a son, but here was her chance to get rid of the only obstacle between herself and her daughters and a vast inheritance. While I was studying in America, my stepmother came to see me and secretly arranged for me to see an American doctor who specialized in transsexuals. He suggested psychological therapy to prepare me for an operation—and for life as a woman. Of course, he didn't know I was already preparing myself by coming here, or going to other clubs like this, every evening. Without my father's knowledge, my stepmother transferred a substantial amount of money to my Swiss bank account. I went through the psychotherapy and hormone injections, and soon I was ready to go to Switzerland for the final transformation."

She gazed at Levanter. He said nothing, and she went on.

"While I was still in the clinic, an anonymous caller, no doubt hired by my stepmother, told my father that I had been disfigured in an accident. Within hours, he was at my side, anxious about my injuries. The doctor lifted the covers and told him proudly that the surgery was successful, his son was now a woman. My father ran out of the room, screaming that he had no son." She paused, as if to swallow the pain in her voice. "Before I left the clinic, an embassy clerk came as an emissary from my father to tell me that I was to be prevented from discrediting my father, his family, and his post in the service of the King. My passport was no longer valid; I had no further right to use the family name, for my father said his son was irretrievably lost. The emissary informed me that my father had secured testimony from various medical authorities to have me declared insane. If I ever returned to my country, I would be apprehended as a self-mutilating mental defective and dumped into a mental asylum. And if ever, anywhere in the world, I publicly reveal who my father is, his men will make certain that I won't live to slander him again."

It was clear to Levanter that she did not doubt her father's threat.

"My banks immediately informed me—" Foxy Lady stopped, then began again. "The day I met you, in fact, my banks had just notified me that I was deemed legally unfit to be responsible for my share of the family's oil revenue left to me by my grandfather, all my foreign and domestic bank accounts were closed, my weekly allowance was stopped, and all my savings and income reverted to my father."

She touched Levanter's arm and looked up at him. Her eyes were as sad as her voice.

"That's how it all happened," she said, sounding as if her story were as much of a shock to her as it was to him. "In a matter of days, my transformation was complete: Once a man, I was now a woman. Once rich, I was rich no more. Along with my manhood, I had lost both my father and my country. I had become a vagrant whose residence in any nation is secure only as long as I can support myself and pay for the medical treatments that I continually need."

A good-looking young woman, slender and long-legged, her breasts set high on her chest, walked toward them. Foxy Lady stood up, and they greeted each other with a kiss. Levanter rose, and Foxy Lady introduced him to the other woman, who gave him a whimsical, teasing smile and walked away, swinging her hips.

Levanter glanced at Foxy Lady. He was crushed to think of the hopelessness of her condition, yet he knew that at this moment he must consider only himself.

"Same breed!" Foxy Lady exclaimed when the woman was out of earshot. "I don't think there is a God-made woman in this place. This one was once a clerk in a big city bank." She laughed. "Half the time behind the counter, a man in a business suit. Nobody in the bank knew about the other half of his time, spent as a grand lady here. Finally he left the bank, took hormones, grew breasts and long hair. All the lady needs now is a bank loan for her final cut. And they say only secret agents live in disguise!"

She saw that Levanter was looking around, making no effort to hide his discomfort.

"We think of ourselves as ideal lovers," said Foxy Lady, "each one a sum of passions both of a man and of a woman. But in fact, all we combine are the vanities of both. After all, if not the vanity, what else could sustain us, except maybe the fun. All kinds of things happen here," she said. "Occasionally, an unsuspecting out-of-towner drifts in, thinking he's showing his wife the big city. She'll go to the ladies' room to fix herself up, and there they'll all be—a troop of man-made women in high heels, skirts hitched up at a row of wall urinals, or comparing breasts, cosmetics, fancy stockings, and, reluctantly, their not-so-atrophied 'tumors.' The out-of-town lady takes one look at them and, shocked out of her skull, rushes away as fast as she can. Meanwhile, at the bar, her all-American husband is being conned by a young thing showing off her brand-new boobs."

She paused. Then she moved toward Levanter, nuzzling his neck, kissing his cheeks and eyes.

"During those in-between years," she said, "whenever a man or a woman made love to me I kept wondering whether I was wanted as a woman or as a man. Or was I merely being used to help other people make up their minds? Even when I knew my lover wanted the woman in me, the male part of me stood in the way, denying who I was and mocking what I felt. There was only one way out of my dead end and I took it."

She stopped again. Upstairs a glass crashed to the floor. The voices rose, then quieted again.

"You, George, were the first straight man who knew me only as a complete woman. I was a virgin with you," she said. "When you first came to me in that no man's land, you personified the whole of manhood which I had cut myself off from forever. You were the challenge I had to meet from then on."

She looked at him. Levanter saw once again how beautiful she was, the skin on her face radiating light; her eyes, like her hair, appeared jet black; her breasts felt firm against him. He put his arms around her, but for the first time he felt no desire to touch and possess her. It was strange not to want the body that he had enjoyed for so long, but Foxy Lady now seemed incapable of providing him with the view of the world and of himself he had so desperately wanted from her.

"I do wish you would stay with me," Foxy Lady whispered. "Even if I didn't tell you the whole truth, I didn't lie to you. And, after all, what's important in sex is to be excited and to stay excited—to be yourself. With you I always am."

Levanter felt the warmth of her breath on his neck. He was silent for another moment. Then he asked, "What will happen to you now?"

She disengaged herself and pulled him toward the staircase. "Come upstairs with me."

They entered a large, dimly lit room. Several waiters, young effeminate men in white sailor uniforms, navigated between the tables carrying trays of drinks. Dense smoke from tobacco, hashish, and marijuana filled the air.

Levanter noticed that most of the tables were occupied by older women dressed in gaudy gowns, or leather jackets and short skirts, with black silk stockings suspended from satin garter straps and puffy feet squeezed into stilletto-heeled shoes. The few male customers also seemed old. Many of the people in the room already appeared to be in a state of drunken or drugged dreaminess, prevented from falling asleep by the loud music blasting from two corner speakers.

Foxy Lady pulled Levanter into the room. Several women looked up, arching their plucked-out, penciled-in eyebrows. They called to Foxy Lady, admiring her dress and hairdo but paying no attention to Levanter.

In the hazy light of the room, the women seemed old. Yet when he looked into their faces, he discovered they were barely middle-aged. No joy showed in their eyes. Under the thick make-up, their skin was coarse and wrinkled, their dyed hair was thin and scanty with balding patches, which some tried to cover with wigs. Almost all of them were obese, with fleshy necks, fatty shoulders, shapeless thighs and overdeveloped calves. Their artificially overblown breasts had become soft, and flapped like pancakes on their barrel chests. Their hands, covered with brown spots, were unnaturally broad, nearly square; their fingers, the nails bright with polish, seemed uniformly thick.

Slowly, Levanter turned and left the room. Foxy Lady followed.

"That's what we call the Menopause Room," she said. "It's where we pause after being men—the only menopause we get. And those are some members of our self-made generation," she said, forcing a matter-of-fact tone. "Hormonal imbalance. Metabolic disorders. Mental impairment. No sex drive. And no money for doctors or a decent life. Sleeping most of the day in their cold-water flats, drinking most of the night here to wash down an endless supply of uppers and downers. Their only salvation is that the club owner remembers them as foxy ladies, young and fresh and lovely, and gives them dinner every night without charge. Then, of course," said Foxy Lady, "in a country as large as this, there are still some customers willing to go on a blind date with them."

They went downstairs again. As she was helping him on with his coat, he saw some men in the cloakroom leering at her. She saw them too.

"Let them look," she said. "They've known all along what you've learned only tonight. They want me, yet they think I've made the worst sacrifice a man can make. And for what? For no more than a short appearance just for them. Until I end up upstairs too!"

Alone, missing the company of Foxy Lady, Levanter turned for company to his old friends. JP was one of them. In the world of sport, JP was a legendary figure. Three-time world fencing champion, Olympic gold medalist, winner of scores of other international meets, JP ranked as the greatest saber fencer of all time.

As was customary for star athletes in Eastern Europe, JP was given the pro forma rank of lieutenant colonel in the army and assigned to a Ministry of National Defense troop-training program.

He had come to a competition in New York and invited Levanter to his hotel room. JP sighed and shifted in his chair as he told Levanter that intelligence-service officials had proposed that he act as military attaché in his country's Brussels embassy, using his social and sporting connections in Western Europe to penetrate the high command of NATO.

"They want me to become a spy for the Warsaw Pact military forces," JP said.

Levanter was astounded.

"When they first spelled it out to me," said JP, "my mouth went dry. I couldn't say a word." He stopped for a moment. "Fencing is my whole life, you know that. The saber is the national symbol of my country, and at home I am a hero to every man, woman, and child, a source of national pride. Why isn't that enough?"

"What did you say to them?" Levanter asked.

"I said I only know how to fight in the open. Then a general present at the meeting shouted that I would be ideal for the job because in the West they worship me so much they don't watch my hands. 'You're wrong, General,' I said. 'I'm a fencer. If they worship me, it's because they do watch my hands.' And I stormed out of the interview."

"What happened then?"

"Nothing at first. Then my address books and notebooks would disappear for a while, only to turn up later in places I would never have put them. Some of my friends were interrogated. One time I was fined a third of my salary for arriving late at a training session." He laughed bitterly. "As there's no one better— or even as good as I am—for a sparring partner, I fence against my own reflection in a specially constructed triple mirror. And several times they fined me for being late to train against myself!"

JP stood up and walked across the room.

"Then this," he said, taking a book from the top of a bureau, "was the biggest blow. And it happened right before I left on this trip."

He handed the book to Levanter. It was a copy of *The Olympic Gold,* his newly published autobiography.

"Fresh from the State Publishing House," he said wistfully. "Delivered to me just as I was boarding the plane to New York." He paused, obviously upset. "Without my knowledge, unidentified state censors have deleted many passages from the book and seriously altered many others. The name of my fencing coach, whom I had mentioned dozens of times, now doesn't appear even once. The man taught me all I know. I guess they took him out because he's Jewish," JP said. "Things have been added also—attacks on high military and sports officials, dragging me into their political infighting."

Anxious to help JP, Levanter called on his friend, the Arab diplomat.

"What would you like me to do?" the diplomat asked.

Levanter did not hesitate. "Can you find out whether JP will be in danger if he returns home?"

A few days later, the diplomat phoned and told Levanter to meet him at a men's public baths in mid-Manhattan. At first he was surprised that the Arab would choose such a place. But once he was inside, it occurred to him that the diplomat probably frequented such establishments for sexual purposes, and possibly used them for the privacy they afforded for secret political activities.

Wrapped in towels, they walked along the dark corridor without speaking. Music seemed to flow from every corner—slow and sentimental, it combined with the dim light and the scent of marijuana to create a sense of insistent intimacy. The doors to most of the rooms they went past were open; inside each room, under weak blue lights, lay naked men, some sleeping, some posing, some sniffing drugs from small atomizers, and others blatantly gesturing to them to enter. They went downstairs, passing a large shower-and-bath room, with large bottles of red mouthwash and stacks of paper cups piled high over each sink. A younger man approached from the opposite direction, and just as he was about to pass them, his extended hand touched the diplomat's groin. The Arab patted the young man's cheek. "Not now, not now," he said. Smiling, the young man walked away.

"It's too bad," said the diplomat, "that you Westerners, when pressed by desire, rely on the gesture. In my culture, men first talk about their sexual wants in great detail; words carry no shame. You must visit us sometime," he said to Levanter as the two of them entered the dormitory, a large room with dozens of cots.

Men cruised the aisles, watching each other, their limbs posed as invitingly as their faces might be in ordinary daytime encounters. Every now and then, one would edge closer to another, seeking the other's flesh, first with his hand, then with his mouth. In the far corner of the room, two naked men lay in a tight embrace. There, sitting together on a cot, in the eerie light of the bare red bulb, amidst the quiet music and the hum of whispers and sighs, Levanter and the diplomat discussed JP's fate.

The diplomat told Levanter that JP had voiced his opposition to certain methods of troop training adopted by the military, claiming they were too harsh and inhuman. Because of his status as a national hero, his views attracted many supporters. The Party, fearing the growing role of the military, was clearly setting the stage for JP's arrest. Consequently, the diplomat told Levanter in hushed tones, East European intelligence agents were spreading rumors in Western sports circles that the fencer was a member of a gold-and-antiques smuggling ring. And more recently they seemed to be working up a charge of Zionist conspiracy.

The diplomat also explained that several hotels in Paris, London, and New York were indirectly owned or controlled by East European state security agencies. Certain suites reserved for important guests were equipped with sophisticated monitoring devices so that the authorities could keep track of the activities and contacts of traveling officials, scientists, sports stars, actors, and writers, all of whom were assigned to hotels by their embassies. Thus, their trips abroad served not only as a reward for loyalty to the state but also as a further test of this loyalty.

It was from the New York hotel where JP often stayed that his government had obtained the most incriminating evidence against the fencer, the Arab diplomat said. They had complete recordings of all JP's conversations with his Western friends, including one with the man they considered an open enemy of their state: George Levanter.

The diplomat strongly advised that JP not go home. Whenever the state went to such lengths to find evidence to incriminate a man, he said, it always found that evidence without difficulty. In fact, JP's government had already prepared its lists of national world sports record holders for distribution at the forthcoming World Championships—and JP's name was not on it.

Levanter wasted no time. He had JP meet him in a park near his hotel. When JP heard what Levanter had learned from the diplomat, he appeared stunned.

JP thought for a moment. "This can't be true," he said. "Of all people, why a national hero?"

"You must not go back," said Levanter. "You belong to fencing, not to the government. Stay in America. Fence here. Teach fencing. Write."

JP reflected. "I never considered defecting," he said. "I belong to my nation; my saber helps shape my people's national pride. Everybody in the government knows that. They can't touch me. I am going back."

Some weeks later, the Arab diplomat got in touch with Levanter to give him the news about JP. As the fencer stepped off the plane from New York, he had been arrested and held incommunicado in a military fortress.

For a while there was silence about his fate. Then the first ominous sign appeared. In one of the country's official publications, a well-known Party hack published a cartoon showing JP as a hooded, trench-coated, saber-rattling spy, superimposed on a graph of military secrets, his weapon broken, his leg chained to a ball. The word was soon out that JP had refused to cooperate and play into the hands of his accusers. With some sense of relief, Levanter reflected that in a small country of soulless bureaucrats, no secret can be kept, not even in a fortress.

From various leaks and rumors, the following picture of JP's interrogation had reached Western intelligence: JP had been seated in a chair in a large, stark room, the diplomat told Levanter, and had been grilled under glaring lights. After a long session of loaded questions clearly designed to wear him down, the fencer had pointed to his arm and shouted, "You can't destroy what this arm stands for. It belongs to the people!"

The officer in charge got up from behind his desk and entered the circle of light to stand behind the fencer. "Is this the arm you speak of?" he asked calmly, tapping JP's right shoulder.

JP swung around in his chair to face him. "Yes, Colonel, this is the arm," he said, extending it with pride.

The officer looked at the outstretched arm. Swiftly he grabbed it with both hands and, putting all his weight on one leg, pushed the chair away with the other. Like a peasant breaking a twig in two, the colonel bent the fencer's arm over the back of the chair, then pressed down. The elbow snapped with a loud crack, and the arm went limp. JP howled and tried to pull free, but the colonel twisted the broken arm sideways and brought the wrist down over the back of the chair. Now the wrist cracked, and the hand went as limp as the arm. Moaning, JP slid from the chair onto the floor. "So much for the arm of the people," said the colonel, returning to his desk.

A military tribunal, meeting in closed session, decided to deprive JP of property and all civilian rights for life as punishment for acting against the highest interests of the state. In addition, he was sentenced to twenty-five years in a maximum-security prison.

Levanter was filled with outrage. Twenty-five years for JP the fencer, he thought, while most of the leaders of the Third Reich received shorter sentences from the international tribunal at Nuremberg. He determined to conduct a systematic survey of the hotel in New York where JP had stayed.

With the diplomat's aid, he obtained a long list of JP's compatriots who had been booked into the same hotel and were punished when they returned home: a novelist who failed to recount his meeting with an American intellectual had his forthcoming book withdrawn before publication; an actress who saw her uncle in New York but had never admitted having a relative in the United States was not allowed to travel abroad again; an architect who overlooked mentioning a professional fee he had received from his American colleagues for an industrial design was assigned to work on collective projects only. There were dozens of other such victims.

Several times, under different names and wearing various disguises, Levanter rented rooms in the hotel. He was looking for surveillance devices, and soon he found them. By scrutinizing the hotel employees responsible for selecting and assigning the rooms, he narrowed his search to a senior clerk, the man in charge of booking visitors from Eastern Europe.

The clerk, Levanter learned, had worked in the hotel for over ten years. After observing him for some time at his job, Levanter followed him one evening to his house in the suburbs. Then, when the man and his wife went away for a weekend, he broke into their home and found a large basement workshop filled with electronic equipment. Several of the components matched those Levanter had discovered in the hotel suites regularly assigned to guests from behind the Iron Curtain.

Levanter checked with the Arab diplomat, who confirmed a few days later that, according to his sources, there were sufficient indications that the senior clerk was one of the minor East European operatives active in North America.

Levanter telephoned the man at the hotel one morning and, in a rehearsed stutter intended to make his speech unforgettable, introduced himself as a well-to-do retired businessman from out of town. Levanter explained that he had obtained the clerk's name from a travel agency whose clientele included many East Europeans. He was concerned about the fate of certain men and women from behind the Iron Curtain, he said, some of whom might wish to defect to the United States. He pointed out that these visitors were often advanced in age and not fluent in English, and that they might therefore hesitate to take such a decisive step without aid and encouragement. Levanter explained that several freedom-minded American businessmen—he mentioned half a dozen names the clerk would be sure to recognize—had just established a special tax-deductible fund for long-range assistance to potential defectors.

He and his associates needed someone trustworthy and knowledgeable to cooperate with them; for obvious reasons it couldn't be anyone too visible who might put such a clandestine human-rights project in jeopardy. Would the clerk be interested in helping them? Or did he know of anyone who might? There would be substantial remuneration for any professional risk incurred, and financial arrangements could certainly be worked out to their mutual satisfaction. The clerk expressed interest and was willing to meet with Levanter to discuss the matter further.

Levanter apologized for not having a private club in New York where he could take his guest, but said he had thought of a convenient spot where they could meet privately. Besides, he said, he had a bad lower back and needed a sauna. Could they, therefore, meet at the Cavalier Baths, in midtown, where they could enjoy a measure of seclusion and anonymity? As he had to fly home the next morning, Levanter said, he hoped the clerk could meet him that day, perhaps after lunch, when the baths would not be crowded.

The clerk eagerly agreed, and Levanter, who remembered the layout of the baths from his previous meeting there, outlined a plan. To save them both time and insure that they did not miss each other, he suggested, the clerk should rent a room at the baths, prepare himself for a sauna, and then come to the room Levanter had reserved, number 101. Then they could proceed together to the sauna and converse discreetly there.

Levanter had just two hours to prepare himself for the meeting. He put on a pair of chamois gloves and picked up a saber he had bought some weeks earlier and a heavy household hammer with a thick leather protective cap over the iron head. Wrapping each in a woolen scarf, he put them into a strong shopping bag, added a coil of rope, took off the gloves, and threw them into the bag.

In the strong light of his bathroom, he carefully fitted a gray theatrical wig over his hair and glued on false eyebrows, a mustache, and a short beard. In minutes, he had become unrecognizable.

He left his building through the service entrance, hailed a taxi, and arrived at the baths, his raincoat draped casually over the shopping bag.

He approached the cashier, a sleepy old man with a sallow complexion and puffy cheeks, and, in a low voice, said he had reserved room 101. Scarcely raising his eyes from his newspaper, the cashier handed Levanter a bracelet with the room key and two towels, murmuring that the price of the room covered twelve hours of rental time.

Room 101 was located upstairs, at the farthest end of the corridor, next to the central air-conditioning unit, which was so noisy that Levanter was sure that anyone cruising the corridor would turn back before reaching the end.

Levanter put on his gloves before opening the door and then locking it behind him. Lit only by one dim bulb, which barely dispelled the darkness, the room contained a wooden bunk with a mattress, a sheet and two pillows, a chair, a locker, and one small bed table. Levanter slipped the saber under the bunk and put the hammer on the table. He undressed, hanging his clothes in the metal locker next to the bunk, taking off the gloves only after unlocking the door. Then, wrapped in a towel, he went downstairs, leaving the door slightly ajar. He sat in the area where customers came to cool off after the sauna. From here he could watch the main entrance.

The hotel clerk arrived alone a little ahead of time and rented a room. Levanter went upstairs after him and returned to 101. He hid his room key in his raincoat pocket and put on the gloves, then lay on the bunk, listening to the music from the corridor. In a few minutes there was a gentle knock at the door. Levanter rose, picked up the hammer with his right hand, and, holding it behind his back, opened the door with his left hand.

Stuttering, he greeted the clerk and invited him in. The clerk seemed uncertain, self-conscious, and timid in his towel, and said he would rather wait in one of the lounges downstairs. Levanter explained that he had just come up; there were too many unsavory types downstairs, he said, old men openly trading pep pills and snorting coke. He himself, he added, did not like to be exposed to such goings-on, but if the clerk was interested, he was certainly free to go. That remark did the trick. The clerk denied any such desire and, as the voice of Judy Garland floated in from the corridor speaker, he fumbled in the semidarkness to the chair beside the bunk. Levanter pushed the door closed with his left hand while with his right he hit the man's head with the leather-covered hammer. Stunned, the man slumped, his towel fell off, and he collapsed onto the edge of the bunk. Levanter grabbed him by the legs and lifted his entire length onto the mattress. He pried the man's mouth open and gagged him with a towel, then removed his room-key bracelet and put it on his own wrist. He turned the body face-down and, twisting the rope around the man's neck, waist, knees, and ankles, he tied it securely around the length of the bunk.

Levanter dressed carefully, making sure that he forgot nothing. He put on his raincoat, wrapped the hammer in the scarf, and placed it in the shopping bag. He bent over the clerk and pinched him: a shudder ran through the man's trunk; he strained, but he was too tightly gagged to utter a sound. Levanter reminded himself that what he was about to carry out was impersonal revenge, as simple as the verdict of a military tribunal.

He slid the saber from beneath the bed. Weapon in hand, its polished blade glistening in the blue light, Levanter stood at the foot of the bunk. He reached over the naked man and brought the tip of the saber to the narrow passage that, like a shadow, divided the man's rump. He inched the end of the sword down the passage, until its tip touched the larger opening in the flesh.

Levanter leaned over; supporting himself with one hand, he thrust forward and, as if sheathing the weapon, plunged the blade deep into the opening. An intense spasm convulsed the body, followed by a shudder. When the entire blade had penetrated, the corpse lay motionless. Levanter covered it with the sheet.

He turned off the light and pulled the door tightly shut as he left the room. He put the gloves in the bag and, without hurrying, walked through the corridor. A few men stood embracing in doorways or inside dim rooms, their doors left open.

On the way out, he dropped the bracelet from his wrist onto the counter. The cashier, still absorbed in the afternoon tabloid, did not even raise his head as he mumbled a perfunctory response to Levanter's quiet good-by.

Walking home through the park, Levanter slowly

peeled off the wig, then the eyebrows, mustache, and beard, and threw them, one by one, into the bushes.

He thought about the public consequences of his personal deed. Both the authorities and the media would demand a direct connection between the crime committed and the reason for it. They would keep looking for a plot, and to look for a plot in this killing would be as useless as grooming a bronze horse; no one would be able to untangle the web of circumstances and motives that had led to the clerk's death.

Back in his apartment, Levanter felt safe and secure. Scarcely an hour had passed since the clerk had entered Levanter's room at the baths. But what had taken place there had already receded into a remote corner of his memory. It was nothing but an old Polaroid snapshot; no negative, photographer unknown, camera thrown away.

Knowing Jacques Monod did not have much time left, Levanter decided to go to Cannes to be with him. When he arrived in town, Levanter discovered that the annual Cannes Film Festival was taking place at the resort. Although Monod had been born and raised in Cannes and in later years spent most of his vacations there, he told Levanter he had never been to the Festival. As Levanter spent part of every day with Monod, he persuaded him to attend a few film events; and he introduced his ailing friend to some filmmakers, hoping they would provide amusing distraction.

After a film screening one afternoon, Levanter noticed a starlet staring at Monod. She approached them and asked guardedly whether Monod was one of the famous stars, like Charles Boyer, who were said to have come to Cannes for the release of *Hollywood, Hollywood!*, a selection of fragments from their old films. Monod was about to introduce himself when Levanter cut in and said that Monod was indeed a famous star, but from another galaxy.

"Another galaxy?" asked the wide-eyed young woman. Levanter nodded. She apologized for not having seen *Another Galaxy* yet, but assured him that she would as soon as it was released.

Later a distinguished French movie director saw

Monod on the hotel terrace and recognized him instantly. He greeted him respectfully and introduced himself. "We don't see many Nobel Prize winners here!" he exclaimed solemnly. Then he introduced Monod to his companion, a statuesque brunette. "This is Doctor Jacques Monod," he said, "the author of a book that influenced me tremendously."

The woman smiled coyly but said nothing.

"You know *Chance and Necessity,* that book you saw on my night table?" said the director in a tone of reprimand.

The woman extended her hand. "But of course! I'm delighted to know you, Doctor," she said, placing the other hand on her hip and leaning slightly toward him. "Are you in Cannes because of the film based on your book?" she asked, obviously pleased with herself for thinking of the question.

Monod, visibly amused, was prepared to answer. But the director, rolling his eyes in frustration, grabbed the woman by the arm and yanked her away.

At a gala after one of the films, two starlets asked Levanter who his handsome friend was. Levanter asked them to guess.

"He's handsome enough to be a movie star," said one, glancing at Monod coquettishly.

"Couldn't be," the other argued. "He's too distinguished-looking."

"The head of a film studio?" the first guessed.

"Too self-assured," commented the second. "Studio heads only try to look self-assured. He really is."

"A director?"

"Too natural and too well dressed." She looked at Monod intently. "He might be a scientist," she said after a pause.

"Why would you think that?" asked Levanter.

"He looks at you with such analytical eyes," she murmured.

They talked and joked in the afternoon sun on the verandah of Monod's family home. Levanter picked up his camera to photograph Monod. Only from behind the viewfinder did he dare to focus on the barely perceptible evidence of Monod's illness. There was no startling change, yet certain physical clues, uncharacteristic tiredness, suggested that the disease had made further inroads on his health.

Later in the day, Monod escorted Levanter to his car. "Until tomorrow then?" said Levanter from behind the wheel. Monod stood beside him but did not answer. Levanter raised his eyes. The two men looked at each other. Levanter knew it was for the last time.

"Farewell, my dear boy," said Monod, finally breaking the silence.

Levanter could not speak. Mute, dispirited, he started the engine. Without pausing to look back, Jacques Monod walked away. As he started to climb the steps to the house, the last rays of the setting sun wrapped him in their glow.

The dark-haired woman stepped off the boardwalk and strode through the sand to the last empty lounger, just next to where Levanter sat. She untied her robe and slipped it off as she lay down. Like most women on the hotel's private beach, she was going to sunbathe naked. Her body was evenly tanned; her skin was smooth, unbroken by fat or wrinkles. She raised her head toward the sun.

Levanter looked at her face. A slight thickening at the top of her nose made her face familiar.

He moved his lounger closer and leaned toward her.

"Forgive me, Signorina," he said, overlaying his French with an exaggerated Italian intonation to mask his own accent.

She turned her head in his direction. He could see that she was annoyed. "Yes?" She opened one eye.

"I can't help admiring your face. Your nose fascinates me particularly," he said.

She sighed. As she opened the other eye, he noticed that her irises were as dark as they had seemed in the black-and-white snapshots he had seen years ago. He knew who she was.

"Here I lie naked, Signore," she said, "yet all that fascinates you is my nose? I should be offended." She closed her eyes once again.

"There is drama behind that irregularity at the bridge," Levanter went on. "Perhaps your nose was injured in a lovers' quarrel?"

She didn't respond.

"When I look at you lying near me," continued Levanter, "I can almost see this handsome, strong man—your boyfriend, perhaps—as he enrages you. I see you fighting him, scratching his face. He slaps you hard. You fall, bleed. Then the hospital. They fix the bone—but leave a small bump. Charming, really charming."

He waited for her to react. Still, she did not.

"I see this man who broke your nose wanting to leave you. And you don't want him to go, even though he hurt you. You cry. You make love. You fight again. He gets letters, many letters, urging him to leave. Then he leaves." Levanter paused. "I see him among tall buildings and villas and beautiful people—then I don't see him anymore. He vanishes. Maybe he is dead? Now I see you alone."

Slowly she sat up and turned to him. "You are the first fortuneteller I've ever known who reads not from the palm but from the nose," she said. "Unless my nose is only a pretext?" She caught him glancing at her body. "What else do you see?"

Levanter closed his eyes and pressed his fingers against his brow. "I see another man, in America. You never knew him, but he saw pictures of you. I see him writing to your lover, begging him to go to America, to leave Europe—and you—behind. I see you in another fight, angrily tearing up these letters. I see him leaving you, and I see that man greeting him in New York." Levanter paused and glanced at her. She was lying down again. Her eyes were shut, but her head was twisted in his direction. He closed his eyes once more. "Ten years have passed. I see you sunbathing naked in Cannes. I see the man who wrote the letters. He sits beside you on the beach."

She sat up again and faced him. She put on her sunglasses and studied him. "Then you must be that man: George Levanter," she exclaimed. "Levanter!" she repeated. "How I once hated that name!"

"Only the name?" asked Levanter. They were both speaking their native Slavic language now.

"That was all I knew." She turned and lay down on her front, her chin resting on one hand. She looked straight ahead and spoke in an even voice. "When I met 'this handsome, strong man'—Woytek—you had been in America for years."

"Woytek often told me you were the most beautiful girl he had ever seen," said Levanter. "He said you were still in grade school when he met you and that he started sleeping with you right away. Was that true?" he asked.

She shrugged. "It was and it was not. Who cares? He was my first lover. Later, you started writing to Woytek, urging him to defect to the West. Your letters turned our life upside-down. Suddenly, all Woytek talked about was Levanter—his closest friend, already settled in America, while he was wasting his time with me. He imagined himself with you in Paris, London, New York, Los Angeles. With a successful investor for a friend in the West, how could he fail? And how could I, simple flesh, compete with such a vision? So I lost him to you, Levanter. And to Gibby, that American

heiress you found for him. And look how it all ended!"
She took her suntan lotion out of her bag and handed it
to Levanter. "Could you put some on my back?"

He took the tube, stood up, and leaned over her.
He squeezed the cream onto her shoulders and began
spreading it. Her skin felt warm and smooth. When he
reached her waist, she looked back over her shoulder at
him. "There was a time," she said, smiling, "when if
any man touched me, Woytek would take him apart."

As Levanter spread the lotion over her hips and
thighs, he found himself thinking back to the time
when securing Woytek's future in America was his main
concern.

Levanter had telephoned Gibby and told her he
had to see her alone to talk about Woytek. They met at
a café near Central Park.

"How is Woytek's English coming along?" he
asked.

"It's improving," she said. "But surely you didn't
ask me to meet you to talk about Woytek's English."

"I didn't. It's about the two of you."

Gibby looked apprehensive, almost panicky. "Did
Woytek ask you to talk to me?"

"No."

"What is it then?" She stared at him, her eyes
magnified by the thick lenses of her glasses.

Levanter was having difficulty beginning.

"I know you and Woytek have no secrets from
each other," she encouraged. "You're his only close
friend in New York. You can be direct with me."

"Ever since I introduced you to Woytek," said
Levanter, trying to sound casual, "you and he have
lived in the same tiny West Side studio. Yet you have
unlimited charge accounts at all the best shops in town,
your wardrobe is made by the finest designers, and your
jewelry is worth thousands of dollars. Woytek doesn't
have a penny. If he wants to buy a pack of cigarettes,

he has to borrow money for it from his friends. He's wearing the clothing he arrived in from Eastern Europe because he can't afford anything new. It looks to me as if you've suddenly turned into a penny-pinching shrew, acting as if you were on your own."

Gibby shifted in her chair. "What's wrong with being on your own?"

"Nothing. But you aren't exactly on your own. You come from one of the richest families in the country and have a trust fund that yields a great deal of money. On top of that, there have been large financial gifts and inheritances over the years. Still, with all your wealth, you won't help Woytek, the man you love."

"I won't give Woytek money, if that's what you mean. I don't want people to think that the one man I want is the one I have to pay for," she said stubbornly.

"Are you going to live your life with Woytek according to what other people might think?" asked Levanter.

Gibby looked away. For a moment, Levanter thought she wasn't listening. He grew impatient.

"If you're so concerned with what people think, why do you tell them everything about yourself? Why do you say that before you met Woytek your life oscillated between drinks and sweets, with pot in between? That, intellectually, Woytek is the first man you haven't had to talk down to? That only with Woytek can you be open and honest?"

Gibby interrupted. "Woytek loves me for what I am. What I do with my money is my own business."

"But not what you do with Woytek," said Levanter. "I feel responsible for him. I arranged a blind date for you and Woytek so he could have someone intelligent to speak French with, since that was the only other language he knew then. I didn't expect him to be destroyed. With you, he's vegetating, but he loves you too much to leave you. It seems to me that you are preventing both of you from enjoying your money and the life it could offer: the world of travel, of new experience, of ideas, of people."

"I don't want Woytek to be known as a man without a profession, living off my money," said Gibby. "I don't care what kind of work he does, as long as he supports himself like everybody else."

"But he's your lover, and you're not like everybody else," Levanter said sharply. "You are unusually rich. You and your lover are thereby excluded from the fate of the ordinary. Woytek was once a wealthy and educated man. Then he became a refugee. He's been here only a year—half of which he's lived with you. He doesn't know English well enough yet to pursue his profession. You quit your own job when you fell in love with him. Why do you want him to work? Don't you understand that getting a job would keep him from studying English? And what do you suppose he could do? Don't try to answer me," said Levanter. "Just listen for a minute."

Gibby glared at him.

"All Woytek is suited for at the moment is menial labor: parking cars, scraping paint off ship decks, cleaning bars, something like that. He could earn about as much in one month as you spend in one week on restaurant tips when you take your rich cousins to lunch. And it costs you more to pay your monthly phone bill for long-distance calls to your college chums than Woytek would make in an entire year."

Levanter paused. Gibby did not speak.

"What is your reasoning?" Levanter asked. "Do you believe that as long as he's penniless everyone will think Woytek stays with you for yourself, whereas if you give him money, everyone will think he loves you just for the money?"

Gibby remained silent.

Levanter went on. "Woytek was a superb athlete. He used to play soccer and basketball and was one of the best swimmers in his country. He loved company and enjoyed being surrounded by creative people. Now he's cooped up in your ground-floor apartment where he can't even see daylight, and he can't afford to go out. You've made him your prisoner."

"Maybe I should take him to California," Gibby said, more to herself than to Levanter. She went on without waiting to hear Levanter's opinion. "My family is there, and Woytek knows people in Hollywood. There are also those film directors he knew in Europe," she mused. "Near them, Woytek might regain his own sense of accomplishment and pride—and possibly find work."

She looked at Levanter, expecting some response, but now he said nothing.

Levanter was in Paris one summer researching the prospects for the marketing of a new American-made ski safety binding. Just before he was to return to New York, he received a long letter from Woytek. He and Gibby were staying in California with their friend Sharon, whose baby was due soon. Sharon had invited Levanter, whom she hadn't seen for a long time, to join them for the rest of August.

New York would be every bit as hot and empty as Paris, Levanter knew, and Sharon's house, a large Beverly Hills estate overlooking the center of Los Angeles, offered an inviting escape. He reserved a seat on a flight from Paris to New York, with a connecting flight to Los Angeles, and he cabled Woytek: ARRIVING FRIDAY AFTERNOON STOP ANXIOUS TO SEE YOU ALL.

At the airport he asked the airline clerk to arrange for three of his bags to accompany him and three to be unloaded in New York and held for his return at the end of the month. The clerk handed him a baggage form, which he filled out and returned to her.

"You've made a mistake here," she said. "You wrote a New York address, but we need your return address in Paris, in case your luggage is not claimed."

"My home is in New York," said Levanter, "and that's where the luggage should be sent if something happens to me and I am unable to claim it."

"But you have to claim it," the clerk insisted.

"What if I die?"

"Death finds you without a return address," the woman said impatiently. "Your luggage does not."

"I can only repeat that my return address is New York."

"As you wish, Monsieur," she said with a smirk.

During the New York stopover, a stewardess checking his ticket for the Los Angeles flight looked at Levanter's baggage stubs. "I see that all your luggage has been unloaded in New York," she said. "Are you continuing to Los Angeles without any baggage?"

"I have a lot of luggage," said Levanter. "Three of my bags were supposed to be transferred to this flight."

"There must be some mistake, sir," the stewardess said. "All your luggage was labeled in Paris for unloading in New York. No transfer has been indicated." She phoned the baggage dispatcher. "Your suitcases are already on their way to the inspection ramp," she said. She checked her watch. "I'm sorry, sir. You won't have time to go through customs before this flight takes off."

Levanter realized that he should not have argued with the airline clerk in Paris. Once again, he thought, he had been defeated by the French character, as once again the French had somehow confused logic with the facts of human existence and emotion.

He went through similar ordeals each time he was in France, and each time strove to defend himself against the French bureaucracy of the mind. His comprehension of the French language far exceeded his ability to express himself in it. Consequently, the French treated him in one of two ways: if he succeeded in making himself understood, he was just a foreigner treated with contempt for not having been born French;

if he failed, he was a mental invalid to be brushed aside for being incapable of even verbal communication.

One day, he decided to by-pass altogether the dilemma of language. As an investor, Levanter was required to retain all receipts and bills as proof of his business expenses for the United States Internal Revenue Service. Therefore, each time he bought stamps at a French post office, he would politely ask for a receipt. And each time the French postal employee would routinely refuse, claiming that at the time of purchase he had to submit two copies of a letter of request on his firm's official stationery, addressed to the specific post office. But there was no room in Levanter's life for filling out forms in duplicate.

Stumbling and jerking, he entered a crowded post office in the center of Paris that day, going straight to the front of the line. As he twitched past the men and women who stood waiting their turn for service, he peered at them defiantly; they looked at him, then, uncomfortable, dropped their gaze, as if ashamed to be staring at a pathetic cripple.

He pounded the counter several times and an alarmed clerk raced over. Mumbling incoherently, and spitting saliva through his twisted mouth, Levanter managed to communicate his need for a pencil and paper. Then, his left hand grabbing his right as if to guide it and prevent it from shaking, Levanter wrote that he wanted three dozen air-mail stamps. He pushed the money toward the clerk, who averted his eyes from the cripple's distorted face and promptly slid the stamps to him. His left hand once again guiding the right, Levanter scribbled down his request for a receipt. The clerk hesitated. Levanter again banged the counter with his fist. The supervisor approached, glanced at Levanter's note, motioned him to calm down, and, whispering that the man might be a French war invalid, ordered the clerk to issue the receipt.

Now it occurred to Levanter that he should have

thought about this, and many other such experiences he had had in Paris, before engaging the French airline clerk on the subject of his return address. Now the French bureaucracy of the mind was having its revenge—all his luggage was in New York.

Dispirited, he left the plane, claimed his luggage, cleared customs, and went to his New York apartment. He would fly to Los Angeles the next day. He tried to phone Woytek, but there was no answer at Sharon's house. Exhausted from the journey and the mix-up, he fell into a sound sleep.

The next day, Levanter's phone rang, waking him. A man's voice said, "Los Angeles Police Department, Coroner's Office," and asked to speak to the next of kin of one George Levanter.

"There are no relatives," Levanter told him.

"How well did you know this Levanter?"

"Better than anyone else," he said. "I am George Levanter."

"Are you the George Levanter who sent a telegram about arriving yesterday in Los Angeles?"

"I am."

A long silence. At the other end people were talking in muffled voices.

"Then why didn't you arrive?" asked the man.

"My luggage was misdirected. I'm flying out today."

Another silence. Again a chorus of faraway voices.

"Were you coming to Los Angeles to visit friends?"

"That's what I'm going there for," said Levanter.

"Haven't you heard the news?" asked the man, his voice hushed and uncertain.

Levanter thought perhaps Sharon's baby had been born prematurely. "What news?"

The man hesitated. "There was a tragedy here," he said. "Sharon and her houseguests are dead. They were

all murdered last night." Mechanically, he listed all
their names in full. "Also killed was a stranger, a man
whose identity we still don't know. He must have driven
up at the time the others were being killed. When your
telegram was found, we assumed he was George Levanter."

Levanter felt his heart lose its rhythm. He fought
for breath. His mind was in chaos. All he could think of
was how strong Woytek was. He whispered, "Woytek?"

The man seemed to know what Levanter was asking. "Shot twice. Struck on the head thirteen times.
Stabbed fifty-one times."

"And Gibby?" Levanter murmured.

"Twenty-eight stab wounds. No more questions,
please," the man added quickly. "I shouldn't even have
told you this much. You can hear the rest on the news."

As he listened to the radio reports, Levanter stared
at a stack of snapshots Woytek had sent him recently of
himself and Gibby with Sharon and other friends. Then
he looked at the collection of college diaries that Gibby
had given him, and reflected that from now on her
clean, slightly square handwriting remained his only
connection to her.

Levanter thought back to the first time he had met
Woytek. Several boys were playing "Name the Jew" in
the schoolyard. In that game, one boy stood in the center while the others slowly circled around him. He was
"the Rabbi," and he had to guess which boy had been
designated "the Jew." Each time the Rabbi guessed
wrong he was fined a penny or a possession. The sooner
the Rabbi found the Jew, the fewer fines he had to pay.
Everyone had a chance to be Rabbi, and the Rabbi with
the fewest wrong guesses won all the fines lost by the
others, becoming "the Greatest Taker of Them All."

As Levanter was walking past the group, the
Rabbi spotted him and called him into the circle. He
refused to play the game, and the Rabbi ordered him to

be brought over by force. Three or four boys rushed toward Levanter. He pushed the first one away and had almost managed to escape from the others when two more boys cut him off. Suddenly a tall boy whom Levanter did not know came alone; although he was not a Jew, he said, he found the game disgraceful. Single-handedly, he knocked down two attackers, the rest backed off, and the game was over. This tall boy was Woytek.

Levanter had visited Woytek and Gibby when they first moved to Los Angeles. One afternoon, the two men went for a drive in a car Woytek had borrowed from one of his wealthy friends. They drove through Beverly Hills on their way down to Sunset Boulevard, passing the lavish bungalows and sprawling villas. Shiny automobiles stood in the curved driveways, apron-clad gardeners manicured the grounds, strings of invisible sprinklers sent up fine sprays that turned sunlight into rainbows. No sound broke the serenity of the hills and the private enclave.

In minutes they were in Hollywood. Groups of haggard young men and women in shabby jeans, many barefoot, strolled aimlessly along the crowded sidewalks or lounged on the pavement. Vacant looks on their faces, they seemed to have little to say to each other, nothing to do, no place to go.

"In other countries," said Woytek, "people like these would be starving, and they would join the Party to fight the rich."

Levanter was suddenly aware that his friend's English had improved so greatly that it was now the language they spoke even with each other.

"Here they're not hungry," Woytek continued, "so they have no need to join anything. They sleep through the day and in the evening crawl out to the streets. I call them Crabs of Sunset. But they're not like nature's crabs, because Crabs of Sunset are out of balance with their world. I think they may be the missing link between man and robot."

Woytek steered the car through the traffic, stopping from time to time to watch the sluggish mass crossing in front of them. Levanter noticed with some amusement that Woytek looked pleased when several young men and women enviously eyed the expensive custom-built sports car he was driving.

"Had California been an independent country," Woytek said, "it would long ago have gone fascist— Left or Right, it wouldn't matter. For the Right, Crabs of Sunset would become the fuel for the draconic measures that would be used to get rid of them; for the Left, they would be the ignition for the revolution that would swallow them later. As it is, the State of California has become the embodiment of their mental state: neither Right nor Left, with no shape or direction, a giant amoeba. Here everything stretches—nature and people."

They turned around, heading back toward Beverly Hills.

"You know," said Woytek, "one night, when they are hungry, these Crabs of Sunset may stretch out as far as their neighbors in the hills."

"Why do you suppose that hasn't happened already?" asked Levanter.

"They simply haven't had time to stretch that far yet."

"And the people in the hills? Don't they fear the Crabs might come?"

"Those are rich people," said Woytek. "They think they always win. But in fact they're losing twice: once while they're alive, because with so much to lose they never really take chances; and once when they die, because being rich they lose so much."

They were back up in the hills again. Sumptuous homes stretched on all sides.

"Some of these people take only the most naïve

precautions," Woytek said. "This house, for example." He pointed out of his window. "It's probably equipped with every conceivable electronic safety device, and every person on the staff may be armed—even those two little spaniels might be wearing sound transmitters on their collars."

Levanter chuckled. "Isn't that sufficient security?" he asked.

Woytek shook his head. "I once asked a man who lives near here, 'What if Crabs of Sunset stop you in your car, outside your fancy fortress? These hills of yours,' I said, 'have everything but pedestrians who would hear your screams and rush to the rescue. You might not have time to activate your Citizens Band radio.' The man said he thought I had a sick imagination."

Levanter asked, "What about the police?"

"They don't have homes in the hills, you know. Police will show up the morning after. To collect the bodies and fingerprints, and to talk to the reporters about the supposed motive."

"Yet you and I are not afraid here," said Levanter.

"We are not," said Woytek, "because we've known greater fear in other places."

The news reports went on all day. Levanter kept imagining it was the night before and he was with his friend.

Woytek is alone in the living room, looking out the window. Way below, as far as he can see, the boulevards and freeways of Los Angeles stretch like a thousand runways of a giant airport. It is twilight; he is waiting for Levanter to arrive. The blinking lights of the city are beginning to fuse with the blinking of the stars. Perhaps, Woytek thinks, that's why the city was named Los Angeles. From here on Cielo Drive, the drive of the sky, it almost seems one can look down on the angels. He thinks of Levanter; his departure from Paris must have been delayed by one of those French strikes. Paris, he muses, Left today, Right tomorrow, or the other way around.

It is getting darker. Gibby is in a bedroom reading. Sharon is resting in her room. Jay, an old family friend, is elsewhere in the house. Levanter is on his way to Los Angeles, the city he likes so much. Woytek stretches out on the sofa. All is quiet. A peaceful house on Cielo Drive, he thinks, a peaceful hill, far above the caves of the scruffy hordes of Crabs of Sunset. He dozes off.

He is awakened by unfamiliar voices. He opens his eyes. A gun is pointing at him. It is in the hand of a pale young man who has a solid swelling under his cheekbone. Three teen-age girls stand next to him, each holding a knife and loops of rope. In their limp cotton skirts and loose hanging blouses, they seem lost in the room, unsure, and they glance occasionally at the solid walls and the massive beams of the ceiling. All four stare at Woytek vacantly. Crabs of Sunset, Woytek thinks.

"What can I do for you, sir and ladies?" asks Woytek sarcastically.

The man motions with his gun. "Don't move, pig. We're here to kill you all." His stare remains fixed and indifferent.

"What are you, ghosts from a Boris Karloff movie coming to meet your maker?" says Woytek, stretching up slowly. "This is Cielo Drive. Old Boris's ghost lives on Bowmont."

Like a stiff-jointed dummy, the man steps forward and hits him on the head with the butt of his gun. Woytek hears the crack and for a moment loses his balance. He wants to jump at the attacker, but the man holds the gun to his head. Woytek lies down again, feeling a trickle of blood from his forehead.

His gun still trained on Woytek, the man turns to one of the girls. "Tie him up," he snaps. "And bring all

the other pigs to this room," he orders the other two
girls, who trot off like trained retrievers.

The one assigned to Woytek tucks her knife into
her skirt and edges toward him, a stubborn look in her
eyes. As she leans over him to tie his wrists behind his
back, he smells her unclean body and sees her face covered with blemishes, the pus ready to be squeezed out.
Woytek's blood smears onto her, but she ignores it. Under the gaze of the pale young man, the girl goes to the
other end of the sofa and starts to bind Woytek's ankles.
He watches her; she seems to be following a script prepared by an invisible agency monitoring her from afar.

"What is it you people want?" asks Woytek.
"Money? Love? Fame?" He is suddenly conscious of
his foreign accent.

The man with the gun turns away and, without a
word, leaves the room. The girl has finished her job;
she looks at Woytek with no passion, no fear, no excitement. His blood is soaking through her blouse and
Woytek wonders whether it is seeping onto her small
breasts. She catches his gaze. Suddenly, she grabs her
knife and stabs Woytek in the leg, then, rapidly, in the
chest and belly. In sudden pain, Woytek jerks away,
howls, and almost rolls off the sofa. Sneering, she pokes
him back into place with the knife.

Blood oozes from the wounds, clinging to his jaw,
wetting his clothes, staining the sofa. The girl stands
over him. His bleeding and pain make no impact on
her. He tries to reassure himself that women are accustomed to the sight of blood because they menstruate, and
that the girl is only trying to intimidate him. His leg
goes numb. Still, behind his back, he is trying to wiggle
his wrists free. To distract her, he turns his head to the
side and looks at her bloodied skirt. It could almost be
her own blood, he thinks. Again, the girl catches his
gaze. She raises her knife, lunges forward, and drops
her hand, digging into his chest. As the shriek tears out
of his throat, Woytek feels the blade hitting a rib, which

stops it from sinking farther. His legs kick spasmodically, and she withdraws the knife. Fresh blood gushes out. He no longer doubts that she intends to kill him. Woytek weakens and for a moment feels weightless.

He is about to give in to this sensation when he hears Gibby scream. He turns, raising his head, and sees her on the staircase, being urged down by one of the girls, who keeps jabbing her with a carving knife.

Gibby's face is bruised and pale, her glasses have been knocked off. There are red marks on her white robe. Does Gibby have her period? He can't remember. There was a time, he recalls, just after they became lovers, when she couldn't bring herself even to talk about it. She was ashamed of her body, ashamed of going to the bathroom, too shy to show affection, too proud to ask for it. But that is all past now. She has learned to give generously of herself. Her body is free; she is not afraid to receive pleasure or to give it. Their love has survived its harsh beginnings: they are finished prompting each other with hard drugs; at last they are at ease together.

Gibby is shaking and crying. The girl behind her swings her hand down and, pitching forward, stabs her; the red marks on Gibby's robe grow larger and blood is streaking down her legs. Gibby is falling down the stairs. She crashes against the railing, then gets up and tries to run, but she falls again. The long knife is flashing in the girl's hand. She brings it close to Gibby's neck to show she is ready to slash her throat. The redness spreads all over Gibby's robe.

Woytek hears Gibby offering the girl money and credit cards. He hears the girl's cackling laughter. She says she does not want Gibby's paper and plastic.

"Gibby, run!" he shouts, his voice tearing through his body as the pain mounts in his chest.

Spinning violently, the girl beside him rams him with her knife again. It sinks deep into his groin. There is so little time left, he thinks, howling. He closes his

eyes, pretending to faint. Gibby should try to bluff her
way out. She should tell the attackers who she is—they
must have seen her name in thick bold letters on cans in
every supermarket they've ever been to. She should tell
them they can gain nothing by killing her; she is rich,
among the richest in this rich land, and she can give
them money if they will let her go. She should tell them
who she is, tell them about her money. Anything to stop
them. He thinks of shouting all this at them himself, but
his mind is tired, clutching at the thought: one wrong
phrase and Gibby may again think he's trying to use her
money to pay off other people. He is growing confused:
his thoughts drift back and forth from his native tongue
to English; he cannot anchor them in one language or
the other. As he writhes, he feels the rope loosening on
his wrists. He has one chance only; he waits for the appropriate moment to make his move. He keeps his eyes
closed, even when he hears the screams of Sharon and
Jay and the sounds of a scuffle. He hears the man with
the gun order one of the girls to keep watch outside. He
hears Gibby scream again, then Sharon pleading for her
baby. Jay yells for Sharon and Gibby to get out if they
can.

Woytek finally looks. He sees Gibby tied to a
chair. Sharon and Jay are tied together, lying on the
floor. Jay's entire face is a red raw mass, yet he strug-
gles free of his ropes and manages to get up, when the
man points the gun at him. A shot explodes. Jay's head
lolls to one side, his knees bend, he slumps lower and
lower, silent, shrinking into himself, his neck squeezed
between his shoulders, a froth of blood on his mouth.
Gibby and Sharon shriek. Jay's body folds into the pool
of blood and does not move.

The man plays with his gun and smiles. He threat-
ens to shoot the rest of them if they are not quiet. Then
he and the girl who has been guarding Woytek ponder
aloud whether to shoot him; they decide to save the bullets for later. The man points at Woytek and says to the

girl, "The big pig is yours. Finish him off." He strides over to Sharon and Gibby.

The girl stands next to the sofa. She still holds the bloodied knife. Behind his back, Woytek's hands are now free. He is ready to spring up. Just then he hears a car pull up to the main gate. For a moment, the killers panic; the man with the gun runs out. Levanter must have arrived, thinks Woytek. He knows there is nothing he can do to save his friend.

The girl beside him fidgets. Rocking from side to side, she raises her knife. Woytek suddenly sits up and butts her in the chest with his head, knocking her to the floor. Grabbing her by the hair, he holds her on the floor with one hand while he unties the rope around his ankles with the other. He feels dizzy; blood pours out of his body with each move, but he keeps pulling her head by twisting her hair around his wrist. She yells to another girl to help her. Gibby and Sharon start to shout and throw themselves about, and the girl guarding them begins to stab them randomly. Woytek increases his pull, and the girl strains and jumps. The blood from the wounds on his head blinds him for a moment. Kicking herself away from the sofa, the girl pulls Woytek down onto the floor. He pounces at her throat. They roll together, knocking over chairs, gripping each other in a tight embrace. Woytek's blood spills over the two of them, as their heads and knees and elbows bang against each other in the frenzied wrestling. He feels his fingers in the girl's mouth, and he pushes his hand deeper, tearing at the slippery mucous surfaces. Yet, even with his hand at her throat, she keeps on stabbing him, and he cannot stop her. Woytek sees Gibby suddenly wrench herself free of the chair and run across the room toward the door to the garden. Her captor catches her, blocking the door with a knife. Panicking, the other girl pushes Gibby outside and follows Woytek to the garden door.

As he crosses the threshold, the girl overtakes him, stabbing him time after time in the back. Fresh blood

warms him like sweat. He hurls himself outside. The
girl falls upon him, stabbing and stabbing. As they
grapple on the mist-wrapped lawn, she yells and
screams for help. Woytek scrambles up and breaks
away from her, running toward the fence, across the
lawn, falling, getting up, falling again, and again getting
up. In the spotlights, he sees the other girl stabbing
Gibby and sees Gibby collapsing onto the dewy grass.
Woytek strains to call out into the darkness for help,
but his breath whistles in his throat. The man with the
gun steps out of the dark and hits him over the head
repeatedly. The girl stumbles over and, with a downward motion of her arm, sticks her knife into him again.
He feels no more pain. The man points the gun at him;
Woytek falls to his knees. As he crawls over the lawn,
two bullets hit him in the leg. Something snaps inside
his chest. Quivering, he can feel only the clumps of
earth on his lips. He looks up and sees four silent figures bent over him, but he no longer knows who they
are or what they are doing so near him, so close to the
sky that spreads behind them like a black fan.

Woytek's final image, is of himself as a boy making an anonymous call to the Secret Service. For
months they have been holding his father. Woytek says
he has an important tip for them. In an old abandoned
factory on the outskirts of town, on the top floor near
the elevator shaft, some young people have stored a
cache of arms and explosives. An agent takes his message and he hangs up. Hours later, Woytek waits on the
top floor, hiding near the elevator shaft. An unmarked
car arrives. Through the window he sees two agents in
gabardine raincoats running toward the entrance, guns
in hand. He hears them on the decrepit staircase. They
reach the top, they are near him. He holds his breath.
As they look into the shaft, he jumps from behind and,
arms spread, gathers the two men against each other,
pushing them into the open shaft. They fall scream-

ing—a long double howl, then silence. He must vanish from the factory. He runs. As he is running, he is older, and a beautiful girl is running beside him, but he is faster, leaving her behind. In a house on Cielo Drive, high above Los Angeles, he is finally safe.

The shaft of the abandoned factory. The girl behind. All this was and was not. Who said that to him? It was and it was not.

The death of his friends was incomprehensible to Levanter. He tried to make himself believe that they had all died in a crash in a sports car or were buried in a house in one of the landslides so common in the area.

He was too restless to stay home alone, too restless even for company, yet he had a need to be among people. He walked the city streets, stopped for a drink at a bar, rode a bus or subway, and he kept looking into the faces of strangers, considering how impenetrable they were, asking himself whether these were the faces of victims or oppressors, whether they were people capable of murder. In every place, there were always several people he wished he knew, several he wanted to talk to, to learn about.

Were people all cruel by nature, he wondered, and would they be amused by the games he had seen in some European cities? Would they enjoy the colorful ducks tapping a frenetic dance on a metal platter if they knew the platter was connected to a battery that sent electric shocks through the bird's body each time the webbed feet stepped on it? Would they be entertained by the man who tucks his trousers into his boots, then slips two fierce-looking rats into his baggy pants, buckles up, and waits while blood begins to seep through the fabic? The bystanders move away in horror, sure that his flesh is being eaten away by the rats. He bleeds more and more, and when everyone around appears convinced that he will bleed to death, he smiles and opens his fly: two dead rats fall out, and behind them jumps a little ferret, its jaws still full of hunks of rat meat.

Staring into the faces of strangers, Levanter regretted that in his profession individuals were perceived only in relation to the grand schemes of their business undertakings, in which profit was usually the sole incentive. He should have been in a profession which allowed him to analyze one single human being at a time. For this, he was envious of one of his friends, a famous plastic surgeon.

The surgeon spoke about all his operations as if they were routine. For each patient, however, the surgery might be the major event of his or her life—whether it was correcting a harelip, rebuilding a nose or hand, tightening facial skin, giving new contours to breasts, hips, buttocks, or thighs, or smoothing over scars left by diseases or accidents.

Levanter watched several operations: steel penetrating living tissue, cotton sponging up blood, chisels sculpting bone, scalpels etching in skin. He marveled at the surgeon's skill, his ability to remold features, lifting the skin so far off the muscles of the face that his gloved hand could vanish inside it as if slipping into a pocket. Levanter observed as open veins were cauterized and droplets of hot fat spurted out; as globs of fat, shiny and yellow like buttery popcorn, were pried away; and as rows of tiny threads were knotted by fingers moving faster than those of a seamstress.

Levanter spent hours in this operating theater, elated, curious, fascinated, watching the surgeon respond to physical reality. His friend's investment required no explanation; the motive was implicit in the result, and the result was obvious for everyone to see: the defeat of blind nature by rational man.

In order to close a complex deal that involved companies on both coasts, Levanter rented a house in the canyons of Beverly Hills, not far from Cielo Drive, and commuted between it and his New York apartment.

He was reluctant to become part of the busy social life of Los Angeles, still preferring to rely on chance encounters. One day, in a UCLA bookshop, Levanter noticed a young woman. She walked between the shelves of paperbacks, scanning them as she went by, slowing down now and then to read a title. Walking behind her, Levanter felt there was something indefinably girlish about her, although she looked old enough to be a university student. She stopped to pick up a book. He was passing her when she turned and looked him straight in the eye.

"Are you following me?" she asked.

Levanter was taken aback. "Yes. That is"—he hesitated— "I've been watching you."

She did not look away. "Why?" she asked.

"I want you, but I don't know why. I am sorry you are not for sale in this shop. I'm trying to find out the source of my need."

She looked at him quizzically. "And have you found out?"

"Not yet. It takes time," said Levanter.

She replaced the book and glanced at the clock over the cashier's counter. "You have almost three minutes before I leave," she said playfully.

"May I follow you?" asked Levanter.

She turned back to him, smiling. "You may not. I'm not free tonight." She kept looking at him. "But one day, when I'm free, perhaps I'll call you."

"I might be in New York."

"I might be there too," she said.

Levanter wrote his name and telephone numbers on both coasts on a piece of paper. "I have answering services for both numbers," he said.

"I don't leave messages," she said, putting the paper in her purse.

"What's your name?" Levanter asked.

"Serena."

"Serena who?"

"Serena! How many Serenas do you know?"

A car horn honked twice. She walked out of the bookshop toward the chauffeur-driven sedan. Levanter noticed how gracefully she slid into the rear seat. She did not look back at him as the car made the turn onto Sunset Boulevard.

Several days later, when he was in New York and had begun to doubt that he would ever hear from her, she phoned.

"Have you found out?" she asked.

He did not understand. "Found out what?"

"The source of your need."

"I have," said Levanter. "You are."

"How do you know?" she asked.

"You resemble a girl I made a pass at in a summer camp once."

"Then she is your source, not I."

"You are," said Levanter. "When can I see you?"

He could hear no sound at the other end and was terrified that she had hung up. Just then she said, "What's your address?"

Serena called about once a week, and only when she was ready to see him.

He might have been planning to go to the theater that evening with some friends who were soon to pick him up. But his decision was always instantaneous: for Serena he was available at any time. When she summoned him, he would telephone his friends and say that urgent business had come up and he couldn't join them for the evening after all. His friends would be disappointed: they might have invited a date for him. He would apologize: here he was an investor, he joked, who wanted to be master of his fate yet couldn't even master his leisure time.

When the house intercom buzzed and the doorman announced a young lady on her way up, Levanter's heart would quicken. By the time she entered his apartment, he had usually managed a semblance of calm.

There was an air of confidence about her. She never wore make-up and her clothes were selected with care; she appeared to be the well-bred coed dressed for a date in the big city. When she came to embrace him, she always seemed fresh, unspoiled. Each time, like a curious child, she would flip through the business letters on his desk, take a look at the pile of books on his bed table, turn the tape recorder on and off, examine the photographs of him skiing that hung on the walls. She'd go toward the bathroom, Levanter close behind, and turn on the tub for a bubble bath. Then she would study herself in the mirror and check his medicine cabinet, picking up some of the vials and reading aloud the names of the drugs and the doctors who had prescribed them.

As she climbed into the full tub, she would ask Levanter to plug in the whirlpool machine, which she set between her legs. Levanter remained in the bathroom, watching her until she stood up and handed him the bottle of scrub granules. He poured some into his palms and let his hands slide slowly over her back, her belly, her breasts and nipples, until all the sandy granules had worked up into suds. To keep her balance, she clutched the shower-curtain rod, facing him, her lips parted, eyes closed. Her body would be taut, her legs spread wide. He kept stroking her, first gently, then harder and rougher; the lather foamed on her skin, hiding her flesh and his fingers from view. Her body, stirring under his touch, seemed to be suspended from the rod. He would increase the friction, letting his fingers play and circle and wander over her, until the foam subsided. Levanter would help her out of the tub and, with a fluffy towel, rub her until she was dry and cooled off.

After her bath, holding his robe tightly around herself, she sat in his rocking chair, waiting for him to put a mood into her, as she called it. She loved to be aroused by listening to a man talk, she claimed, and she knew that her arousal would then excite him. She insisted he tell her things about himself, stories that would break the routine of her life.

Sometimes he would be telling her about an incident that took place a few years earlier at the time of some headlined public event and Serena would draw a blank, reminding him that she was too young to know of this. She was just a little girl when some of these things happened, she would say, rocking back and forth and looking at him as if he should feel guilty that he was old enough to remember them.

She would never tell him anything about herself. Not a passing reference to her family, her school, or her friends. Levanter had examined her belongings and found out that she carried a lot of cash but no driver's license or any document that could identify her. She refused to answer his questions about her life away from him, dismissing them as utterly irrelevant to their sporadic meetings. For a while Levanter thought that, like Gibby, she came from a wealthy and distinguished family and did not want her origins to affect her relationship with him. Later, it crossed his mind that she might be kept by a rich, older married man who was a public figure.

But though she would reveal nothing about her private life, Serena always wanted to know about him, his friends, his business acquaintances, his interests in things other than herself. Soon he began taking her to cocktail parties and dinners, and all his male friends were delighted with her.

One night, after a party attended by well-known political people and celebrities, Serena asked why he was interested in her when he had so many more fascinating contacts.

"To friends who have known me for years," he told Serena, "I try to be what they want me to be. Only with strangers like you am I what I really feel myself to be."

Serena was a good listener, and as she sat spellbound she reminded Levanter of a game he had participated in as a student in Moscow.

One autumn, Levanter and several other students were assigned by the university to give lectures at a collective farm near the capital, traveling to and from the farm by train. There were always peasants taking the train to a farmers' market on the way, and they invariably listened in on the young people's conversation. A student who was a good storyteller would begin a tale; as the train approached the market station, the drama would mount, with the narrator piling incident upon incident of comedy and tragedy, of betrayal and passion, of happy reunions and incurable illnesses. The peasants would stand open-mouthed, swallowing every word, laughing or crying or gasping with terror. The train would stop at the market, but they were so engrossed, so afraid to miss a word, that they never moved. As the train pulled away from the platform and began to pick up speed, the story would end abruptly. The peasants would then suddenly become aware that they had missed their stop. But they were never disappointed and never failed to thank the student for his story. The farmers' market would always be where it was, they said, but a storyteller took their minds to places where they could not travel. Each day a different student would tell the story, luring another group of peasants, who would also miss their station. At the end of the week, the student whose storytelling had caused the largest number of peasants to miss the market stop won the game.

Serena had contempt for any predictability in love-making. She was upset when she triggered Levanter's orgasm too soon. To her, an orgasm was a failure, the death of need. What touching was to the body, desire was to the mind: all she wanted was to sustain the passion, to make desire flow incessantly.

Often, when her body wriggled under his tongue, she seemed so engrossed in sensation that he thought she would not even feel it if he bit into her flesh.

For Serena, just as passion was demonstrated by gesture, desire was expressed by language. She would ask him continually about his feelings and responses. When his mouth was on her flesh, she wanted to know whether he felt that his tongue was shaping her. When she kept him aroused, she asked if he was aware of her giving him pleasure, or of himself, or only of the pleasure. And each time they were together, she kept demanding that he tell her what it was that made him want her so much.

Levanter could not link his need for Serena to any particular attitude, to any particular yearning. When she was not with him, he was an objective witness to his own need, viewing it as if it belonged to another man. When she was with him, he was devoted to her, like a criminal who could not part company with an accomplice.

He wondered whether it was her body that he wanted or simply her way of perceiving him, of giving him a sexual reality that he had lacked before. He recalled a young woman he had once met in Switzerland. Then, as with Serena, he did not understand the nature of his desire.

He had just walked into a drugstore in ValPina. A nurse was pushing a large pram toward the exit, and he peeked in. Only a face showed above the blanket. Levanter was surprised to see that it was the face of a woman in her early twenties. He thought it was a special kind of wheelchair and tried to see how her body was fitted into it. The body outlined under the blanket was no bigger than a baby's. The woman seemed to be conscious of his curiosity and smiled at him. He smiled back at her and was astonished by the beauty of her features. The nurse cleared her throat to get his attention, then threw him a look of reprimand as she pushed the carriage out of the shop.

The proprietor of the drugstore, who had observed the encounter, told him that it was a woman in the baby carriage. She was twenty-six years old, the child of a well-known, prosperous foreign family. As an infant, she contracted a bone disease that left her grossly deformed; the doctors did not expect her to live, but the family was able to provide the best possible care and she had survived. Her head was of normal size, but the rest of her body was stunted and she had no legs.

Thus she had to be fed and cared for by others. Even though she was so greatly handicapped, the proprietor said, the young woman was intelligent and had been living a rewarding life. She went to school, spoke four languages, and was about to receive an advanced degree from one of the best art schools in Europe.

Levanter asked whether he could be introduced to her; as an investor, he explained, he was interested in the concrete predicaments that life set for each of us. The proprietor agreed to introduce him and the next day telephoned to ask him to a party given by a friend's son, who went to the university with the young woman and had invited her.

It was a crowded party; she arrived about an hour after it began. Wrapped in a short blanket, she was carried in without much effort by a young man, who propped her on the sofa between two pillows. As most of the guests knew her, her arrival caused no unusual commotion. Several students came over to say hello; two or three sat around her on the sofa, others came and went. Slowly, Levanter made his way toward her. Soon the person who had brought him to the party introduced them. The girl smiled and, in an even, soft voice, said she recognized him from the drugstore.

Levanter was struck by the scope of her deformity. Short, twisted arms, with no elbows and unbending, barely mobile, fingers, stuck from her tiny torso like the forelegs of a baby toad. Under the blanket, her body appeared to be not much larger than the head it supported.

"I understand you are a student," said Levanter. "What do you study?"

"History of art," she answered.

"Any particular period?"

"A particular subject," she said. "The role of the human head in Christian art." She smiled thoughtfully. "As you can see, I have a vested interest in my studies."

"I'm sorry I stared at you yesterday," said Levanter.

She laughed. "Don't be sorry. I like being noticed. I've spent years trying to persuade my nurse that the only unkind ones are those who don't want to look at me. But she still disapproves of the staring." She paused, then laughed again. "She should see the stares I get when I hitchhike!"

For a moment, Levanter thought he had misunderstood her. "When you what?" he asked.

"Hitchhike," she said. "Each summer a friend takes me to the main highway and thumbs a ride for me. Of course, I always have money and my papers with me. Eventually, someone—a man or woman, a couple, or even a family—comes along who does not mind picking me up. After that, I'm on my own—passed from hand to hand, from car to car, traveling across Europe."

"Aren't you afraid?" asked Levanter.

"Afraid of what?"

"Of strangers. Someone could hurt you."

She looked at him. "Hurt me?" She seemed surprised. "Most of the people I meet are protective of me. They are even reluctant to let me go, afraid that people they pass me to won't take care of me as well as they have."

Her voice was weak, and Levanter moved closer to hear her better. The fate that had mangled her body took nothing away from the wholeness of her face. The features were singularly expressive, giving trace to the nature and intensity of her thoughts and feelings.

"When I first began hitchhiking," she said, "my parents were afraid I might be kidnapped and held for ransom. But that never happened. I'm sure even professionals couldn't bring themselves to kidnap just a head. After all, isn't it the head they threaten to send back when their demands are not met in time?" She laughed again.

The young man who had carried her in approached them. She introduced him to Levanter as her boyfriend. He carried her off to the buffet.

Levanter realized he had been imagining himself as her lover. He examined the feeling carefully and found nothing morbid about his craving. What fascinated him about this young woman was that she had incorporated her deformity into the totality of her life. She was a woman, and her view of herself in the world was that of a woman. Her view was as mysterious and exciting to him as that of any woman he had ever desired. He wanted to become an object of her emotions and her passions, to enter her world and be given her knowledge of it.

Later in the evening, Levanter asked the girl for a date. She told him politely that she was too emotionally committed to her boyfriend to see anyone else.

Levanter's New York apartment was in mid-Manhattan, on a high floor, with a terrace overlooking one of the city's busiest intersections. Occasionally, to amuse themselves, he and Serena would aim his powerful garden hose over the high wooden fence on the terrace and shoot a stream of water down onto the avenue below, trying to hit hansoms carrying tourists from the big hotels toward Central Park. The perfect score was to strike the passengers but not the horse and the driver; when the passengers were soaked, they would scream, and the driver, uncomprehending, would instinctively stop the carriage; by the time he started up again the passengers would have received a double drenching, but still would not know where it came from.

One summer night, a Hollywood studio held a giant reception for the New York première of a film in the new marble mezzanine of the subway station under the intersection. A crowd of spectators, press photographers, and a televison crew had gathered on the sidewalk. The entrance to the subway was directly under Levanter's terrace, and he and Serena, their hose ready, were able to see the event both in immediate view and, as the event was nationally televised, in close-up on the television set Levanter had moved out to the terrace for the occasion.

First, an actor known for his macho performances stepped from a long black limousine, waving to the crowd, which roared in response. Just as he was blinded momentarily by the floodlights, Levanter and Serena turned the hose on. In seconds, they could see their torrent on TV, washing over the man's rugged features, upsetting his smooth toupee. As his make-up began to dilute right in front of the zoom lenses, he covered his head and ducked into the subway.

A famous Hollywood golden-youth couple emerged from their sleek auto and embraced before the cameras. They were just about to kiss for the benefit of millions of fans when the first dose of water blasted their perfect profiles. Dripping wet, they scurried to the subway, colliding at the entrance.

Levanter and Serena accomplished several successful dousings before the police, the cameramen, the press, and the crowd, all laughing, looked up to see the source of the stream; nothing was visible in the dark but endless rows of indistinguishable windows and terraces.

Once, after they had soaked several carriages, Levanter and Serena noticed the doorman from a building across the way pointing to the pool of water in the middle of the street. He kept motioning toward the sky as he talked to a group of curious passers-by. Levanter and Serena went down and walked over, pretending they had just noticed the puddle.

"It hasn't been raining, has it?" said Levanter to the doorman. "Where did the puddle come from?"

The doorman looked at him and Serena. "I can tell that you folks don't live here in the city," he said with a wise grin.

"No, we don't," said Serena.

The man gestured at the surrounding high-rise apartment houses, hotels, and office skyscrapers. "It's quite a place down here, as you can see," he said solemnly. "All these tall buildings generate a lot of magnetism. Every few days that magnetism makes a little cloud, right about here." He pointed straight above the pool of water. "A small cloud, it's true, but it produces enough rain to make this puddle and sometimes to sprinkle on hansom cabs going by." Proud of his explanation, he looked at his listeners for some sign of appreciation of his knowledge.

Levanter and Serena nodded thoughtfully.

"On different days, that little cloud may move just a couple of feet to the left or maybe to the right," the man continued. "There's no end to nature's mysteries," he concluded as another knot of people gathered around to hear his theories.

Serena phoned. She was flying into Los Angeles and was free to spend the night with him, she said. He immediately canceled his other plans and agreed to collect her in three hours at the airport. Almost automatically, he asked where she was.

"There is no message," she whispered.

Levanter took a taxi to the airport. He was half an hour early and dismissed the cab. He wandered through the lounges, watched the departing passengers lined up to pass through the gates of the electronic surveillance gadgetry, had a cup of coffee, and finally went to stand at the entrance of the terminal, where he was to meet her.

She appeared, looking pleased to see him there. Behind her, a porter carried a dress bag and a soft fabric suitcase. Neither piece had an airline baggage tag. Outside the terminal, the dispatcher was trying to hail a yellow cab for them when Levanter noticed a black limousine parked at the curb. It looked far more spacious and comfortable and appeared to be for hire. He gestured to the driver, a short, middle-aged man, who quickly jumped out and came to pick up Serena's luggage.

Opening the trunk, the driver tossed both pieces inside. Serena saw that he had thrown the suitcase on top of the dress bag and spoke to him sharply about crushing her dresses. He glanced at her and, without saying anything, rearranged the luggage. Then he closed the trunk, got behind the wheel, and waited for his passengers to get in.

Levanter gave the driver the address, asking whether he knew the way to the spot high up in Beverly Hills. The man looked at him in the rearview mirror and, again without a word, started the engine and drove off, accelerating as he reached the freeway.

Serena moved closer to Levanter. She put her leg over his, and he felt the pressure on his groin, the force of her hip against his. His right hand slid over her thigh, moved higher, caressing her, until she stretched over him, tense and excited. He put his left arm around her, and as she rested her head on his shoulder, he traced the outline of her breasts, then began stroking her through the thin fabric of her dress. Under his hands, she shivered and pressed against him.

The car turned off the freeway and sped along an empty road. Levanter saw that they had taken the wrong exit. He disengaged himself from Serena and leaned forward to tell the driver that he had left the freeway too soon and would have to go back and continue to the Beverly Hills exit. But the driver seemed to be in a daze. He did not answer, did not even look up into the rearview mirror. Instead, he accelerated suddenly, screeched across Sunset Boulevard, and started to climb along one of the dark roads of the canyon. The sudden turns and speed seemed to agitate Serena. Visibly frightened, she was about to say something when Levanter squeezed her arm, signaling her to remain silent.

From where he sat, Levanter could see three fourths of the driver's face. The man's hair glistened with perspiration, droplets of sweat streaked along his cheeks and neck and dripped from his eyebrows; Levanter wondered why he was wearing a heavy woolen jacket over his shirt. The driver made another rapid turn; one tire mounted the sidewalk and the front fender scraped the embankment. They were still going up the steep hill, and the engine, throttle fully open, was straining, its whine alternating with the screech of the tires.

At an intersection, the driver speeded up and barely avoided running into a car making a turn. At another intersection, he slowed down so suddenly that the car behind almost smacked into them.

Pushing herself rigidly against the backrest, her feet on the back of the driver's seat, Serena clutched Levanter's arm. She held her breath and, staring over the driver's shoulder, kept her eyes glued to the road.

Assuming an even, almost joking tone, Levanter asked the driver to take it easy, saying that the constant slowing down and speeding up was making him and his companion dizzy. But the man did not respond. Gripping the wheel tighter with both hands, he made another rapid turn. For an instant, two tires lost their hold on the road; in reaction, the driver jerked the steering wheel the other way and the tires banged back onto the road. As they soared over the crest of the hill, Serena screamed and started to shout abuses at the man, but he only went faster. Frantically, she tried to open the car door as they sped down the other side of the hill, but Levanter restrained her. She trembled and cried.

The man had made no threats; he had waved no weapons and did not seem to be concerned about whether his passengers had any. Still, Levanter felt he had to stop him. He could grab the driver from behind and choke him, but there was the danger that, fighting back, the driver might press even harder on the gas pedal and kill them all in a crash.

Again Levanter spoke to the man. In a calm, conciliatory voice he asked him to slow down, to stop for a moment. He said that he and his companion would not mind being discharged at any house; they could phone for a local taxi that knew the way through this maze of unlit canyon roads. But the driver paid no attention to him. He kept the car racing at top speed. Levanter slowly slid off his seat as he spoke. He rested his hand tentatively on the driver's shoulder. The man did not react. Levanter felt the rough surface of the sweat-soaked wool and, in a friendly manner, remarked that it was hot and he might be better off without his jacket. With Levanter gently patting him, the man seemed to lose some of his determination. He was slowing down.

Suddenly, Serena pushed Levanter sideways. He lost his balance and fell to the floor. Screaming, she threw herself forward, a shiny object in her hand. In an instant, she jabbed it into the driver's neck. The man yelled, and the car jerked forward, picking up speed. Serena withdrew the object—a metal rat-tail hair comb—then stabbed the man in the neck again. He

howled, twisting in his seat, and once more she plunged
the sharp metal into him, this time under his jaw. He
began to mumble, but the words died in his throat. Serena twisted the comb sideways and pushed it deeper; his
sounds became a gurgle, and he sank lower on the seat.
The car veered off, ran into the side of the hill, and
stopped, its engine still running.

Levanter scrambled to his feet. He leaned over,
pulled the comb out, and let it drop on the floor of the
car. Blood gushed from a ripped artery, spilling over the
back of the seat onto Levanter's suit and shoes. He
opened the door and, dragging Serena with him,
stepped out and ran to the driver's window. He reached
in to turn off the engine. He looked into the man's face:
the driver was dead. Blood was pouring from his mouth
and spilling over his chin; the eyes, still open, were
fixed on the rearview mirror. Serena sobbed quietly.

It was after midnight; the canyon was quiet. On
the other side of the road the palm trees stood motionless in the moonlight. Far away a dog barked, and another answered from below the hill.

Calmly, Levanter remarked that they must leave
everything untouched and summon the police.

"I don't want police," Serena blurted out. Her
mouth twitched; she was barely able to speak. "Let's get
rid of all this," she said, pointing at the car. "Anything
but the police."

"But there's nothing to worry about," said Levanter. "You acted in self-defense. We were being abducted by an insane man. He might even have a previous record of instability."

Serena grabbed his arm with surprising force. Her
face was twisted with rage. "I told you: no police," she
whispered. Levanter gently attempted to free his arm.
She let it go. "It's not just for my sake," she said. "It's
for yours too."

"For mine?"

"You know nothing about me. The police will

make a murder out of this." She was shaking as she spoke.

Levanter put his arm around her. "But we were being abducted," he said again. "There was no way we could have stopped him without violence."

"Your fingerprints are now on the murder weapon," she said, gesturing at her comb on the car floor. "The victim's blood is all over you. And for a witness"—she stopped and pulled away from him— "you have me. A convicted prostitute. A streetwalker, arrested more times than she cares to remember." She looked at him. "And how do you know, Mr. Investor"—her tone was mocking and defiant; he had never heard her speak like this before—"that this man," she said, pointing at the body, "was not a pimp I worked for? Or that he wasn't working for me?"

What she said slowly sank in, and Levanter didn't know which affected him more: her admission and the contempt in her voice or the body of the dead man in the car. His impulse was to leave, to walk away from her and from the body. But he thought of his fingerprints all over the car and recalled the phrase that the Impton Police Chief had used: "that special clan of the fingerprinted."

Serena waited for Levanter to say something, but he did not speak.

She went on. "Will any jury believe that you, my lover for three years, did not kill him in an argument over me? And why did you choose his unmarked car when there were so many regular cabs at the airport?" She spoke in the exaggerated tones of an accuser. "And the murder weapon—a steel comb with the longest possible rat-tail handle, sharpened to a fine point, like an ice pick? I was arrested when I cut a guy with a comb like this because he took my money after I did what he wanted. Would they believe it was just a coincidence that I had the same kind of comb in my purse tonight?"

Levanter looked away. She waited for a moment, to give him time to digest what she had said.

"You've introduced me to some of your friends," she continued. "Would the police, or a jury, believe that you don't even know my name, where I live and with whom, and how I make my living?" She seemed about to end her argument. "And you don't know what I might say to them."

She got into the car, slamming the door behind her. Levanter could not see her face in the dark.

He removed her luggage from the trunk, placed it on the rear seat beside her, and motioned for her to pick up the comb. He carefully pulled the body to the edge of the seat and, like a weightlifter, crouched beside it and tilted it until it rolled into his outstretched arms, the head cradled against his shoulder. Blood from the man's wounds soaked into his clothes. He dumped the body into the trunk, its head bouncing on the spare tire. He closed the trunk, got in behind the wheel, turned on the engine, and slowly backed the car out onto the street again. He drove all the way down to Sunset Boulevard and then up again, to his house high atop another hill.

In a few minutes they were at his house, and he pressed the button on the remote-control gate opener he carried in his pocket. As the gate opened, a series of lights went on automatically, spotlights playing on the trees that sheltered the house on all sides and illuminating the lawn and swimming pool.

As he pulled into the driveway, the lighted house stood before them like a freshly unwrapped toy. He picked up Serena's bags and she followed him inside.

In the living room, he told her to fix herself a drink. He was going to get rid of the car, he said, and hoped to be back with her in a short time.

He drove around to the side of his garage, away from the bright driveway, got out, and opened the trunk. He reached for the body. It felt heavy and warm.

He carried it to the front seat and propped it against the door on the right, then took a large plastic canister of gasoline from the garage and placed it on the seat between the body and himself. He drove out, the gate opening once again at the command of his remote-control device, then closing behind. He steered the car to the top of the hill, only a few hundred yards away, and turned into a construction site. He pulled onto a large reinforced-concrete platform that rested on stilts planted into the side of the hill—a house had yet to be built on it. Below, the hill dropped at a steep angle all the way down to the ravine. He extinguished the headlights. In the distance, the lights of the city shone like a mammoth fairground.

Levanter sat for a moment listening to his heart over the hum of the idling engine. After the earlier excitement, he felt in control again. He was pleased that he still had the athlete's ability to slow his heart down for the final sprint. He took out his handkerchief and wiped the fingerprints off the steering wheel, then stepped out of the car and wiped his prints from the trunk and the door handles. Reaching into the car, he pulled the dead man onto the floor, until his shoulder was resting on the accelerator. He removed the canister from the seat, opened it, and carefully poured gasoline over the entire length of the body and onto the rear seat, tossing the empty canister into the car.

Leaning through the window, he pressed in the car's cigarette lighter, and when it was heated he pulled it out. In one quick motion he slipped the gearshift out of Park and into the Drive position, dropped the lighter onto the body, then jumped back.

The car lurched forward. The flames inside flickered timidly as the black mass dove from the platform. He heard it smash into the hill, thundering as it rolled down, loosening rocks, which tumbled in its wake. He could see an explosion of flames in the ravine, and within seconds all was quiet again.

He walked away from the site, trying to stay close to the hedges, in the shadows, out of the direct moonlight. He was calm; his heart settled to its normal rhythm.

He had no reason to doubt what Serena had told him about herself. He was willing to accept that she was a prostitute. He had had prostitutes before and he would have them again. A prostitute was a stranger pretending to be a lover; she turned sex into a single act. Serena was a lover pretending to be a stranger; keeping Levanter perpetually on trial, she turned her single act into sex for him. Since he never knew whether to expect her again, he could not grow apprehensive about her absence. And every time she left; he knew that nothing he had done or said could make a difference: either she would return or she would not. With all her unpredictability, Serena provided the only real break in his life's routine.

In the time they had known each other, they had never been together more than three or four times a month, and there were many months when they hadn't seen each other at all. He doubted that he would have felt differently if he had seen her every day for three or four months and was then separated from her for over three years only to run into her again today. It was her absence that hurt him, not the presence of other men in her life.

There were, however, practical considerations. He had not suspected what her profession was, but now he realized that she could have infected him at any time. It would never have occurred to him to have a special blood test, and, as he traveled in various climates, he was accustomed to disregarding temporary skin eruptions and mouth lesions; he might have overlooked the fast-healing sores that can be the early physical symptoms of a sexual disease.

Perhaps the disease was already in a more advanced but quiescent stage, invading his spinal fluid and the tissues of his brain and nervous system. Maybe it was just about to manifest itself: headaches, slight lack of concentration, barely perceivable loss of memory, occasional vertigo. Going about the business of life unconcerned, he might soon start to go into an extreme depression, show hesitancy in speech, exhibit poorly coordinated movements. Then there would be euphoria; he would become reckless, impulsive, and aggressive. He would start to forget details of recent events while recalling the past with vivid detail.

One day, he imagines, he is in the bathroom, washing his face, his eyes shut. Suddenly his body starts swaying, even when he stands with his feet wide apart, and his hands seem to float about him. He opens his eyes and sees in the mirror that his pupils remain dilated, that they are not contracting in the light.

In the hospital, his disintegration follows quickly. Terrified by death, he sits for hours huddled in a corner of the psychiatric ward, making no attempt to change position, constantly recalling the inscription—EVERY HOUR WOUNDS, THE LAST KILLS—on the antique sundial at the swimming pool of his Beverly Hills house, but unable to concentrate long enough to know what the phrase means.

He was close to the brightly lit house and Serena. Now that the night had turned chilly, he was anxious to be indoors. His past was a matter of regret, his future was haunted by premonitions; only the present still gave value to time.

Serena was in the living room and had already started the fire. As he moved toward her, he saw himself in the large mirror. Covered with splotches of blood, pale and perspiring, he looked sinister.

She greeted him eagerly, saying she was relieved that he was back. Dried blood covered her right hand, and her blouse and skirt were smeared. She ran her fingers through his hair, then brought the bloody fingers to her lips, and, hesitating at first, tasted the blood on them. She began to nuzzle his hair, mussing it with her lips. Soon the blood covered her face, and when he kissed her he could feel it on his lips. His face became pasty with the dead man's blood, and she kept licking it off as she kissed him.

Her excitement mounted, and he also felt aroused, giving himself over to her mood of freedom and abandon. She drew him down onto the floor, by the fireplace, hurriedly undressing herself and tugging at his clothes. Her bare skin glowed pale orange in the light of the fire. She stretched out on the carpet and began to roll over his bloody pants and blood-soaked shirt, pressing them into her breasts, squeezing them between her thighs; the blood smeared her skin, and her movements quickened. She pulled Levanter onto the pile of soiled clothes and, hunching over him, weighing him down, she put him inside her and threw her body over his. She grabbed his shoulders and started to shake him. Her tense limbs slowly loosened; she began to moan and cry, as if she were being ripped apart. Staring at him with glassy eyes, she moved up and down, opening and constricting, relentlessly groping for her release as if her flesh were pouring away. She inched deeper onto him. All at once, the tightly wound chain inside her seemed to snap. Suddenly still, she slid down beside him on the floor.

Like a child ready to be lulled to sleep, she curled up on the carpet. As she lay watching him, Levanter stood up, gathered their blood-soiled clothing, and threw it, piece by piece, into the fire. After his clothes had burned, he emptied Serena's dress bag and suitcase, both of which were stained with blood. There were at least a dozen outfits, crumpled negligees, several pairs of shoes, evening bags, and a jewelry case. He was about to place the suitcase on the fire when Serena stopped him. From under the lining she pulled out a concealed bulky envelope bound with two thick rubber bands. Putting it into her handbag, she joked that she refused to burn her money, even if there was someone's blood on it. Then she gave Levanter the comb; he threw it into the fire, and they watched it blacken in the flames.

In the morning, Levanter removed the remaining blood spots from the living-room carpet and mixed the fireplace ashes with the garden fertilizer. In order to be alone with Serena, he telephoned the part-time maid and gardener and gave them the day off.

The sun had reached the swimming pool. Levanter had just set up a breakfast table at the pool when Serena came out. Her satiny black tank suit contrasted with the whiteness of her skin. Standing in the shadow, lit by sunshine reflected off the water, she looked luminous. She sat down at the table across from Levanter. For a moment they just looked at each other.

"You were right last night," said Levanter. "No jury would believe that I could have known you for any length of time without knowing anything about you. And anyone would wonder why you even called me that first time." He stopped. "Come to think of it, Serena, why did you? And what made you keep coming back?"

"I liked your act: your stories and games."

Levanter turned his face toward the sun. "On our second or third date," he said, "when you were in the bathroom, I looked into your handbag, hoping to find something—a driver's license, a credit card, a check—with your name or address. Instead, I found about eight hundred dollars in cash." He paused. "And so I thought you were the spoiled daughter of well-to-do parents." He turned back to her.

She laughed. "If it was only eight hundred, I must have cut my workday short for you," she said.

Levanter returned to his sunbathing. "Who are your customers?" he asked.

"I go out with anyone in a decent business suit. As long as he's not drunk or sick or too creepy."

"How do you meet them?"

"Hotels. Bars. Conventions. Any city that planes fly to, I fly there too."

"Do you keep all the money?"

"Why do you want to know? Thinking of investing it for me?"

"What do you do with it?" he asked, not allowing himself to be provoked by her remark.

"I keep most of it," she said. "One day I might buy my way into a regular business."

"How do you feel about getting arrested?"

The glare was making her squint; she put on her sunglasses. "It doesn't happen too often. My only curse is that my brother is a cop. He and his buddies hate my guts and give me a hard time every chance they get."

They both watched a self-propelling skimmer as it noiselessly scooped up leaves and dead insects from the surface of the pool.

"You may be infected," said Levanter, breaking the silence.

"I take pretty good care of myself," she said.

"Still, any customer you've had since your last blood test might have infected you."

"So what?"

"So, by now, you might have infected me too."

She fidgeted, apparently annoyed. "I might have. But so might anyone else you sleep with. Any customer of mine could be a lover of one of your women."

She had finished her breakfast. Two police cars passed by on the other side of the hedges, their sirens blaring. Levanter thought of the burnt-out wreck down in the ravine. The police could not possibly connect it to him, a respectable tenant in this peaceful estate, lounging at poolside, accompanied by a delicate, charming, young woman. He was about to doze off when Serena took off her glasses, then removed her swimsuit. Naked, she dragged a mattress to the edge of the pool and lay

233

down on her back. He was aroused and wanted her, but now he was reluctant to show it.

"There was once this lawyer," she said, "a widower who put up the bail when I was arrested." She spoke in a quiet, offhand manner. "To keep up his interest, I went out with him a few times. Then I had had enough. But he had gotten involved. He started to pester me to stay with him. He tried following me, and when I managed to lose myself, he bribed some detectives to trace me. Finally I'd had it."

She appeared to be losing herself in her recollections. When she went on, she was talking more to herself than to Levanter.

"One evening, up at his place, he was all sex and so was I. When we finished, he started filling a bubble bath for himself, with his whirlpool ready to be plugged in. I got dressed, then said I had to go to the toilet, and he left the bathroom. I took out my rat-tail comb and split the thick electric cord of the whirlpool machine, peeling back the rubber until all the wires were exposed in the water. The foam of the bubble bath covered the split. I came out and he kissed me good-by, letting me out of his apartment and locking the door."

She paused. Her voice sounded almost weary when she spoke next.

"They say that when a prisoner gets the chair, all the lights in the building dim as the electric current flows through the body. I walked down the hall and pressed the elevator button. As I waited, the lights in the corridor flickered. Later in the week, I read his obituary."

She turned sideways, and he could see her profile. She seemed fresher and more girlish than the first time he had seen her. As he listened to her, he was thinking that she could have been a coed griping about her exams and term papers.

"One of my regulars is an older man," Serena said, her tone slightly sharper. "He's been around for years and sees me often. As long as I've known him, he has always wanted the same stuff, but each time he gives it a different name or describes it in a new way or has another reason for wanting it. And each time I do it to him, his need for it gets deeper and deeper. He can't live without it."

Levanter expected her to tell him what it was the man wanted, but she went on with her story.

"One night, he was getting tired, but he couldn't get enough. When he was right above me, I looked up at him and saw him straining. And then his eye—I guess from stress—his eye popped out and slid out of its socket! It rolled out, like a freshly laid egg, hanging by its slimy root. It stopped midway down his cheek, dangling like a yo-yo. His eyelid sank into the empty socket and, when he opened it, a black hole gaped at me. I jumped away, screaming. The old man bent over, the eye nestling in the palm of his hand beside the socket, and screamed for me to help him squeeze it back in. But I just stood there, afraid to touch him, afraid even to look at him."

Serena rose from the mattress and slowly came to Levanter. He felt powerless and defeated, teased by her nearness. The feeling grew stronger and his mood shifted. He saw himself knocking her off her feet with one blow of his head, gripping her by her hair, forcing her to the ground, and shoving himself into her, smashing her again and again onto the cement until her face turned into a pulpy mass. But he did not move. She seemed to know she had defeated him and she stepped away.

"What if I were to open a three-year trust which would support you in luxury on the condition that you spend at least six months of each year with me? Would you agree to such an arrangement?" he asked.

"I can earn as much money as I want, no strings attached," she said. "You'd have to be a millionaire to buy me out."

She turned and glanced at the sundial. "Don't invest in your vice," she said, after a moment's reflection. "It's a losing business. Of course, if you marry really rich, maybe then you can afford to own me."

Another siren sounded in the distance. The spinning light on a police wrecker flashed behind the hedges.

She picked up her swimsuit and started to walk toward the house. He knew she was going to leave him for the last time. He made no move to stop her.

Levanter's article on the role of chance in creative investment, first published in *Investor's Quarterly*, had been condensed and reprinted by various newspapers and magazines. He received a number of responses from readers. One letter, on elegant stationery from the Hôtel Ritz in Paris, was sent by a Mrs. Mary-Jane Kirkland. The subject of his study interested her greatly, she wrote, and she referred to several innovative investors she had known. She collected privately published case studies and suggested that Levanter might like to peruse them in the library of her New York apartment. Mrs. Kirkland explained that she was not planning to return to New York for two more months, but she could instruct the guard to allow him to use her library.

Levanter was considering a follow-up to the article in *Investor's Quarterly* and was anxious to review the case studies, which in many instances were otherwise inaccessible. He wrote to Mrs. Kirkland, thanking her for her invitation and accepting it.

Her apartment was in one of the oldest cooperative apartment houses on Park Avenue. The doorman looked Levanter over carefully, and the elevator operator waited until he identified himself to the armed guard at Mrs. Kirkland's door.

The guard led Levanter into a white-marble hall

with a wide, curving staircase and a crystal chandelier. They walked through a set of double doors into the library, a large room paneled in wood and lined with shelves of leather-bound books. A life-size portrait of an elderly gray-haired man hung above a marble fireplace.

"Who is that?" asked Levanter, pointing to the painting.

The guard stepped back and gave the portrait a respectful look. "That is Mr. William Tenet Kirkland," he exclaimed, "founder of Kirkland Industries." He appeared surprised that Levanter, a guest in the house, did not recognize it. "Mrs. Kirkland's late husband," he added. "A very fine gentleman."

Levanter examined the portrait. "How old was he when he died?" he asked.

"Mr. Kirkland passed away two years ago, sir," said the guard. "It was just days after his eighty-fourth birthday." He opened the cabinet that contained the case studies Levanter had come to read and left the library, closing the door behind him.

Levanter settled in to work. The studies provided him with some valuable information and insight, and he returned every day for the next three weeks to pore over the firsthand reports, memoirs, and diaries of a wide range of investors and their associates. When Levanter was finished he wrote Mrs. Kirkland to tell her how much his new study would owe her, and he wired a bouquet of flowers to her in Paris.

About a month later, Mrs. Kirkland telephoned. She was back in New York, she said, and wanted him to know she was touched by the flowers and pleased that he had found her library helpful. She asked Levanter to come and have dinner with her. He said he would like to repay her generosity by inviting her out to dinner. Mrs. Kirkland suggested the following evening.

Levanter made a reservation at one of New York's most expensive restaurants. He knew the service would be reliable and the food of the highest quality. He explained to the maître d' that his guest would be an older lady, not in the best of health, who might be on a restricted diet, and asked that their table be in discreet proximity to the toilet.

He was afraid his own car might be too low for Mrs. Kirkland, so he hired an old-fashioned limousine, which would be easier for her to get in and out of.

At Mrs. Kirkland's apartment, a maid ushered him into a vast living room. The furniture was upholstered in brocades and velvets, drawings and paintings hung on the walls, and glittering objects were displayed on every table. Levanter felt as if he had stepped into a museum. He was awed by these riches and by the thought that they served as simple decorations in someone's home.

As he waited for Mrs. Kirkland, he rebuked himself for not having telephoned her just before he arrived, to be certain that she was well enough to go out this evening.

A woman dressed in a tweed skirt and jacket came into the room. Judging by her age and her manner, he guessed that she was a secretary to Mrs. Kirkland.

"Good evening, Mr. Levanter," she said, extending her hand, She seemed to be looking him over. Afraid he was not dressed properly, Levanter shifted uneasily, then shook her hand.

"It just occurred to me that I should have called Mrs. Kirkland to confirm our date," he stammered. "It would be perfectly understandable if she were somewhat tired after her trip. It mustn't be easy to travel at her age."

The woman smiled. "It's very considerate of you, Mr. Levanter," she said. "In fact, Mrs. Kirkland wanted me to come down to see you. I'm with Mrs. Kirkland. My name is Miss Saxon, Madeleine Saxon," she continued. "Mrs. Kirkland is still eager to meet you, and she hopes to mobilize herself. Unfortunately, at her age—" She spread her arms in resignation.

"I do understand," said Levanter.

Miss Saxon offered him a drink, and they sat down. There was a pleasant softness to her looks.

"If you don't mind, Mr. Levanter," she said, "Mrs. Kirkland suggested that you and I go on ahead to the restaurant, and the minute she feels better her driver will bring her there to join us."

"I'd be delighted," murmured Levanter. "The reservation can easily be changed to three." He named the restaurant and mentioned that he had made special arrangements for their table.

Miss Saxon seemed impressed. "It's very considerate of you to be so concerned," she said. "In fact, Mrs. Kirkland is not sufficiently conscious of how old she is."

"Is she disabled?" asked Levanter.

The woman hesitated. "She has been restricted for years, particularly when she was married to such a powerful man." She paused. "Then, after Mr. Kirkland's death, she became a bit secluded."

"I can imagine," said Levanter. "Were they close?"

"Very close."

Miss Saxon stood up, ready to leave. Levanter followed her. Outside, she complimented him once again on his thoughtfulness in providing a special limousine. Mrs. Kirkland, she said, would not have thought to order such a comfortable car for herself.

In the restaurant, Madeleine—as she had asked him to call her—reassured Levanter that Mrs. Kirkland would enjoy the restaurant's subdued atmosphere. After apéritifs, she said she was anxious to find out how Mrs. Kirkland was and went to the phone. When she returned, she told Levanter that Mrs. Kirkland regretted not being able to join them that evening but hoped to see Levanter very soon.

During dinner, Madeleine told him she had been born in the Midwest, an only child. Her father had died when she was six and she had to work her way through college. She studied foreign languages, stenography, and small-business administration, and found a job with the Kirklands.

More than twelve years had passed since then. In spite of obvious limitations imposed on her life by the nature of her work, they had been rewarding years, she said. She always had enough free time to pursue her interests and learned a great deal about herself and about the world of industry and power. Even though she now suddenly found herself nearly middle-aged, she felt no remorse for the years that had passed her by so quickly.

She gave Levanter a fascinating sketch of William Kirkland and his achievement: the creation, during his lifetime, of the fourth largest industrial conglomerate in the country. She had admired the man from the day she met him, she said. It was William Kirkland who, in a mere sixty years, built a small one-man investment outfit into a billion-dollar financial empire and took on the most powerful adversaries—a handful of Presidents, countless Congressional committees, and the whole financial industry.

Until his last days, William Kirkland remained youthful and determined, Madeleine explained. When he knew that uremia was ending his life, he summoned all the directors to his apartment for a regular board meeting. None of them suspected how ill their board chairman and chief executive officer was. He had had special ventilating equipment installed; silently, the air in their meeting room was purified before any of the directors, corporate secretaries, or stenographers could detect the odors that emanated from his diseased body. Minutes before he called the meeting to order, William Kirkland had received his last blood transfusion. An expert make-up man had overlaid the yellow-tinted skin on his face and hands with the natural-looking tones of a Florida tan. When William Kirkland entered the room and greeted his board, no one would have questioned his ability to make binding decisions.

In the cordial and healthy atmosphere of the meeting, she said, William Kirkland admitted with regret that he was finally ready to give in to age. He resigned his official function and passed the stewardship of his company to the men he had chosen so carefully, and the directors unanimously approved his appointments. The meeting ended as it had begun, on a note of optimism. Still cheerful, William Kirkland had escorted his directors to the door. But before they had reached their suburban homes, the memory of his firm handshake still fresh in their minds, William Kirkland had died in his bed, with his wife at his side.

As long as William Kirkland was alive, Mrs. Kirkland's life revolved completely around him. She entertained his associates, his political friends, and often his staff and their families. She had to be ready to leave New York at an hour's notice to accompany him to any of their numerous homes—on Long Island, in Florida, the Caribbean, Beverly Hills, London, and Paris— traveling in Kirkland's yacht, *Nostromo,* anchored at Palm Beach with its crew of seventeen, or *The Night Flight,* his four-engine transatlantic turboprop, fitted out like a small apartment, kept in a hangar in New York.

William Kirkland's last will made Mary-Jane Kirkland one of the major beneficiaries of his estate, Madeleine said. The estate and its trustees were to pay for all the households, the plane and the boat, maintenance and insurance for all their art collections, as well as Mrs. Kirkland's personal expenses, regardless of where and how they were incurred. However, when she died, she could make no bequests other than her most personal belongings. Thus Mary-Jane Kirkland could never forget that, even though he was gone, it was William Kirkland who held the reins of her existence.

Levanter regretted that he had not known the personal history of William Kirkland when he wrote his initial article for *Investor's Quarterly*.

The waiter brought the check.

"As I was imposed on you, may I at least share the cost?" asked Madeleine.

"Where were you when I dined here a few years ago and needed such an offer?" Levanter asked, chuckling. He paid the waiter, then stood up and held her chair.

It was still warm when they left the restaurant. Levanter dismissed the limousine and they began to stroll.

"What happened at that restaurant a few years ago?" Madeleine asked.

"Soon after I arrived in America," Levanter said, "I received a fellowship for my studies—about two hundred dollars a month, for a year. I had been parking cars until then, so this was quite a break, a lot of money. To celebrate my good luck, I made a date with a girl I'd just met. She lived right over there," he said, pointing to an old brownstone. "When I picked her up, it was pouring and there wasn't a bus or even a taxi in sight. We huddled under my umbrella and dashed across the street to that restaurant. I thought it was a perfect place, small, intimate, unobtrusive—and French."

Madeleine smiled at him. "It is all that," she said.

"We were seated at a corner banquette and, after drinks, were handed menus. For some reason—possibly to be closer to my date—I looked at her menu with her, leaving mine unopened. No prices were listed on her menu, and I thought that so unassuming a restaurant had to be inexpensive as well, possibly offering a fixed-price dinner. We ordered hors d'oeuvres, soup, main course, wine, salad and cheese, dessert, coffee and cognac."

"Sounds lovely," said Madeleine.

Levanter nodded. "It was lovely. It was still pouring outside, the restaurant felt warm and cozy, I liked the girl. We had another cognac. A perfect evening." He laughed. "Then the waiter slipped the check on the table. I glanced at it and called him back to tell him that he must have accidentally given us the check for the table for eight across the room. He apologized and removed the check. The maître d' came over and asked us most courteously whether we had enjoyed our dinner. We told him we had. Smiling, he handed me our check, assuring me that he had gone over it carefully. I looked at it: the total was the same as before. I pondered aloud that perhaps, as it was a French restaurant, the amount was given in French francs and you had to divide by about five to get the price in dollars. The maître d' laughed. Everything in his restaurant was French, he said, except the figures on the check. I still didn't understand how dinner for two could cost almost as much as I had to live on for a month. The maître d' politely informed me that his little restaurant was justly known to be not only one of the very best in this country but also—because of its insistence on French excellence—one of the most expensive. My date and I had about thirty dollars between us."

Madeleine laughed. "Poor you! How did you pay for your dinner?"

"The maître d' took me aside and he agreed on a ten-month installment plan. It was my first lesson in the relativity of riches in America," said Levanter.

They had walked to the East River. A three-masted schooner glided slowly toward the South Street Seaport, its lights flickering against the far shore. On the boat's afterdeck, a solitary figure played a guitar, and its faint sound carried across the water. Madeleine and Levanter leaned against the balustrade. Below, the first waves made by the sailboat lapped against the embankment.

"Over the years, the Kirklands' way of life has become mine," said Madeleine. "If I weren't with Mrs.

Kirkland, I would be on my own and I would have to learn such a lesson myself."

"Have you ever thought of having children? Of marrying?" asked Levanter.

"I have. But I'm not brave enough to have a child without a husband. And I'm reluctant to marry. The men I know are always afraid that after my life with the Kirklands I would never be satisfied living on an ordinary income. Or, if they're rich, they think I've been contaminated by exposure to Mr. Kirkland's wealth and would sell myself to anybody just for the money." She paused. "There have also been other men, young, handsome, bright, who pretended to be in love with me. But they really only wanted to gain access to Mrs. Kirkland's bed and, after Mr. Kirkland's death, to marry her."

The schooner seemed out of place, a relic of another world. Levanter found himself thinking of the millions of people who had never cut across ocean waves on a luxurious liner. The world of such experience was as foreign to them as the world of Mary-Jane Kirkland was to him. For a moment he felt bitter as he viewed the woman standing next to him. How arbitrary it was that sheer chance had allowed Madeleine Saxon into the world of the rich, while so many others who strove all their lives to enter it wouldn't ever catch so much as a glimpse of it.

"In your letter to Mrs. Kirkland, you mentioned your love of the Alps," said Madeleine. "I've never been there."

"I thought you traveled everywhere with the Kirklands," said Levanter.

"I did," she said. "But Bill Kirkland would never go anyplace except on business, and Mary-Jane didn't want to travel without him. She has never been to the Greek islands or the south of Italy or Spain—dozens of other countries."

The subject seemed to make her uneasy. She appeared dispirited, defenseless. Suddenly, he felt tender toward her and gently took her by the arm. She did not stiffen. They started to walk crosstown and soon were west of Fifth Avenue.

"That's my apartment," said Levanter, pointing across the street toward his terrace, "where I live and work."

"How large is it?" she asked.

"Two rooms, a kitchen and bath," said Levanter. He imagined Madeleine's quarters in the Kirkland houses and felt slightly embarrassed that his were so small.

Madeleine was puzzled. "Two rooms? But if you work there, where do you sleep?" she asked earnestly.

Her surprise was authentic and Levanter couldn't help laughing. "You've been with Mrs. Kirkland for too long!" he said. "If you were a Russian actress, I would ask you to come upstairs and see my photographs, as a pretext to get you up to my apartment."

"What pretext would you find for me?" she asked, challenging.

"To come have a drink. To learn how a lonely bachelor can work, live, and entertain a lady all in two rooms." He smiled.

She took his arm. "A perfect pretext," she said as they crossed the street.

In his apartment, she admired how economically he had used the space. He pointed out the *Amerykanka,* his convertible sofa, which he kept in his office room as a souvenir, and told her about the predicament that the prospect of opening it had once presented. He jokingly wondered how she would react.

She laughed and said that anything mechanical made her nervous.

He looked at her. Her face was round, unmarred by a single wrinkle. She had a narrow nose, delicately outlined lips, and wide-set blue eyes, which gave her an innocent expression. Levanter suggested that they go for a ride in his car. There was little traffic, and in minutes they had passed the lights of the George Washington Bridge and were climbing up the steep, dark lanes of Fort Tryon Park to the Cloisters, a millionaire's whim brought from another time and another place. Levanter drove her back downtown through Harlem, which Madeleine had never seen before.

As he stopped the car in front of her building, Madeleine said, "Mrs. Kirkland or I will phone you about that dinner." She hesitated. "Meanwhile," she said, reaching into her jacket pocket, "I stole this from your apartment. A memento." She opened her hand, but he could not see in the dark. "It's a turnstile token. To enter one of the Alpine cable cars, no doubt," she exclaimed.

The metal caught the light. "It's a New York subway token," he said, laughing. "There's nothing like it in Mrs. Kirkland's collection."

She leaned toward him and quickly kissed him on the cheek, then ran to the building's entrance. A doorman rushed to open the door for her.

Two days later, he received a card from Mrs. Kirkland. She apologized for missing him the other evening and invited him to dine with her and a few friends on Saturday. A delicate postscript indicated black tie, and Levanter promptly sent his old tuxedo to be pressed.

The maid showed him to the library. Madeleine Saxon left a group of guests and came to greet him. Levanter asked whether Mrs. Kirkland was again not well enough to come down. Before Madeleine could answer, the butler offered a tray of drinks and she stepped aside.

One of the guests turned to talk to Levanter, politely asking how long he had known Mary-Jane. Levanter was about to tell him he hadn't met her yet when Madeleine introduced another couple.

"I enjoyed reading your piece in *Investor's Quarterly*," the man said. "Mary-Jane sent it to me. First-class work."

Levanter bowed slightly. "I have been looking forward to talking to Mrs. Kirkland tonight," he exclaimed. "I hope she will be well enough to dine with us."

The man raised his eyebrows. "Well enough? Why? Isn't she well?" He turned to Madeleine Saxon, who was talking with some guests nearby. "What's wrong, my dear?" Madeleine turned around. "Mr. Levanter wonders whether you're feeling all right? How do you feel, Mary-Jane?" He took her hand and kissed her fingers with the fondness of an old friend. She moved closer and stood between him and Levanter.

"How nice of you to worry about me, George," she said, patting Levanter on the arm. "Ever since we met, George has been worried about my age. Haven't you, George?"

Levanter was speechless and felt he was blushing.

Dinner was announced. In the dining room, the round table was set for twelve. Levanter was seated at Mary-Jane's right. She kept glancing at him, laughing quietly, letting him know how pleased she was with her practical joke. In a pale pink evening gown, which masked her large hips and accentuated her slim waist and sloping shoulders, and with a simple square-cut diamond on a fine silvery chain hanging between her small breasts, she looked almost beautiful.

During dinner, as he talked to the other guests, he felt Mary-Jane's eyes upon him. When he chatted with her and she leaned close to him, he could tell that her friends were scrutinizing him and the butler and waitresses were exchanging anxious glances.

Occasionally, he found himself staring at the paintings that covered the walls, trying to sort out his discomfort: he was unable to determine whether he resented seeing such masterpieces in a private home, where the public could not share them, or whether he was simply envious that he did not own them himself.

After dinner, as coffee and liqueurs were being served in the living room, Mary-Jane took Levanter aside. "When I said I was with Mrs. Kirkland, I merely added the 'with,'" she whispered. "Saxon was my maiden name. Madeleine was a name I used as a child with my pen pals! I hope you're not angry."

Levanter had gotten over the embarrassment of being tricked. He smiled at her. "You look stunning tonight," he said softly.

She studied him for a moment. "I benefit from the Kirkland setting," she murmured, bowing her head.

At nidnight, Levanter was leaving with the last of the guests. Mary-Jane stopped him. "If I were a Russian actress, I would ask you to come see the rest of my apartment," she said. "This would be a pretext to get you to stay for a drink."

"What pretext could you find as Mrs. Kirkland?"

"To stay and see how a widow can live all alone in an old Park Avenue triplex."

After the others had left, Mary-Jane showed him through the maze of rooms with obvious pride. The third floor of the triplex was her personal domain: her bedroom all in pink taffeta, two dressing rooms, a bathroom with gold-plated fixtures, and a small pink-marble swimming pool.

Levanter studied the photograph of William Kirkland on the night table while Mary-Jane went into a dressing room. She came back wearing a long purple silk robe that made her look taller and more stately. She phoned downstairs for tea and sandwiches.

"Mr. Kirkland was so much older than you," he remarked.

"Bill was in his early seventies when we met," she said.

She sat down at the edge of her bed and kicked off

her shoes. Levanter was sitting on a small bench at the foot of the bed.

"I had just started working for the advertising department," she said, "and he came in to approve some copy. The attraction was instantaneous—and mutual."

"How do you explain it?" asked Levanter.

"For Bill, it was my youth," she reflected, "and, in spite of it, my maturity." She smiled. "For me, it was his power. We began meeting secretly. We wrote to each other every day, and used outside messengers to deliver the letters."

She stared at the photograph, then turned to Levanter.

"When we met, Bill was married and had two grown sons, both in their forties, both on the board of Kirkland Industries. Within a year, Bill divorced his wife—with the largest settlement anyone had ever heard of. By the next year, we were married."

The maid brought the tea tray.

"As a husband and as a corporate executive, Bill was always a very proud man," Mary-Jane continued. "He saw himself as guardian of Kirkland Industries, not its master, and as master of his family, not its guardian."

She glanced at the photograph.

"One day, his sons made some insulting remarks about me. Bill summoned the corporate secretary and a sworn-in stenographer and asked his sons to repeat the remarks they had made to the Chairman of the Board of Kirkland Industries. These men, both about twice my age then, told their father, 'You made a fool of yourself when you married that child whore!' Bill immediately assembled the rest of the board, and his proposal that the two of them be dismissed passed unanimously. Bill's sons were sure their father would reverse the decision, so they didn't take any legal action or look for jobs with a competitor. Both apologized to me, and I begged Bill to put them back on the payroll. He asked me never to mention their names again."

She stopped, apparently upset by her memories.

"Shortly before that final board meeting, I took a chance and summoned them. I hardly recognized them—they both looked aged and haggard, and one was half drunk. I told Bill his sons had come to see him. 'I have no sons,' he said. 'My company has no business with those it has fired.' He waved me away. When I told the sons, the two aging men, they wept in front of me."

In another room a clock began to chine. Levanter looked at his watch. Mary-Jane lay back against the pillows, her legs thrust forward, her knees spread. There was an aura of gentle sensuality about her, and he was reluctant to leave.

He stood up, breaking the mood.

"Can't you stay?" she asked.

He slowly focused on the opulence of the surroundings. The thought of making love to her had never quite taken shape in his mind. Becoming her lover would be simple; yet he was afraid of overstepping his limits.

"I want to stay," said Levanter. "But I can't help wondering whether I would want to stay if you were Madeleine Saxon."

"I will never be Madeleine Saxon."

"Would I stay without the benefit of this setting?" he asked.

"You'll never know," she said quietly.

He did not move or change his expression as he stood examining his emotions. She was open to him, all frontiers gone, waiting for a sign or a word.

Mary-Jane suggested they get married. As soon as she said it, Levanter felt almost fearful that marrying her would be a step toward creating their own fate. A superstition lingered in him that if they did so chance might turn from a benefactor to the ultimate terrorist, punishing both of them for trying to control their own lives, trying to create a life plot. This fear, he thought, must be a remnant from his childhood, when he had read one sentimental novel after another, assuming that if novels reflected life and he could easily detect their plots without even reading each incident, then life must also have a plot that could be detected.

They were on *The Night Flight* on their way back to New York from a vacation in Mexico. Mary-Jane said that if he agreed, they ought to marry in a city that did not require a license and blood test in advance, as she did not want the press and gossip columnists alerted. They should marry soon, she felt, because she was tired of hiding the fact that they lived together and of taking separate suites when they traveled—all to preserve the dignity of the Kirkland name.

She went to the galley to check on lunch. Levanter looked down through the window. If chance were going to punish him for marrying Mary-Jane, he wondered, wouldn't it have punished him already for living with her for almost two years? Why should he try to guess his future, when the outcome of the imminent moment was often uncertain?

He recalled a morning when he was feeling most confident about his image in the home of his wealthy mistress. He was shaving, naked, in Mary-Jane's bathroom. He dropped the razor blade and it got stuck between the marble counter and the wall. He couldn't reach it from above, so he crawled under the wash basin, headfirst, but still couldn't find it. To get a better look, he turned onto his back, raised his legs, and pressed his feet against the underside of the basin to push his head as far up behind it as he could. He found the blade. But he couldn't get out. He had squeezed himself in so tightly that his legs were jammed against the underside of the basin. He needed someone to pull his feet from another angle. Mary-Jane had already left for an early appointment. He shouted for the butler, but from under the basin his voice did not carry well. Mary-Jane's personal maid, an elderly French woman, came to the bathroom. The instant she saw his bare body, she exclaimed, "Pardon, Monsieur," and disappeared. He screamed again, but no one came. He had the feeling that the maid had gone off to warn the other members of the household staff that Madame's beau was performing some formidable exercise in the nude and ought not to be disturbed. He was folded up under the basin for hours. Only at midday, when Mary-Jane returned, was he rescued.

He phoned the pilot, asking him to radio for information on the nearest city on their route that had a jetport and permitted marriage without prior application. In a few minutes, the pilot had an answer: Birmingham, Alabama, less than two hours away.

Lunch was served. Levanter told Mary-Jane they could get married in Birmingham. She summoned the pilot to land in Birmingham.

Mary-Jane and Levanter went to visit an old friend of Bill Kirkland's, a successful businessman who had recently retired to the privacy of his sumptuous Long Island estate, Blackjack.

They traveled by helicopter and landed on a grass-covered pad. Their host came out to greet them and to show his atomic shelter to Mary-Jane and her foreign-born husband. As the helicopter took off, clearing the pad, the man pressed a button in a small electronic device hooked onto the belt of his trousers and a steel plate under the pad slid sideways, revealing the entrance to an underground passage. As they walked down the stairs, the plate automatically sealed above them, activating equipment to purify the air and guard against the transmission of radioactive dust.

Descending the staircase, they passed through an elaborate system of doors and compartments. The host explained that he could enter his shelter through several such entrances in the house and elsewhere on the property.

Levanter was expecting something similar to the bomb shelters he had spent so many days in as a child in Eastern Europe at the outset of World War II. Instead, he and Mary-Jane and their host entered a faithful replica of one of Manhattan's most fashionable restaurants, complete with bar, rows of round tables, high-backed chairs with red leather seats, wall mirrors—even the tablecloths and cutlery were duplicated to the tiniest detail.

The host pressed a button, and part of the wall slid sideways, revealing another staircase. The lower level, he explained, consisted of several bedrooms, bathrooms, a library, a dining room, and a kitchen. A generator constantly supplied fresh air, instruments monitored radioactivity levels within a twenty-mile radius, and a series of radio and TV monitors and transmitters maintained contact with the world outside and provided a means of communication within the shelter.

The host told them that the stock of food and medical supplies was sufficient for eight people to subsist for six months and thus outlive the immediate danger of an atomic war, and he continually revised the list of people he would invite to join him.

Patting Mary-Jane's shoulder, he said, "You've always been one of them, you know." Mary-Jane kissed him affectionately on the cheek.

Later, when she was absorbed in looking through the shelter's library, the host took Levanter aside.

"I'll square with you, George," he said in a cordial tone. "You're not on my list, even though you're married to Mary-Jane."

Levanter nodded politely.

"If you're cooped up underground, six months is a long time," said the host, "and you have to know all about someone you're going to be cooped up with."

"I understand," said Levanter.

"It's not that you aren't likable, George," he said emphatically. "On the contrary. You are. It's just that one wonders if you haven't made a career out of being so likable."

"I don't follow you," said Levanter.

"You're a survivor, George. The war. The Russkies. Parking cars. You've survived it all. And look at you now." He paused, as if to let the implication sink in. "Married to Mary-Jane, the nicest girl there is, who also happens to be one of the richest widows in America, with the most powerful friends around."

"Mary-Jane and I met on a blind date," said Levanter.

"Sure you did, George," he agreed quickly. "But have all your survivals begun on blind dates?" He looked at Levanter, then continued, his lips pursed. "What if there was some deed, some awful price you had to pay to emerge unscathed? How do we know that there wasn't?" He glanced at Levanter and, as if afraid he might have hurt his feelings, quickly added, "Take me, for instance. Like every other WASP, I'm completely documented: city, state, federal records exist for every facet of my history; schools, hospitals, clubs have files on me; and there are people who have known me at every stage of my private and professional life. But where can one find out about you?" He lowered his voice. "What does Mary-Jane, your own wife, really know about who you are?"

Levanter did not know what to say.

Mary-Jane ended her tour of the library and rejoined them. Lunch was to be served here, prepared entirely from food stored in the shelter, in circumstances approximating the period after an atomic alert.

Walking to the shelter dining room, Mary-Jane fell. She said she must have caught her heel on the rug. She fell again the following day while playing tennis, and again explained that she had tripped on something.

This time, Levanter was certain that she had fallen backward, as if her sense of balance had suddenly failed her.

When they were back at their New York apartment, he mentioned that he was worried about her. She admitted that she had fallen several times in the last few weeks but claimed she was just absent-minded and clumsy. Levanter insisted that she have a thorough medical checkup and, reluctantly, she agreed.

In a week they had a diagnosis: a growth in her inner ear. Soon they had the verdict: the cancer had already begun to spread to her brain; surgery was out of the question.

Within weeks Mary-Jane was bedridden, and there were only a few rare moments when she recognized him. These lucid periods came unanticipated, and they left as unexpectedly as they came. At such times, the nurse would discreetly leave the room. Mary-Jane would start to talk to Levanter as though he had just come in, as though it was he who had been away and had only now returned to talk to her, while she was always waiting for him. He sat on the edge of her bed, and they looked at each other with the spark of rediscovery that comes after a long absence.

She was aware of her disease and of the prognosis. She cried only once—when she told Levanter that her illness had cut off what she saw as her mission: to expand his freedom, to offer him a life that he might have lived had he inherited such great wealth himself. She said she wanted him to enjoy her money without the sense of entrapment and guilt such affluence usually brings its heirs, and to pursue whatever interested him most in life.

"Instead, you're married to a vegetable," she said, "and the law won't let you divorce me for at least seven years, because legally I'm your mentally incapacitated spouse. What if I keep wilting for years? You'll be imprisoned by me, unable to marry, to have children."

"You've given me the best moments I've ever known," said Levanter.

She looked at him, lost in thought, and then the thoughts drifted. Her eyes still looked at him, at the room, but her mind was elsewhere. Her body was alive, but she was indifferent to it. The nurse returned to the room and resumed her post at Mary-Jane's bedside.

Levanter spent his days in the apartment, waiting for any sign of perception, staring into the eyes that remained open but did not see. Occasionally, he fed Mary-Jane and walked her to the bathroom, her head resting against his shoulder, his arm supporting her. He dressed and undressed her, combed her hair, helped to bathe her, to rub her dry, and to put her to sleep. At these times, she was his infant child.

The last traces of life left her body as quietly as the thoughts had left her mind. He felt he was losing his only child, becoming an orphan himself. He moved back to his old apartment, which, as a gesture to chance, he had kept as an office while they were married.

Each time his eye caught the photograph of Mary-Jane on his night table, the words "it was and it was not" returned to him.

Walking past Carnegie Hall one evening, he saw a familiar face staring at him from a row of posters. The bold black letters of her name contrasted with her light hair and pale eyes.

The concert was already in progress and the box office was closing. The ticket seller looked at him and mechanically announced that the concert was sold out. Saying nothing, Levanter took out pencil and paper. He made himself tremble. His left hand clasped his right wrist, restraining and guiding the hand over the paper, and he wrote in large uneven letters that he had to go in because he suffered from fits that only music could subdue. The woman read his note. Before she had a chance to refuse his request, he jerked his right hand free and spastically slapped his ear several times. The woman looked nervous, as if she feared he was about to have one of his fits. Hurriedly, she reached under the counter and passed him a ticket that someone had reserved but had not yet picked up. Levanter paid her and, still shaking, rushed inside.

The hall was filled with the sounds that sprang from under the pianist's fingers. The music she played elated him. His mother had played this piece, and he recalled how he had often listened to recordings of it, as if the music itself could bring back the emotion it had so often aroused in him in the past.

His seat was near the back of the hall: he could hardly see the pianist's features and seemed to be looking at her through the wrong end of opera glasses. He remembered clearly how he had felt the first time he heard her play. Yet he was no better able now than he had been then to define the sensation.

He glanced around at the audience. People sat motionless, absorbed in the music that rushed at them, intimate and immediate, pure spirit without words, without gestures. No one stirred until the concert had ended.

He could still hear the applause for her encores when he went backstage. He walked confidently past the guard, and, murmuring that Madame expected him, asked her maid to let him sit down in the dressing room. Stagehands brought several large baskets of flowers into the room; Levanter could see a crowd of admirers gathering outside.

Pauline opened the door but stood with her back to the room, facing a group of photographers in the corridor. She autographed some programs and entered, closing the door behind her. Her face and neck were flushed with excitement. Midway into the room, she noticed Levanter. At first she looked surprised, then she simply asked him to open the wine on the table beside him. He filled two glasses. She dismissed her maid, sat down in a chair on the other side of the table, and took a sip of wine.

"Another great success," said Levanter.

She smiled distantly. "A good audience. But the audience is gone now. All that's left is the recording, a memory."

"But it's a memory with feeling, which can be listened to many times," said Levanter.

"It can," she said. "But only as a source of reflection; no more magic of the spontaneous." She paused. "In that cavern in ValPina," she said, "you told me about a baseball player who killed the girl he once loved."

Levanter nodded.

"You told me about him for a reason. What was it?"

"I hoped you would remember the story. And possibly you would remember the person who told it to you."

"How do you want to be remembered?" She looked in the dressing-table mirror outlined in white bulbs and patted her hair.

"As a memory with feeling," he said.

"Without the magic of the spontaneous?"

She stood up and went to examine the baskets of flowers. She read the cards and telegrams with them, smelled the blossoms, rearranged some leaves. As he gazed at her, he feared that he might lose courage.

"I live half a block away," he said. Then, before she had a chance to react, he forced himself to plead, "Come there with me. Please."

She bit her lips. Without a word, she went behind a screen and came out moments later in a simple dress. She reached for her coat, and he helped her on with it. Behind her back, he brushed his face lightly against her hair.

As they walked out into the corridor, Pauline gently touched his arm and stopped him. "Why?" she asked.

Levanter felt at ease now. He reached for her and drew her close, his lips grazing her neck, his face buried in her hair. She folded her hands behind his neck, and he felt her body against him, pliant and vulnerable.

"Why?" she repeated.

"I'm afraid of losing you," he said. The sound of his words brought him a faint memory, so faint that he dismissed it.

"Why?" she asked again.

"I want you to fall in love with me," he said, "to want me as I am now. Somehow, I think you're my last chance."

She disengaged herself from his embrace and stepped back.

"Your last chance? For what?"

"To be wanted, rather than remembered. To have a fresh emotion, a sensation that isn't just a ricocheted memory. To be part of that spontaneous magic."

When they stepped from the elevator and approached his apartment, he noticed that the door had been painted while he was out. The paint had already dried, but when he inserted his key into the lock it would not turn; paint had seeped in and hardened inside. He was going to lose her because of a drop of paint, he thought.

Pauline was amused. "Are you sure you live here?" she asked.

Levanter was fighting the lock. It would not budge. "You wouldn't happen to have any nail-polish remover on you, would you?" he asked.

"I don't even have a nightgown," she answered.

Levanter didn't know what to do. It was nearly midnight; the superintendent did not live in the building.

Pauline came to his rescue. "Where would the painters keep their supplies?" she said.

They went down to the basement. Among the broken refrigerators and vacuum cleaners, the mops and pails, Pauline found a can of turpentine and Levanter poured some into an empty bottle lying nearby. Back at his door, Pauline handed him her comb and he dripped the turpentine down the handle, straight into the lock. He inserted his key. The door opened.

He turned on one small lamp. The dim light outlined the contours of the desk, bookshelves, TV set, copying machine, two armchairs, his old convertible sofa, and the small rocker.

Pauline took off her coat and placed it on the sofa. Quickly, Levanter stacked some of her recordings on the stereo; the first clicked as it fell into position. He drew the curtains over the windows and the terrace door, took off his jacket and laid it over her coat, then went to her, backing her against his desk. He slid to his knees and gently raised her dress up around her waist. He tugged her panties down and she stepped out of them. Mutely, he found her flesh hidden in the silky fur between her thighs. It was moist and fragrant, and he pressed tighter against it, warming it with his breath. When he felt her hips quiver, he opened her with his fingers, and his tongue moved inside.

Images of her in ValPina whirled through his mind: in the hotel lounge, on the midstation terrace, at the underground lake. He remembered trying to catch her eye, hoping she would respond.

She started to shiver; a wave of tremors ran through her and she shoved her flesh into his face. Then she pulled away, almost lifting herself onto the desk with her hands. He kept his mouth over her, as he pushed her thighs against the desk. She put her hands on his shoulders. Then, just when she seemed ready to surrender to her own passion, she shrank back, whispering. "I can't, I never could."

He continued to kiss her, sensing the yearning that coursed through her. Her hands clutched his shoulders, caressed his neck and hair. Writhing and jerking, she again seemed on the verge of giving in to her own surging when, in despair, she repeated, "I can't." He stopped touching her. She slid onto the floor with him, her arms around his neck. He began to undress her, slowly, tossing her clothes onto an armchair. Then he quickly took off all his clothes.

He took her hand and led her to the rocking chair. He sat down, spreading her legs, and guided her over himself. The chair rocked gently, its movement bringing him deeper into her, making her straddle him more tightly. He clasped his arms around her hips, and she rested her hands on the back of the chair behind his shoulders. Heat from their bodies filled the narrow space between her breasts and his chest. In the gleaming light, he saw her eyes, wide open, fixed on him. His lips brushed hers, the taste of her flesh still on his tongue, and when he felt her tongue upon his, he realized that it was the first time Pauline had kissed him.

The chair rocked, and they clung to each other, rising and falling. Her eyes remained open, anguished, staring at him. The next record dropped onto the turntable. They rose from the chair, and he led her slowly to the bedroom.

She lay flat on her back, her legs apart, her arms at her sides, and she watched him as he walked over to the closet, opened it, and pulled out a full tie rack. He selected several ties, one after another, choosing only those which were soft enough.

He returned to her and she did not move. He raised her hands above her head and tied each wrist to a bedpost, taking pains not to knot the ties too tightly. She did not stiffen when he tied them, nor when he fastened each ankle to a post at the foot of the bed. She was spread-eagled. He pushed two pillows under her, lifting her body in an arch, her chest rising, her belly concave, her thighs flat, her flesh open. He picked up one more tie and an elastic band; gathering her hair into a ponytail and securing it with the band, he slipped the tie through and attached her hair to the railing of the bed. He put a small pillow under her neck.

Levanter began to trace his fingers gently along Pauline's neck, the underarm, down to her thighs, then up again, diagonally, over her belly and breasts. His torso brushing against her breasts, his flesh against her hips, he hovered above her like a bird of prey, descending only to nip at her skin, biting until it swelled, pressing his flesh against hers, then lifting himself until only the tip touched her skin. A ripple went through her, and his hands followed it. He kept teasing her until her body was taut; her whole being seemed to be a thin membrane he could pierce at will. He started to enter her, then to leave, to enter again, and leave again; he remained stilled inside her, then twisted, at times bulky and stiff, at times slender and pliant, drawing himself tightly into her, contracting and releasing. She strained, the veins in her neck and arms swelling, the ties threatening to cut through her, and she drew her body up, attempting to pull free, her eyes blank, unseeing, her mouth open but uttering no sound. He crouched between her thighs and wedged his fingers into her flesh. His hand parted it, slowly feeling the tender cords. She tensed and contracted, trying to pull back, but the bonds held her tightly in place. Like a burrowing animal, his hand crept into her, his fingers twisting, spreading the slippery tissues, probing deeper and deeper. She shivered, and he waited for her to ask him to stop but she did not. He pushed his hand farther in, and as her muscles gripped his wrist, he could not tell whether he felt her pulse or his own. Her body rose higher. Her face tightened; she moaned, "No!" A sudden current ran through her like lightning; then, just as suddenly, the tension that gripped her dissolved. He lost the feeling of his own shape; in the ultimate moment, when his vision shrank, he heard her whisper, "Yes!" and, as its sound ebbed, her body softened, freed from its own bondage, no longer struggling against any restraints.

He took his skis from the gondola rack and walked to the start of the run. He was the only passenger in the last PicSoleil gondola on the final day of the skiing season. All the other lifts were already closed, and the attendant warned him that no skiers had come up that day. This would be the first time that he had the mountain range entirely to himself. The Aval was his favorite run, and he could ski it blindfolded. He would be in ValPina in less than half an hour.

He felt exhilarated. The unbroken whiteness of the endless slopes staggered him with their permanence and grandeur. A descent was like life: to love it was to love each moment, to rejoice in the skill and speed of every moment. Soon, skiing down these fields, he would appropriate them as if they had been set there just for him, to be fleetingly possessed, the possession vanishing an instant after it took place. Finally only the memory of having possessed the mountain would be his.

The air was unusually still, with only occasional cold streaks. To the right, over the plains, the sky was filled with slowly churning dark brown clouds. But to the left, over the miles of glacier, where storms formed, the sky was blue, the sun bright, and the faraway white peaks seemed to grow straight out of the ice. He was sure he could reach the first valley of the Aval before the fog from the plains slowed him down.

He put on his skis. The bindings clicked. As always before a long nonstop run, he did a few limbering-up exercises: he bent his elbows and knees several times, twisted his torso back and forth, sat down on the back of his skis and got up without using his hands. He pushed off. A sudden gust of wind sent him skidding sideways; for a moment he almost lost his balance.

The wind changed direction and pushed him from behind. He was speeding toward the ridge, skis rattling on the crusty snow. His sunglasses steamed a bit and an unexpected cold blast chilled his body. The slope was getting steeper, and he was still gaining speed.

The wind changed direction again. It came in gusts, blowing against him, slowing him down. He was surprised to encounter cold wind coming from the vineyards, which were already turning green. The temperature seemed to be dropping rapidly. He was wearing only a light racing parka over his shirt, thin gloves, and no head covering. Visibility decreased; he could no longer distinguish the distant peaks and could barely make out the ridge.

When he turned to look across the valley toward ValPina, he saw a funnel of brown mists steaming up at him like the fumes of industrial wastes. In seconds, the frosty dew had enveloped him and even the tips of his skis were hidden from view. But he kept going down. He was only a short distance from the ridge.

Under his skis he could feel the frozen traces of other skiers. He knew he had reached the ridge, even though he could see only inches in front of him. Beyond the ridge opened the first valley of the Aval, protected on two sides by massive slopes, dropping steeply toward the second of the three valleys. He expected the visibility to improve in the valley and the strength of the wind to decrease.

He crossed the ridge and discovered that he had been mistaken. He was in the center of a boiling, hissing cloud. He remembered the route well and assumed that he could find his way to the bottom of the valley, below the center of the storm. He had gone a few hundred yards when a mass of savagely icy air came from below at great speed. He fought it obstinately, and only when he was not able to move forward one more inch did he stop skiing. The turbulence around him increased and he began to fear that he would be swept down onto the rocks lining the slopes. The wind, pumped by invisible bellows, lifted him, then pushed him against the fall line, throwing him to the ground. He understood that he was caught in one of those spring storms that might end in hours or last for days. Shivering, struggling for breath, he knew that to crawl down was to risk falling into a crevasse or being trapped in the valley by an avalanche. He had no choice but to abort the descent, to spend two hours climbing back up to the PicSoleil gondola station.

There were no pockets in his parka, and he had to keep rubbing his hands together to maintain the warmth. His face went numb and his neck became rigid with cold. He could not move his lips; his nostrils were filling with icy flakes. He touched his ears but could not feel his hands on them. To bring the blood back, he bent down and, with hands that now felt nothing, picked up a mound of snow and began massaging his face and ears. He twisted in pain and stopped the scrubbing. Closing his eyes, he forced himself to remember the dead German soldiers he had seen as a child during the war, their chins, noses, and ears missing, their teeth flashing through the holes in the frostbitten cheeks. The image was more agonizing than the pain he was causing himself, and he kept rubbing until sensation returned.

He started to walk uphill to find the ridge and the large rock that stood next to it, thinking that behind it he might be able to shelter himself from the wind. But he had lost his sense of direction and suddenly feared that he had walked too far up. He was probably above the ridge, he thought, traversing a giant slope that was taking him farther and farther away from the ridge and from the only path to the gondola station.

I must keep climbing, he repeated to himself. I must keep climbing. He dragged himself up in the fog, aware of losing all sense of time and distance, trying to detect by the sound his skis made on the icy sheet whether he was still following the tracks of other skiers.

Each time he thought he had lost the track, he took off his gloves and, with his skis spread, bent down and trailed his fingers over the crusty surface, seeking the traces. Soon his hands were too cold and he could not tell what he was touching. But he kept plodding uphill, step after step, convinced that if the clouds lifted even for a second he would find out where he was.

I must keep climbing, he thought. But this time there was a gap between the "I" and the "must." Behind the white tapestry of snowy space, "I" was still a word that made sense; "must" was a vague command from somewhere else and was as useless as the sunglasses that pressed against his forehead. "I" was still here, on this steep slope blanketed with fog; "must" was drifting away with the wind.

He was tired; he had to sit down, to rest. Perhaps he should even take off the skis and lie down, if only for a moment. He had not allowed himself to panic about the pain he felt under his left arm. His heart had lost its rhythm just once or twice, and at this altitude, with the temperature so low, the winds surging upward at him, a slight tremor was to be expected in a man of his age. Alone in the storm, cold and tired, he deserved a rest.

He always did everything as well as he could, he thought, and if he fell short of his own mark, he worked to improve himself. He once saw a black man, all alone in a Broadway arcade, dressed in rags, playing a ball-and-ramp game and registering the highest score with each roll. Levanter started to play the game at another ramp, but after several attempts still could not score even the lowest number. He went over to the black man and asked if he could pay him for a lesson: he wanted to learn to play the game well, he said.

The black man laughed. "This game?" he asked. "What would you want to learn this game for? Nobody plays this game anymore!"

"You do," said Levanter, "and you get the best score every time."

"I sure do, man, I sure do!" The black man kept laughing as he rolled one ball after another, each ball finding its target easily. "But this game is all I know. So I play it because it makes me feel real good to know how well I play it. But you, man, what would you want to play it for?" He kept glancing at Levanter, his face full of joy, while his hand picked up each wooden ball as it rushed at him from under the ramp, his arm bent, then extended, and he released the heavy ball for another perfect score. He continued to laugh, pleased with himself and pleased that Levanter kept watching him play his game.

Levanter could not catch his breath. The icy wind filled his lungs. He grew confused; drowsily he covered his face with his arms. He had been scoring quite well in the games he played, he reflected, although, like the black man, he knew there were few others who would ever want to learn to play his game. The game was good to him, made him want to play it, yet even a solitary player needs his rest. He leaned on his poles, but the wind threatened to knock him over. He sank down and turned his face away from the wind. Slowly he reached toward the bindings; they were frozen but he managed to open them. He put the skis beside him; his knees and ankles suddenly invited to regain their movement.

He was lucky, he thought, to find this shell of a slope to rest in. The storm might be rolling past him right now, and he might as well sleep through it. Soon the sun would be on him, warming his body as it melted the white walls of this frozen vault.

His rest was not a surrender to the storm, he thought; his striving continued even when he rested. He no longer felt circulation in his legs or hands. To guard the little heat his body had conserved, he unzipped his parka and pulled it over his head. His chest felt tight, gripped by a vest of ice. His heart started to rebel, one beat following another over a block of silence. The ice vest tightened, locking his chest, but as he drifted off to sleep, he thought how snug a bed of snow could be.

Slowly, he began to realize that the cold he felt was of no more concern to him than the heat had been that day in Palm Beach when his friends wondered if it was too hot to stay outdoors. He did not mind the heat. He was observing a young boy on the beach. The boy had wanted to hear a story Levanter had started to tell him. But the boy's mother, an anxious American divorcée, and her suitor, a boring Briton, disapproved of what Levanter was telling the child. They did not want the boy to listen to such stories, they said; he was to enjoy the sea and not to talk to strangers again.

The boy obeyed. He got up and slowly walked toward the ocean. He stood in the knee-deep water. When a wave rolled toward him, he assumed a fencing position and cut at it with an invisible sword. The wave washed by, lapping against the shore. When the next wave came in, he hit it twice before it flattened, foaming at his feet. Like a fencer frozen in a pass, he let the next wave swell on the sand toward him, and then the next. The waves deposited their foam on the steamy sand, one after another, one after another, and the boy, his back to Levanter, watched them mindlessly.

ON KOSINSKI

*Jerzy Kosinski has lived through—and now makes
use of—some of the strongest direct experience
that this century has had to offer.*

TIME

To appreciate the violent, ironic, suspenseful, morally demanding world of JERZY KOSINSKI's novels, one must first acknowledge the random succession of pain and joy, wealth and poverty, persecution and approbation that have made his own life often as eventful as those of his fictional creations.

He was born in Poland. When he was six, all but two members of his once numerous and distinguished family were lost in the Holocaust of World War II. Abandoned, suspected of being a Jew or a gypsy, he fled alone from village to village in Nazi-occupied eastern Europe, working as a farm hand, gaining his knowledge of nature, animal life, farming—and survival. At the age of nine, in a traumatic confrontation with a hostile peasant crowd he lost the power of speech, and was unable to talk for over five years. After the war, he was reunited with his ailing parents (his father was a scholar of ancient linguistics, his mother a pianist) and placed in a school for the handicapped. While on vacation, he regained his voice in a skiing accident, and with renewed self-reliance promptly worked his way through high school.

During his studies at the state-controlled Stalinist college and university he was suspended twice and often threatened with expulsion for his rejection of the official Marxist doctrine. While a Ph.D candidate in social psychology, he rose rapidly to become an associate professor and grantee of the Academy of Sciences, the state's highest research institution. Attempting to free himself from state-imposed collectivity, he would spend winters as a ski instructor in the Tatra Mountains, and summers as a social counselor at a Baltic sea resort.

Meanwhile, secretly, he plotted his escape. A confident master of bureaucratic judo, Kosinski pitted himself against the Establishment. In need of official sponsors, and reluctant to implicate his family, his friends and the academy staff, he created four distinguished—but fictitious—members of the Academy of Sciences to act in that capacity. As a member of the Academy's inner circle and a prize-winning photographer (with many one-man exhibitions to his credit), Kosinski had access to state printing plants, and he was able to furnish each academician with the appropriate official seals, rubber stamps and stationery. His punishment, had he been caught, would have been many years in prison. After two years of active correspondence between his fictitious sponsors and the various government agencies, Kosinski obtained an official passport allowing him to visit the United States under the auspices of an equally fictitious American "foundation." Waiting for his U.S. visa, expecting to be arrested at any time, Kosinski carried a foil-wrapped egg of cyanide in his pocket. "One way or another," he vowed, "they won't be able to keep me here against my will." But his plan worked. On December 20, 1957, Kosinski arrived in New York fluent in several languages though only with a rudimentary knowledge of English, following what he still considers the singular most creative act of his life. "I left behind being an inner emigré trapped in spiritual exile," he says. "America was to give shelter to my real self and I wanted to become its writer-in-residence." He was twenty-four years of age—his American odyssey was about to begin.

He started wandering widely in the United States as a truck driver, moonlighting as a parking lot attendant, a cinema projectionist, a portrait photographer, a limousine and racing-car driver for a black nightclub enterpreneur. "By working in Harlem as a white, uniformed chauffeur I broke a color barrier of the profession," he recalls. Studying English whenever he could in a year he learned it well enough to obtain a Ford Foundation fellowship. Two years later, as a student of social psychology, he wrote the first of his two nonfiction books on collective society. It became an instant bestseller, serialized by *The Saturday Evening Post*, condensed by *Reader's Digest*, and published in 18 languages. He was firmly set on a writing career.

After his publishing debut he met Mary Weir, the widow of a steel magnate from Pittsburgh. They dated for two years and were married after the publication of Kosinski's second nonfiction book.

During his 10 years with Mary Weir (which ended with her death) Kosinski moved with utmost familiarity in the world of heavy industry, big business and high society. He and Mary traveled a great deal—there was a private plane, a 17-crew boat, and houses in Pittsburgh, New York, Hobe Sound, Southampton, Paris, London and Florence. He led a life most novelists only invent in the pages of their novels.

"During my marriage, I had often thought that it was Stendhal or F. Scott Fitzgerald, both preoccupied with wealth they themselves did not have, who deserved to have had my experience. At first, I considered writing a novel about my immediate American experience, the dimension of wealth, power and high society that surrounded me, not the terror, poverty and privation I had seen and experienced so shortly before. But during my marriage I was too much a part of that world to extract from it the nucleus of what I felt. As a writer, I perceived fiction as the art of imaginative projection and so, instead, I decided to write my first novel about a homeless boy in war-torn Eastern Europe, an existence I'd once led and also one that was shared by millions of others like me, yet was still foreign to most Americans. This novel, *The Painted Bird*, was my gift to Mary, and to my new world."

His following novels—*Steps, Being There, The Devil Tree, Cockpit, Blind Date* and *Passion Play*, all links in an elaborate fictional cycle, were inspired by particular events of his life. He would often draw on the experience he had gained when, once a "Don Quixote of the turnpike," he had become a "Captain Ahab of billionaire's row." "Kosinski has enough technical virtuosity to outwrite almost any competitor," wrote *Los Angeles Herald Examiner*, "but few novelists have a personal background like his to draw on." Translated into most major languages, at first his novels have earned Kosinski the status of an international underground culture hero. Official recognition followed: for *The Painted Bird*, the French Best Foreign Book Award; for *Steps*, the National Book Award. He received a Guggenheim fellowship, the Award in Literature of the American Academy and the National Institute of Arts and Letters, as well as the Brith Sholom Humanitarian Freedom Award, and many others.

While Kosinski was constantly on the move, living and writing in various parts of the United States, Europe and Latin America, close calls with death persisted in his life.

On his way from Paris to the Beverly Hills home of his friend, film director Roman Polanski, and his wife, Sharon Tate, Kosinski's luggage was unloaded by mistake in New York. Unable to catch the connecting flight to Los Angeles, Kosinski reluctantly stayed overnight in New York. That very night in Polanski's household the Charles Manson Helter-Skelter gang murdered five people—among them Kosinski's closest friends, one of whom he financially assisted in leaving Europe and settling in the States.

For the next few years Kosinski taught English at Princeton and Yale. He left university life when he was elected president of American P.E.N., the international association of writers and editors. After serving the maximum two terms, he has remained active in various American human rights organizations. He is proud to have been responsible for freeing from prisons, helping financially, resettling or otherwise giving assistance to a great number of writers, political and religious dissidents and intellectuals all over the world, many of whom openly acknowledged his coming to their rescue.

Called by *America* "a spokesman for the human capacity to survive in a highly complex social system," Kosinski has been often labeled by the media an existential cowboy, a Horatio Alger of the nightmare, a penultimate gamesman, the utterly portable man and a mixture of adventurer and social reformer. In an interview for *Psychology Today,* Kosinski said: "And I have no habits that require maintaining—I don't even have a favorite menu—the only way for me to live is to be as close to other people as life allows. Not much else stimulates me—and nothing interests me more."

Traveling extensively, on an average Kosinski wakes up around 8 A.M. ready for the day. Four more hours of sleep in the afternoon allows him to remain mentally and physically active until the early dawn when he retires. This pattern, he claims, benefits his writing, his photography, and practicing of the sports he has favored for years—downhill skiing and polo, which, as an avid all-around horseman, he plays on a team—or one-on-one.

As a novelist and a screenplay writer (he adapted for the screen his novel, *Being There* which starred Peter Sellers, Shirley MacLaine, Melvyn Douglas and Jack Warden, for which he was nominated for the Golden Globe and won the Writers Guild of America Best Screenplay of the Year Award)—Kosinski is frequently interviewed by the press and appears often on television. Thus, he is apt to be recognized, and to obtain private access to public places he sometimes disguises himself; occasionally, he takes part-time employment in businesses and corporations that interest him.

A critic once said of Kosinski that he "writes his novels so sparsely as though they cost a thousand dollars a word, and a misplaced or misused locution would cost him his life." He was close to the truth: Kosinski takes almost three years to write a novel, and rewrites it a dozen times; later, in subsequence sets of proofs, he condenses the novel's text often by one-third. Kosinski said that "writing fiction is the essence of my life—whatever else I do revolves around a constant thought: could I—can I—would I—should I—use it in my next novel? As I have no children, no family, no relatives, no business or estate to speak of, my books are my only spiritual accomplishment."

"Learning from the best writing of every era—wrote *The Washington Post*—Kosinski develops his own style and technique. . . . in harmony with his need to express new things about our life and the world we do live in, to express the inexpressible. Giving to himself as well as to the reader the same chance for interpretation, he traces the truth in the deepest corners of our outdoor and indoor lives, of our outer appearance and our inner reality. He moves the borderline of writing to more remote, still invisible and untouchable poles, in cold and in darkness. Doing so, he enlarges the borders of the bearable."

JERZY KOSINSKI

Winner of the National Book Award, Kosinski is one of the most significant writers of our generation. He is an intensely gifted artist who brilliantly and savagely exposes the nightmare of our contemporary world. Reading his works is an overwhelming experience.